GONE ROGUE SERIES

PATRICIA D. EDDY

If you love sexy romantic suspense, I'd love to send you a short story set in Dublin, Ireland. Castles & Kings isn't available anywhere except for readers who sign up for my mailing list! Sign up for my newsletter on my website and tell me where to send your free book!
http://patriciadeddy.com.

AUTHOR'S NOTE

Hello dear readers,

In this book, our hero can't hear. Because hearing loss has so many nuances, I thought I should give you a little background on why I wrote Griff the way I did.

Please understand that while I do a lot of research before I start any of my books, I'm only as good as the individuals I talk to, the books I read, the websites I pour over. So occasionally, I get things wrong. I think I've done a good job with Griff and his challenges, but if you have a deaf or hard of hearing person in your life, your experiences (or theirs) may not completely align with Griff's.

In part, that's because every person's manifestation of a disability, injury, or chronic illness/condition is influenced by many factors. Basically, no two people are alike.

Griff does not use ASL to communicate very often. There are several reasons for that, including the fact that he only lost his hearing five months ago. ASL is a very different language than English. It has its own set of grammar rules. And it's a two-handed language. While plenty of people who use ASL (whether they're Deaf or want to communicate with Deaf individuals) do sign one-handed, Griff's amputation adds another layer of difficulty to learning the language. Both physically *and* emotionally.

On the subject of his amputation...Griff's prosthetic arm is one of the most advanced ever manufactured. So advanced, it's not widely available, nor would Griff be able to afford it if he didn't have very well-connected friends. But the technology to let him *feel* with his prosthetic hand does actually exist today. There's an amazing book, *Rewired*, by Dr. Ajay K. Seth, that served as my inspiration for Griff's recovery and what he can do with his prosthetic.

However, like Melissa in *Rewired*, Griff is an edge case. He's lucky because he has resources (read: money) and contacts. He can get the best care. He also healed quicker than most, because...well...this is fiction and that's how the timeline came together. His healing speed isn't unheard of, but it is very, *very* fast.

If you're curious about some of the latest advances in upper limb prosthetics, see https://labblog.uofmhealth.org/health-tech/its-like-you-have-a-hand-again.

Formatting note: Technically, when Griff reads lips or reads someone else's words on a speech-to-text program, the editing style guides out there want those words italicized. However, since Griff has long conversations with several individuals in this book, especially Sloane, I made the **choice *not*** to italicize those sections. This is 100% on purpose because otherwise, there would be so much italicized, I'm afraid it would make for a negative reader experience.

I hope you enjoy Rogue Officer!
     Love, Patricia

PROLOGUE

Fifteen Years Ago

Sophiana

My skin crawls as I pull the sheet up to my chest. One of my regulars, Rodney—if that's even his real name—dresses quickly and drops a handful of bills on the dresser. As soon as the door slams, I slip out of bed and scramble for the money. Counting quickly, I curse under my breath.

Der'mo.

Two hundred. That sicko left the bare minimum. He hadn't bathed in days, and the things he wanted? Yet I cannot say no to him. Or any of them.

"You are nothing, cyka! You do what I say, and you get as much out of the men as you can or you are not worth keeping alive."

Dimitri's words play on a loop in my head. Every day, he threatens us. Hits us. So often, starves us. And we can do nothing. Because we are nothing.

Shuddering, I fold the bills and rush into the bathroom. After I hide the cash in a plastic bag underneath the toilet lid, I run the tap and use the rough washcloth to scrub between my legs.

The icy water raises goosebumps along my skin, and the towels are as stained as the sheets. This place is worse than the one room flat I shared with my mama and three sisters back in Penza.

No heat. No hot water. Nothing but dirty sheets, stained carpets, and cockroaches hovering in the dark corners. The only good in this slice of hell? The motel owner hides candy bars in the rooms every day. He knows Dimitri does not let us eat while we are working.

Hurry.

I only have five minutes until my next *guest*, and I snake my hand under the sink, fingers stretched as far as I can until I feel the plastic wrapper. The bar comes free with a single tug and the corners of my lips twitch as I start to salivate.

Snickers. My favorite.

Cramming half the bar into my mouth at once, I continue scrubbing. Tits, pussy, ass. Nothing will make me clean. But I cannot smell like my last fuck when the next one knocks on the door.

The scent of the cheap soap makes my nose burn. If I ever have money, I will buy—*stop it, Sophie.*

Trying to balance on my too-high heels while wolfing down the candy bar *and* wriggling into my cheap polyester-made-to-look-like-silk dress sends me careening into the bathroom door.

The pain sings along my shoulder and back, but I won't let myself cry. I still have to brush my teeth.

I can't focus on my reflection when I brace myself against the sink. If I do, I will see a girl who's too thin. Collar bones sticking out, elbows and shoulder blades like razors. Tits that barely fill a bra. Bruises everywhere.

But mostly, I will see a girl who was so naive, she thought twenty-five thousand rubles could buy her a new life in the United States. A girl who didn't realize the man making that promise would take so much more than money.

This is no life. Dimitri owns me. He took my passport as soon as I landed in New York and tattooed his *mark* on the back of my neck that same night. I will never escape him. Nor will any of the dozen other girls I sleep shoulder to shoulder with whenever I am not *here*. He keeps us locked in a basement on the outskirts of the city. One house among ten he oversees in Philadelphia. We are never free. Never allowed to be outside alone. Forced to have sex with men we do not know, night after night.

The knock on the door makes me choke on the last of the toothpaste, and I hurry to rinse out the sink.

Three more men tonight, then I can shower and sleep. If I earn enough, Dimitri will let me use the hot water. Or finally make good on his promise of McDonald's. Plastering on a shy smile and lowering my gaze, I open the door.

———

IT'S after two in the morning when Anton—Dimitri's driver and our *guard*—pulls the van behind the two-story house in south Philadelphia. "Inside. Quickly," he barks. The twelve of us obey without a sound, barely slowing until we're down the stairs.

I gave Anton enough to earn my hot shower, but before he calls for me, I pull half a candy bar from a rip in the hem of my dress and hand it to the newest girl. Anya is only eighteen, and she still cries before, during, and after every man who buys her.

She sniffles and swipes at her cheeks, her eyes wide as she stares at the forbidden treasure.

"Fast, fast," I whisper. "I hide the wrapper."

"Sophiana!" Anton snaps from the doorway. "Up here, now."

I barely have time to shove the evidence of my rebellion inside the lining of my dress before he calls my name again. A third time and he will beat me.

He curls his thick fingers around my upper arm as he escorts me to the bathroom. But before we get there, the front door bangs open with such force, it flies off its hinges.

"Police!"

"BE GOOD, MY LITTLE SOPHIE," Rodney calls as he slips out of the dingy studio apartment, and I jump off the couch and race into the bathroom. Why, today of all days, did my savior-turned-abuser linger over a second cup of coffee?

My hands shake, and I drop the concealer stick twice, leaving pale beige splatters all over the sink. *Shit.* I have to clean those before I leave. Covering yesterday's bruise in the crook of my elbow is easy. The older needle marks aren't so simple. Then again, at this photo shoot? No one will look too carefully.

It's $500 for six hours, and I cannot say no. I have to save up enough money for a bus ticket. For first and last months' rent on an apartment. In another city. Where Rodney cannot find me.

He was one of my regulars. Six times he came. Asking questions. I thought he was nice—nicer than most of the men who used me, though he rarely bathed and wanted me to do the most horrible things. I thought nothing of his babbling. Some men like to talk, others like to hit.

Until he was one of the policemen who raided the house. I know now, some of what I told him led the Philadelphia police right to Dimitri. Helped them put him in jail for more than twenty-five years.

We were so scared. Terrified we would be deported. Or jailed. Instead, some of the older girls were offered deals to testify. The younger ones were too emotional, but they were given asylum.

I was not. Rodney said they lost my paperwork. That I had no passport. He gave me only two options. Turn myself in to immigration and be sent back to Russia or let him protect me. I made the wrong choice. He arranged for a cheap hotel room for me. Then offered to sleep on the pull-out sofa. To protect me. Even then, I did not fear like I do now.

It took a week for him to demand sex. The day my medical report came back clean.

At least this morning, all he wanted was a blow job. Swishing a double dose of mouthwash, I pull out the phone he gave me. The cracked screen makes it hard to unlock, but at least I can still read the time. Shit. I have to leave in the next two minutes if I want to make the bus.

As soon as I sling my crossbody bag over my shoulder, I race out the door and pray nothing the "director" wants from me will leave a mark.

***

"EXCUSE ME. Are you here for the lingerie shoot?" A smooth, refined voice cuts through my nerves, and I peer up into a pair of bright hazel eyes.

"Yes. Is there a problem?" Instinctively, my shoulders

hunch, and I tug at the hem of my miniskirt. The man doesn't belong in this place. His suit *fits*, and though he wants something from me—it's in his gaze and the way his lips curve into not quite a smile—I think maybe...he is not all bad.

Withdrawing a shiny business card from his jacket pocket, he holds it between two fingers. "I represent the Harvey Ulstrum Agency." With a more genuine smile this time, he sinks into the chair next to me. "You shouldn't be here."

"I was told..." My heart hammers against my chest, and I can't get the next words out. Not in English anyway. Russian tumbles from my lips, faster than anyone but a native speaker could understand.

"No, no. There's nothing wrong. You're not in any trouble. What's your name?"

"Sophie," I whisper, glancing around at all the other girls sitting in the hard plastic chairs lining the hall.

"I'm Max. Max Snood." He offers me his hand, the one still holding the business card, and we shake, but he doesn't let go, his gaze on the crook of my elbow. "Do you want to get clean, Sophie? Have a career you can be proud of? Be able to show your friends what you do?"

Jerking back, I wrap my arms around myself. Men like this are how I ended up here. Alexi was the first. Back in Russia. He sold me to Dimitri. Then Rodney "freed" me only to hide me away. Max is no different. "Leave me alone."

Max sighs, and I tense, ready to run. One call to the police and I will be deported. Or worse. Rodney will know what I've done. But instead of threatening, Max simply stands and drops the business card on the chair. "If you change your mind, my number's on there. You have access to a computer?"

I nod. The library down the street offers free use for an hour a day, and I go often. Though I can speak English well enough, my reading ability is limited to street signs and what I can learn from commercials. Still, I go whenever Rodney is at work and look at fashion magazines, newspapers, and children's books. If they have pictures with the words, sometimes I can read them.

"Go to my company's website. You'll see what we do. If you change your mind, call me."

And then he's gone, striding away with all the confidence I'll never have.

"Sophie Lebedev!" a portly man with greasy skin and bad teeth shouts from the door a few feet away. "Get your ass in here."

After two steps, I stop, turn around, and lunge for the business card on the chair. I don't know why. But maybe…Max will be different.

Sloane

"Are you ready to see the new you?" Dr. Foster asks.

It has been eight months since I called Max, and the last six have passed in a private clinic in upstate New York. Detox, counseling, then four surgeries. A new nose, chin, and cheekbones, and dozens of laser treatment sessions to hide my scars and the tattoo on the back of my neck.

The trees—so green they don't look real—sway gently in the breeze outside my second-floor window. A few minutes ago, two men came to install a mirror in my bathroom—the first one I've seen since I came here.

Max leans against the wall next to the door, a wide smile on his face. "You've outdone yourself, Foster," he says, then turns all his attention to me. "Go ahead, Sloane."

I cannot get used to this new name. According to Max,

Sophie Lebedev cannot ever become a model. Her passport was scanned entering the United States two years ago, and immigration knows she never left.

So I am Sloane Sanders. New name. New face. And now that my surgeries are done, soon I will have a passport declaring me an American citizen.

Every day I have taken classes. How to walk. How to speak without an accent. How to read and write flawless English. I worry what will happen when I leave this place. Will Max turn out to be just another bad man pretending to be good? Can I really pass for an American? Or will everyone I meet see right through me?

Some nights, I lie awake with these fears. But since I fled Rodney's dingy apartment with only my purse and my mother's locket, no one has hit me. No one has fucked me. My room here is small, but I have a collection of books, a brand-new cell phone, a sketchpad, and an expensive set of charcoal pencils. When I told Max I used to draw as a child, he showed up with art supplies the very next day.

Dr. Foster removes the last bandage—the one over my nose —and grins. "Turn around, dear."

I don't recognize the woman staring back at me. It's not only the surgeries. Her shoulders no longer hunch. Her eyes are clear and bright—and blue, thanks to contact lenses—and for the first time, I think maybe Max was right. I will be a model, and I will never have to spread my legs for a man again.

CHAPTER ONE

May

Griff

"What the hell is the Ambassador doing here?" I let the door slam behind me, then fasten the top two buttons on my white dress shirt. My boss, Major General Austin Pritchard, keeps things at the office casual most days. Polo shirts and black pants, the occasional button-up. But we all have a change of clothes on site for occasions like this.

"No fucking clue." Pritchard smooths the wrinkles from his khakis, then unlocks his desk drawer and pulls out a shoulder holster and an M9 Beretta. "But she's headed back to the Embassy in twenty minutes, and we're her escort."

His hazel eyes are tired. We've been here six months, and from what little I've been able to pry out of the man, this assignment? It's punishment for Austin going AWOL from some JSOC publicity tour because his sister needed him.

I know he hates it here, but after my last post in Kuwait,

this is a walk in the park. The CIA set me up in a sweet apartment in a secured building, the food is amazing—while being cheap as fuck—and Austin's a good guy. Haunted in ways I don't understand, but aren't we all?

Pulling out a map—an honest to God paper map—Austin spreads the damn thing across the desk and highlights a ten-kilometer route between our office and the Embassy. "See any pinch points?"

I stare at him like he's lost his marbles. "Yeah. Too many. Two of these streets are under construction, and I think I saw a new sidewalk market setting up on this corner on my ride in. We gotta find another way." When Pritchard gives me the side eye, I add, "Sir."

"Well, this is the way the Ambassador's staff insisted we go. Go convince them otherwise."

"Me? I'm not in charge. Wouldn't this be better coming from you?"

"The Ambassador is friends with my CO. Pretty sure she thinks I'm a fucking idiot." Austin shakes his head, his shoulders slumping with his sigh. His CO, Commander Ivan Clarke, was the one who sent him here, and one late night over a bucket of beers, he told me he didn't expect to have a job when this assignment ended.

"Fine. But make sure Nagan's driving. If I can't change her mind, we'll need a beast behind the wheel."

"BACK THE FUCK UP!" From the front seat of the armored SUV, I twist around, hoping to whatever God is up there the rest of the caravan isn't right up our asses. The Ambassador wouldn't listen when I explained how dangerous this route was. She wanted to see the new school the United States government helped fund.

Nagan wrenches the wheel to the left, but it's no use. We're boxed in. Abandoned vehicles line both sides of the narrow street and ahead of us? Nowhere to go.

The map was wrong. The end of the street is now a bazaar with dozens of stalls and a suspicious lack of women and children milling about. The hair on the back of my neck prickles, and I grab the radio.

"Pritchard! We're blown. Get the Ambassador out of here!"

I'm too late. His reply's lost to the gunfire hitting the sides of the SUV. At least it's bulletproof.

To a point.

One I don't want to test. Pritchard, the Ambassador, her driver, and her teenage son are in the vehicle behind us, and two more of our guys bring up the rear.

Another hour, and we would have been safe. She showed up unannounced five days ago, and we had to scramble to escort her to a dozen different meetings. We thought she was headed home today, but she changed her plans at the last minute and decided to leave tomorrow instead.

Someone doesn't want that to happen.

Nagan slams into one of the abandoned cars, pushing it forward five feet, then throws the SUV in reverse and tries to repeat the maneuver with the car behind us.

"We're sitting ducks!" I snap as I grab a helmet from under the seat. Before I can buckle the strap, the windows in the SUV shatter, and my ears start to ring.

"Bomb!" I can barely hear my own shout and swipe at my cheek, finding it sticky with blood. Craning my neck, I scan all around us.

Fuck. The SUV carrying Pritchard, the Ambassador, and

her son lies on its side, smoke pouring from the engine. "Fall back. We've got to get them out of there."

Nagan kicks the driver's side door open and drops into a crouch with his Colt M4 at the ready. I sling my own rifle over my shoulder and pull the Sig Sauer p228 from my harness with a grunt.

Bulletproof vests are heavy and cumbersome, but you spend enough time in a country where half the population wants you dead, you get used to moving in them.

Pritchard crawls out of the SUV's front windshield, blood staining his collar, then stretches out his arm. "Ms. Ambassador! Give me your hand."

"Austin! Where's the kid?"

"In the back!" he shouts.

With Nagan laying down cover fire, I climb on top of the overturned SUV and pry the back passenger door open. The boy—he can't be more than fifteen—peers up at me, wide-eyed and clearly in shock. A trickle of blood cuts a bright red swath across his arm. "Hand. Now!"

He doesn't move. Shit.

"Are you injured? Benson, answer me. Right fucking now!"

That snaps him out of his fog. He loosens his seat belt and, with a wince, reaches his hands up to grasp mine.

"As soon as you're clear, you get to your mom's side and stick there. Like glue, you understand?"

"Uh huh." He nods, and I maneuver him onto the side of the car. It only takes him thirty seconds to get to his mother, who's hiding behind Pritchard as the man fires at a three-story building across from us.

"Snipers!" he calls, and I take aim.

"Go! I got this!" A flash of a scope in the bright sunlight focuses my gaze, and I pull the trigger, taking one of the snipers down with a single shot.

In my periphery, I see the ambassador and her son, surrounded by her personal security detail, rushing down the sidewalk toward a local mosque.

Nagan and I, along with the other two members of our team, Harrison and Levy, move toward Pritchard, scanning the buildings all around us for more threats.

I'm the first one cross to Austin's side of the street, just in time to see a bullet find its mark in his shoulder. But he barely stumbles and shifts his grip on his pistol.

I turn, searching for the asshole who shot him. Movement to my left. I fire but miss. "Shit!" Something metallic sails in a wide arc from the building above me, landing less than fifty feet away.

Fuck. Time slows to a crawl as I sprint in the opposite direction, but the blast is so close I can feel it in my chest. Searing pain snakes from ear to ear, and the world goes quiet except for a dull hum.

Dizzy, I stumble toward Pritchard. He's backed against a concrete block wall, firing at the snipers across the street, but the wall...something's wrong. Another pipe bomb flies over the concrete, and I race for Austin, tackling him and driving my shoulder into his stomach.

He flies back as the third bomb goes off, but I don't see where. Something knocks me to the ground and drives the air from my lungs.

I can't move. Can't breathe. The sky above me is marred by smoke and dust and when my diaphragm stops spasming and I suck in a breath, the coppery, sweet scent of blood is almost choking.

Austin's face swims in and out of focus. His lips are moving. Why can't I hear him?

"Pritchard," I croak. "I can't feel my arm. Shit. I can't..."

there's something wrong with my ears. It's so quiet. Fuck. Am I dying? Don't let me die, man."

Tears burn my eyes as Austin, his gray dress shirt soaked in blood, grabs for my left arm. Turning my head takes more effort than it should. I'm so tired.

A chunk of concrete sails toward my feet, followed by another, and another. They're bloody. Why are they bloody?

Darkness creeps closer, and the silence terrifies me. "Tell my mom... Austin? Tell her... I'm sorry."

He grabs my shoulders, terror clouding his eyes, and I think he's shouting at me. I can almost *feel* it. But I can't fight any longer.

The light fades away, and with it, the pain.

MY FINGERS ARE CLENCHED so hard, they ache. It's still quiet, only a dull hum somewhere in the background.

Forcing my eyes open, I see nothing but muted beige walls. *Hospital.*

I need to find Pritchard. But when I try to sit up, my left arm sends white hot pain racing all the way to my shoulder. I can't *hear* the sound I make, but I'd guess it's not that different from someone strangling a duck.

The door flies open, and a man in blue scrubs races in. He rests a hand on my right arm and holds me down until I can breathe again. "You...made your point. Not moving," I manage.

Every word I can't hear raises my panic another dozen notches, but what sends me over the edge? Catching sight of my left arm.

And the thick bandage wrapped from the top of my bicep to a few inches above where my elbow *should be.*

Fuck. Fuck, fuck, fuck.

The man hovering over me shimmers as I fight not to lose my shit completely. He picks up a small whiteboard and starts scribbling. I don't want to read it, but I have to.

"I'm Dr. Winster. Both your eardrums were perforated."

"My arm…"

I don't give a shit about my ears. Not when I'm *missing half my left arm.*

The doctor erases the board and starts over as I force myself to breathe.

"Tourniquet above your elbow stopped you from bleeding out, but your arm was crushed, and with no blood flow, we couldn't save it. I'm sorry."

I'm fucked. Completely and utterly fucked.

"Surgery went well. You're a good candidate for a prosthetic."

At the moment, a prosthetic is the least of my concerns. "I can feel my hand. And it hurts like a motherfucker."

"Typical. Phantom pain. The specialist will come see you in a couple of hours. He'll give you some tricks to try to manage it."

"And my hearing? How long?"

Winster writes slower than a turtle, but at least his handwriting is legible. His eyes darken, and a furrow deepens between his brows. *"Not just your eardrums. I'm sorry, Griffin. The hearing loss may be permanent."*

If I had anything to throw, I'd lob it hard enough to punch a hole in the wall. Winster rests his hand on my right shoulder for a long moment, but I can't meet his gaze. Don't want to.

What the hell am I supposed to do now?

THE HAZE from the painkillers is pissing me off. All I want to do is sleep, but no one will tell me a damn thing about Pritchard, the rest of our team, or the Ambassador and her kid.

In the few hours I've been awake, I've at least pieced together a rough timeline. The attack occurred at 1600. I was in surgery until 0400, and the clock on the wall currently reads 14:30.

It's been almost twenty-four hours, and the medical staff is losing their patience with me. At least that's better than their looks of pity at the guy who used to be a capable CIA operations officer but now, will be lucky to ride a desk for the rest of his life.

I had a job to do, and I failed. My emotions swing between anger and depression—proving I'm well on my way through the stages of grief. Denial only lasted as long as it took me to *very* gingerly touch the bandaged stump of my left arm. And bargaining? No amount of *that* is going to regrow the limb.

With nothing else to do, I've been trying to write down every detail of the attack. The CIA and JSOC will want to debrief me soon, and I need to unscramble my thoughts before they do. I'd stop fighting to stay awake, but the nurse comes in on the half hour to check my vitals. If he won't answer my questions this time, I have what I hope is a very effective threat all queued up and ready to go.

Who am I kidding? Hours ago, when they got me vertical so I could take a piss, my equilibrium was so shot to hell I only managed two steps before crashing into the tech helping me. I can't fight a mouse in my current condition.

The light shifts as the door opens, and I drop the pen onto the notebook in my lap.

Oh, fuck.

The man being pushed toward me in a wheelchair looks nothing like Major General Austin Pritchard. He's aged a decade in under a day. Then again, no one's let me anywhere near a mirror. For all I know, I look worse.

"Pritchard."

His right arm is held tight to his body in a sling, and he struggles to sit up straight as he meets my gaze. The pity in his eyes is like a knife to my chest, and neither of us says a word until he nods at the aide behind him, and the man leaves us alone.

"Assuming they told you I can't hear shit?"

He pulls a cell phone from the pocket of the thin hospital robe, taps the screen a couple of times, and then turns it toward me as he angles his head at his right shoulder.

"Speech-to-text is shit, but best I can do. Shot three times. Threatened to crawl in here if nurse didn't help."

I huff out what might be a laugh. "You would have done it, too."

"Damn straight."

What the hell do you say to the man whose life you just saved? Who probably feels like he's the reason you only have half your arm?

"I'd do it again. Even knowing what would happen. That's the job."

From the way his chest stutters with each breath and his eyes water, that was exactly the wrong response, even if it was the truth.

"They won't tell me anything. Did the ambassador make it out?" Distraction. Ignore the big issues. Like not being able to hear. That'll work, right?

Austin nods, then starts speaking into his phone. After a minute, he shows me the screen again.

"She and her son are fine. But Nagan, Harrison, and Levy didn't make it. We killed three of them, but two of the duckers got away."

"Who sold us out?" I try to sit up straighter, but the room tilts on its axis, and I collapse with a groan.

Austin scoots forward in the wheelchair, pain tightening lines around his eyes as he touches my shoulder. "Take it easy."

At least that's what I think he says. My lip-reading skills were never more than passable. Someone needs to get me a tablet so I can practice. Finally, a use for YouTube.

"Easy? Since when is sitting up *not* 'taking it easy'? I can't even get myself out of this fucking bed."

Austin closes his eyes and presses his lips together. His right cheek is black and blue, and bandages peek out from under the hospital gown at his shoulder. Retrieving his phone, he returns to dictating.

"JSOC is sending a special investigations team. Working theory is someone in the ambassador's office, but hell if I know. Or care. I'm out. Retirement paperwork pushed through. Not my choice."

He pauses for a long moment, tugging at the neck of his hospital gown. A hint of red seeps through his bandages.

"Austin, for fuck's sake. You saved her life."

This man who spent his entire career in the armed forces, who worked his way up through the ranks of the Air Force, who has been, by all reports, one of the best commanders JSOC has ever seen, was just fired?

"I failed. Everyone. Especially you."

Looking over his shoulder at the door, he says something—I think. My hearing isn't completely gone. The occasional low-pitched rumble breaks through the silence, and Austin's voice is deep. The guy who wheeled him in returns, and before I can think of anything to say in response, he's gone.

Four Months Later

"AGAIN."

JoAnn, the rehab tech, sits back and crosses her arms over her chest. The coffee cup lies on its side. Thank God she didn't fill it with anything.

"This is useless," I mutter, glaring at the silicone and metal fingers of my prosthetic.

With a massive eye roll, JoAnn reaches out and pokes the thumb with her pen. The sensation is fucking weird.

Pritchard, the bastard, disappeared not long after they transferred me to a hospital in McClean, Virginia, saying he had to "find himself." But he called in a bunch of favors, and after a twelve-hour surgery to rewire the nerves in my upper arm, I have weekly appointments at Johns Hopkins for follow ups and to learn how to use one of the most advanced prosthetics in the world.

The average guy doesn't have a chance in hell at a limb like this one. But Austin's connected. Big time. So are his friends, apparently.

The surgery was a game changer. My phantom pain all but disappeared, and like some kind of fucking miracle, after just a few weeks, the doc could touch a spot on the inside of my upper arm and I'd feel it in my non-existent index finger.

"Less than fifty people in the country have the opportunity you have, Griffin. Don't take it for granted!" From her expression, she's pretty steamed. My lip-reading skills are impressive after four months of practice, but she reinforces her words by writing them down. Along with five exclamation points.

"Don't you think I'm trying? But what's the point? Nothing's going to get me out in the field again."

"You want...your problem?"

She's agitated, and that makes it harder for me to understand her. "Slow down a little, okay?"

Her eyes soften, and she takes a deep breath. "Sorry. Your problem is that your whole identity is tied to your job. You're more than that. It's time you accepted it."

"Maybe I don't want to." Pushing back from the table, I stand and reach for the coffee cup. Anger helps me focus, and the mechanical fingers wrap around the handle. It wobbles a little in my grip, but I manage to set it to rights and release it. "Happy now?"

I don't wait around to see her response. One advantage of being "profoundly hard of hearing"? I don't have to listen to anyone's bullshit. And once I get home, I can unstrap this monstrosity and send Austin yet another email he won't answer.

CHAPTER TWO

Griff

The woman behind the desk flicks her gaze to me briefly, a phone pressed to her ear. Covering the receiver with her hand, she says something, but I can't see her lips clearly.

Great. This is going swimmingly.

"I read lips, ma'am. If you were talking to me, I couldn't understand you."

Cheeks flushed, the woman says something else into the phone, then sets the receiver down and meets my gaze. "I'm so sorry. You must be Griffin Hargrove. Dax is expecting you. Would you like a cup of coffee or tea?"

"No. Thanks." I have no fucking clue what I'm doing here. Austin's ignored every single one of my emails over the past four months, yet he gave my contact info to this guy—Dax Holloway—in Boston and told him to get in touch with me.

"Follow me, then. I'm Marjorie, by the way," she says and smiles. "If you change your mind, just holler."

I don't plan on being here long enough to need something

to drink. Dax's message implied his company—Second Sight— could help me. They can't. If he hadn't dropped Austin's name, I would have ignored the email completely.

Marjorie leads me down a hall and past several closed doors until she reaches the last office on the right. She knocks once, waits a beat, and raps again before she turns the knob.

"Go on in, Mr. Hargrove."

"Griff," I say, but she's already gone. The man behind the desk rises, tugging at the sleeves of his light blue button down as he stares at me.

He doesn't smile—the eyes behind his pair of tinted glasses remain cold. From his expression, I'm not sure he knows how. "Austin told me about the attack in Islamabad. I'm assuming you can read lips or understand ASL, but I'd feel better if you confirmed that for me."

"I can understand some ASL, but I prefer to read lips. As long as you don't talk too fast." I hold out my hand, but Dax doesn't return the gesture.

Asshole. It's my *left* arm that's fucked, not my right. I can still shake hands.

"I haven't heard from Austin in four months. Are you going to tell me where he is and why the hell he won't respond to any of my emails?"

Dax's lips twitch, and he rubs the back of his neck as he returns to the seat behind his desk. "Not sure exactly what he's gotten himself into, but he's in Edgewater with someone he met on his 'walkabout.' Got back from Mexico last night."

"And he called you. Not me. Did the man forget how to type down there? Or FaceTime?"

Dax's shoulders straighten, and he presses his hands flat on the desk in front of him. "He didn't call me. I sent two of my guys down to Edgewater to help him out with a problem, and he gave me an update. Now are you going to sit down?"

"Fine." I drop into a chair and rub my left shoulder. It's humid as fuck today, and the socket is chafing my residual limb something fierce. I shouldn't have bothered with it, but it's a hell of a lot easier to meet new people when I look *normal*. My left hand is covered in a layer of silicone that almost looks like skin—if you're not paying close attention. "Why am I here?"

"Because Second Sight does a lot of things, Griff. We're known as a security and protection firm, but we also work with two companies on the west coast specializing in adaptive tech."

"In what?"

As if he mumbled the last two words on purpose, Dax passes me a tablet *"specializing in adaptive tech"* on the screen.

"So, you put your own speech-to-text program on an iPad. Big deal. Siri already does that."

"You're not looking at just *any* speech-to-text-program," he says, and the words appear in front of me with almost no delay. "It learns. All those words unique to you? It'll catch."

I don't look up. I've watched YouTube videos night after night after night working on my lipreading skills, but the mental load of always translating in my head? It can be exhausting.

"Prove it."

My own words appear on the screen, but unlike Dax's speech, which is in black, my words are in blue.

"Prove it yourself." He sits back and skims his fingers along the top of the desk toward a cup of coffee. The movement's odd, like he's worried he's going to knock it over.

"I don't need a fucking *tablet* to help me communicate with the rest of the world, Holloway. Austin doesn't know a damn thing about my life these days, but as you can see, I'm managing just fine."

His head snaps up, and his entire body goes rigid. "As I can *see?*"

"Yeah." I gesture to my prosthetic arm, then catch sight of the tablet screen. Dax isn't wrong about the software. It even italicized the words we emphasized. And it didn't change fucking to ducking.

Dax sets his mug down carefully, then removes his glasses to reveal scarring all around his eyes. Without the tinted lenses, his irises are pale as the morning sky. "You don't know me, kid. But choose your next words *very* carefully. I'm blind."

Fuck me. Of all the stupid presumptions... I should know better. Anger, shock, and a hell of a lot of shame clog my throat, and I swallow hard before I can reply. "Dammit. No one told me."

"No shit. Austin says you've got the best damn instincts of anyone he's ever met—besides me and my ODA team. Those of us who are still alive, anyway. But you're so caught up in your own shit, you can't see what's right in front of you." He lunges over the desk and holds out his hand. "Give me the goddamned tablet."

Thrusting it at him, I shove the chair back and stand. "I'm sorry for my shitty choice of words. But the rest of it? I don't need your help. I'm managing just fine on my own."

I'm out the door before he can say another word, and when Marjorie waves at me, trying to get me to stop, I ignore her too.

***

STAYING IN A HOTEL? It makes me feel...normal. I turned down the accessible room. It was on the ground floor, and that's just too much risk when you can't hear anyone breaking in.

Even though I didn't lose *all* my hearing in Islamabad, my world's been reduced to low rumbling noises most people would consider annoying. Semi trucks. Trains. And the elevator car as it travels up and down the shaft right next to my room. Strange how what used to be just noise now almost makes me smile.

Alone in the dimly lit room, I sit with my back against the headboard watching the Red Sox on TV. Sports are one of the few things I can follow without closed captioning, and I don't want any more of the broken pieces of my life thrown back in my face right now.

Then why am I emailing Austin?

Pritchard,

When you said you were going off the grid, I didn't think you meant completely. Couldn't have given me a heads up? And what's with sending me to Boston to meet with a blind guy? In case you didn't know, I'm mostly deaf, not blind. Don't try to tell me I can still live a full life. Not until you're walking around without your fucking arm too.

Don't contact me again.

-Griff

Austin and I were never *close*. I was part of his security detail. We had beers once a week. Ate the occasional lunch together. But after the attack, he was there for me. At least for a few days. Until they transferred us from Bagram to separate hospitals in the States. Me in McClean and Austin up in New England somewhere. That's when he went dark, and I tried to ignore how much his silence hurt.

My watch buzzes on my right wrist, and I glance down at the text message.

Open the door.

-Dax

The hell? I didn't tell Holloway where I was staying. And I sure as shit would have noticed someone following me back here.

Sliding off the bed, I check the peephole. Despite being

blind, he's staring right at me—or so it seems—so I open the door.

"Want to explain how you found me?" I ask as I step aside to let him in. His cane sweeps back and forth across the garish carpet, and I add, "There's a chair at your four o'clock."

"So, you're not a complete dick, then." Finding the chair, he sinks down with a grimace and rubs his thigh. "Just angry as fuck."

"Are you going to answer my question?" Closing the door and taking a seat on the bed across from him, I lean forward so I can watch his lips. Why is hotel lighting always so awful?

Dax reaches into his jacket pocket for an eyeglass case and tosses it to me.

"I don't need glasses."

"You do now. Put them on."

There's no arguing with a man like him. He carries himself with a presence that fills the room, and despite his lack of sight, I have a feeling he could still kick my ass. So I do it.

The black frames aren't particularly stylish. Or prescription.

"They're on. Happy now—holy fuck."

Across the top of the lenses, my own words appear.

"They're a prototype," Dax says. Just like on the tablet, his reply is in a different color. "The software's glitchy, the glasses weigh a ton, and right about now, there's probably too much text on the lenses for you to read—or see."

I don't register that he's stopped speaking because seeing the words appear right in front of my eyes with almost no delay is like fucking magic.

"Griff?"

Everything else scrolls away, and my name snaps me back to the present. "This... How?"

"Told you. I work with some of the best in adaptive tech. You got a notepad around?"

I scramble for the pad of hotel stationery and a pen. "Yeah."

"Write something. Anything. Doesn't have to make sense. And hand it to me." He scoots to the edge of the seat and holds out his hand.

I scribble my childhood phone number followed by a handful of random words: cheeseburger, plane, cat, Venus—then pass him the note.

Dax taps the frame of his own glasses, and in under a minute, reads every single number and word back to me.

"How the fuck did you do that?"

His laugh is rough and seems to surprise him. Pulling an earbud from his right ear, he shrugs. "Optical character recognition. Lets me read menus, documents. Slow as fuck, but better than relying on someone else to do all that shit for me."

For the next hour, Dax peppers me with questions. I'm using the tablet now, as the glasses quickly became overwhelming, but this is the easiest I've been able to communicate with anyone since the bombs went off, and I'm talking to a blind man.

"We're done," he says, finally. "Keep the tablet for now. Any software updates my team makes can be delivered wirelessly. Royce—he's our hardware guy—is working on the scroll rate and battery life for the glasses. Pretty sure he even has a couple of frame styles you can choose from. If you can pull that two-by-four out of your ass, come to Second Sight in three days and maybe we can help you get back part of what you lost."

"I don't know what to say. Or how to thank you. But...y-yeah. I'll be there." Dax nods once, and as soon as he leaves, I pick up my laptop and send Austin one last email.

Austin,

I owe you an apology. I don't know how he found me, but

Dax Holloway knocked on the door of my hotel room a couple of hours after I stormed out of his office. The dude is...intense. Asked me questions for-fucking-ever, then told me to show up at Second Sight in three days without the massive stick up my ass.

I guess I'm going. Not like I have anything better to do.
-Griff

CHAPTER THREE

"Are you sure I can't keep my hair down for this shoot?"

The bright lights make the room ten degrees hotter than it should be, and the silk robe sticks to my back. Marina, the makeup artist for all the *Beauty and Style* photo shoots in New York, rests her hands on my shoulders and leans down so we're at the same level. I meet her gaze in the mirror and chew on my lower lip—something I seem to do more and more these days.

"The photographer requested an up-do, sweetie. And come on. I outdid myself today."

She's not wrong. My golden hair shines, with wisps curling along my cheeks to my collarbones. It's organized chaos—Marina's term—and took her more than two hours.

Beauty and Style—a multi-billion-dollar print and online fashion empire—wanted a sophisticated, fancy, and whimsical look for their spring campaign, and Marina delivered. But when she holds up the mirror so I can examine her work, all I see is the cluster of faded dots where once, my neck bore the tattoo of a crown over a barcode and a series of numbers. The evidence of my sordid past, erased for everyone but me.

I brush my fingers over the skin, shuddering at the uneven texture, the lack of sensation.

The alarm on Marina's phone beeps, and she checks the screen. "Twenty minutes until showtime. How do you feel?"

She knows me. Not the real me. The old me. But I'm closer to her than anyone else in my life. "Like I'm about to come out of my skin. I need a pill."

My lips roll together, pressing and pursing, and I tap my fingers on the arm of the chair over and over again. The unconscious movements are getting worse—a side effect of the meds I take for anxiety and depression—but I can't risk switching up my prescriptions now.

Just another couple of shoots, then a potential trip to Zurich for *Beauty and Style's* Christmas Book press junket. After that, I can relax. Take a week or two at a "spa" that's really a mental health and wellness retreat and fix this.

Tardive dyskinesia.

At least my psychiatrist could diagnose me over a video call. One look at me at my worst, and she leaned forward, her brows drawn together, to ask me how long I'd been like this. Admitting the truth—six months or more—had me bawling to her for half an hour, but at the end of the session, at least we had a plan.

Marina hands me a small, plastic case and a bottle of water with a straw. "Once the lip dye goes on, you *can't* chew it off, okay?"

"I'll try." Fishing out one of the Xanax, I wash it down with the chilled mountain spring water and close my eyes. Marina touches up my cheeks, then starts on my lips.

The second the primer wand touches me, I struggle to stay still. While TD movements are technically involuntary, I can control them for a short time if I pour *all* my focus into the effort.

Ten minutes later, I'm barely holding on. The amount of energy it takes to stop chewing off the lip dye is exhausting.

"You're done. Head to wardrobe," Marina says, smoothing her hands down my arms and giving me a quick squeeze. "You have never looked more stunning, Sloane."

"You're biased," I say, rising and giving her an air kiss—can't mess up the lip dye after all.

"Maybe. But I've been in this business for twenty years. Your exclusive contract with *Beauty and Style?* No one and nothing else could steal me away from *Vogue.*"

I pull her in for a quick, tight hug. We only met because *Beauty and Style* pays her to make me look my best—and help keep me calm—but after working together for five years, Marina is one of my closest friends. Maybe my only friend. She sees me at my worst, and other than Max, she's the only one who knows my eyes aren't ice blue, but brown.

"You know I love you, right?" she asks, her voice whisper quiet in my ear.

I nod, though my insecurities rear up and choke any hope of a reply. Everyone wants a piece of me. Max, the *Beauty and Style* marketing department, fans—whenever I go out all made up, anyway. And with my stellar history of choosing the *wrong* people to trust, I worry, even though I know I shouldn't. Not with her.

Marina doesn't ask for more than I can give—most of the time. I'll chew off this lip dye before we're halfway done with the shoot.

"Four outfit changes today, Sloane," a sweet, matronly woman says as she holds out her hand for my robe.

I don't remember her name, but she's quick and efficient, so less than ten minutes later, I'm zipped, taped, and strapped into a shimmering golden evening gown that plunges deep between my breasts. Every step exposes my waxed, moisturized, and body-painted thigh through one slit or another, and though I hate wearing heels, I have to admit...this get-up makes me feel like royalty.

Gliding through the door to the set, I plaster on a fake smile.

"All right, people," the photographer shouts as he snaps his fingers. "Let's see if we can get Ms. Sanders out of here in under four hours, shall we?"

Everyone leaps into action, and within minutes, I'm in another world. One where fantasies exist, and every little girl can grow up to be a princess.

FOUR HOURS, my ass. It's closer to six by the time I pull on the ultra-soft tunic dress I wore to the shoot—designed not to leave a single mark or crease on my skin—and am safely ensconced in the back of the agency's town car.

Here, I can relax. Darius, my driver whenever I'm in New York, knows how exhausting long shoots are, and though he always asks me how I am, he doesn't *do* small talk.

"Any stops tonight, Ms. Sanders?"

"No, thank you. All I want is some time on the stair master, dinner, and a little peace and quiet." Forcing a smile, I meet his gaze in the rear-view mirror.

"Gotcha. I'll have you back to the St. Regis in half an hour."

Despite my words, the idea of spending the entire night locked in my hotel room or at the gym makes my chest tight. I need to get out. To walk. Breathe fresh air. Blend in among the crowds.

Not more than ten minutes after Darius drops me off, I'm

back on the street. Dark glasses dim the beauty of the city, but the energy that *is* New York makes up for it. Disappearing is easy here. A pair of tight jeans, a soft black sweater, running shoes...I look like any other tourist.

If Max knew I was wandering around alone, he'd pitch a fit. Which is exactly why I escape into the crowds whenever I can.

The first time I came to New York City after Max saved me, I was twenty-three, and though I believed most of the world was a horrible, terrifying place, Times Square awed me. It still does. There's a rhythm to this city. A heartbeat I feel deep in my soul.

Maybe it's because I came from such a small town in Russia. Or because in New York, you can be anyone you want to be. Right now, I'm just an ordinary tourist with my scuffed, broken-in Sketchers, a cheap canvas bag, and a freshly scrubbed face free of all makeup.

This is freedom. As much as I ever have since my life belongs to the Ulstrum Agency. At least for another eight months.

Max slides the contract across the table, and though my eyes are puffy from crying through some of the worst of the withdrawal symptoms, I squint at the text until he starts reading it to me. "In public, you'll always wear your contact lenses, and you won't speak Russian ever again. You'll stick to the agreed upon script about your past, how you got into modeling, the loss of your family, etc."

"Will I be able to call my Mama and sisters?" I ask. "I have not spoken to them since I left Penza."

"Yes. But you'll use an encrypted phone, and you'll make sure you're somewhere no one can overhear you." He reaches for my hands and clasps them firmly until I meet his gaze. "This is serious, Sloane. Giving you a new name, a new identity? It's illegal. I'm risking as much—if not more—than you are. If you have

any doubts about this, tell me now. I'll still help you get clean, and I'll arrange for you to return to Russia in a way you won't get in trouble with the authorities. But if you sign this, if we start with the surgeries and the classes, there's no going back."

Max—and my contract with the Ulstrum Agency—changed my life. I should be happy. When I came to this country, I feared I'd be dead before I turned thirty. My thirty-fifth birthday is in three weeks, and I have enough money in the bank to live a comfortable life after I retire. Even return to Russia to see Mama and my sisters.

Most days, I wouldn't change a thing. But when I'm alone, when the pressure gets to be too much, I wish I could be free. Truly free. To bring Mama and my sisters here to visit, to do more than send them money and call once a month.

But if the world found out that Sloane Sanders used to be a trafficking victim and a heroin addict named Sophiana Lebedev ...I'd be deported immediately and I'd never work again.

Still, sometimes, I miss being just...Sophie.

HOME. The little bungalow not far from the beach in San Diego was my gift to myself after eight years of working my ass off—figuratively and literally—as a model. It was a dump when I bought it, but little by little, I've turned it into the perfect refuge.

Leaves rustle overhead as I fish out my keys. Five days in New York and three in Dallas. My body doesn't know what time it is, just that it needs a cup of chamomile tea and my favorite blanket. Once I have those, I can call Mama.

A pile of mail waits just inside the door, and I scoop it up on the way to my bedroom. Despite my exhaustion, I can't simply drop my garment bag on the chair and forget about it.

When you come from nothing, even the smallest possession is too valuable to carelessly toss aside.

Folding the soft clothing I wear to shoots, I set each piece in the hamper. Everything else is dry clean only and goes into a bag to be picked up tomorrow.

After I brew a small pot of tea and turn on the gas fireplace, I prop my phone on my knee and try to reach Mama on FaceTime.

"*Allo, Sophiana!*" Mama smiles at me, early morning sunlight lending a glow to her face.

"Mama, English, please. And Sloane. Remember?" I say, cringing.

Her brows draw close, and judgement lends an edge to her voice. "You are alone. No one will know."

"Mama, please. I'm tired. It was a long trip, and I have to go buy groceries early tomorrow morning. How are you? Did you get the money I sent last week?"

Her eyes dim, even over the poor video connection. "Yes, *Sloane*. Lana was so excited. She will tell you all about the books she bought."

The tea cup rattles as I set it down. My fingers tremble, and I force my lip from between my teeth. "Mama. That money was to fix the car and get your medicine."

"The car work fine."

"There's no heat! Tell me you at least got your blood pressure medicine."

Mama stands with a groan, and the image on screen shifts wildly until all I can see are her old, worn-out slippers as she shuffles into another room.

"Mama, pick up the phone. Remember what I told you about FaceTime?" The swinging image threatens to make me sick, especially as tired as I am, but she doesn't have far to go to reach the kitchen where she picks up a bottle of pills and shakes them.

"I am not stupid. Or helpless. You send money every month, and all we want is to see you. My Sophiana." Her voice cracks, and she squints at the screen. "Are you saying something? Your lips are moving."

Shit. I'm doing it again. Alternating pursing my lips with pressing them together, chewing on them. It's so bad, I can taste blood.

Focus, Sloane. You can hold it together for the next ten minutes.

But can I?

"No, Mama. I'm sorry. My mouth is dry from the plane, that's all. Is Lana up yet?" My sister won't guilt me as much as Mama does. Since she was only three when I left, she doesn't hate me for never coming home, and loves the gifts from the United States I send every few months. Especially the makeup.

With a sigh, Mama calls for Lana. "You spoil her too much, you know."

"You don't let me do enough. I could move you to St. Petersburg. Pay for an apartment there. Lana could get a job—a real job. Have friends. And you would live like a queen."

Mama snorts. "We will not fight today, and you will not mention this again." Lowering her voice, she pulls the phone closer. "You say *nothing* to Lana."

"I know, Mama. I know." Swiping at my eyes, I dash a tear away seconds before Mama hands the phone to Lana, and her smiling face takes over the screen.

"I got so many books!" Her joy fills my living room from halfway across the globe, and for a few minutes, nothing matters but her.

CHAPTER FOUR

Griff

Sitting at my desk at Langley, I rub my left shoulder. The prosthetic, despite being one of the lightest in the world, weighs me down in ways I can't explain. My identity shouldn't be tied to a hunk of metal and silicone, but when I look in the mirror without it, I don't recognize myself.

Quit lying. You don't recognize yourself with the damn thing either.

Recovery and rehab stole a solid thirty pounds from me, only ten of which supposedly came from my arm. Every day, I push myself harder in the gym, and every night, I fall into bed exhausted, sore, and frustrated as hell.

In my periphery, three other information officers enter the room, their voices nothing but unintelligible, soft background noise. I only spare them a quick glance. Last time I did a stint behind a desk, I considered them friends. Now?

Mason: "Thank God we don't have to waste our time scan-

ning all those intel reports from Moldova anymore. Never thought I'd be happy to have a grunt in our midst."

Terry: "I can't believe Hargrove hasn't quit already. This is shit work."

Oliver: "Cut the guy some slack. He lost everything."

The text scrolling across the lenses is a blessing most days. Dax Holloway and the developers at his company, Second Sight, *gave* me the glasses without asking for anything in return. The software recognizes different voices, and my phone lets me assign each one a name. I can even tell the program to ignore certain voices completely.

Unfortunately, now I know exactly what the other officers think of me. I'd chuck the frames across the room, but Dax and his team have done so much for me, the guilt would eat me alive. Not to mention, Dax would kick my ass.

Tapping on the right temple, I send the text scrolling off the lenses so I can focus on the intel reports my senior SSO sent over this morning. I'm lucky. Unbelievably so. Most guys with my injuries would be out on their asses. But *someone* vouched for me—not that I know who—and Ollie gave me a six-month probationary assignment analyzing field reports. It's shit work, and he knows it, but putting a guy out in the field who can't hear anything but the deepest, loudest sounds and isn't weapons certifiable?

No one at the CIA's that dumb.

Except maybe Terry.

My phone flashes next to my keyboard, and I glance at the screen.

SMS: Pritchard

Son of a bitch. Austin remembered how to type.

I enter my unlock code to read the full message.

I'll be in McClean tonight. Dinner?

That's it? Dinner? After almost six fucking months?

Go to hell. Clearly, you're busy with your new life. I'm doing just fine without you.

My finger hovers over the Send button. If I never hear from him again, it'll be too soon. Even if he did convince Dax to set me up with these sweet glasses and got me approved for the best damn prosthetic that isn't even on the market yet.

Fuck. How much of an asshole am I?

Answer? The biggest. Worse than Terry if I keep acting this way. So I delete the message and start over.

Fine. Be at my apartment at 6 pm. You bring the takeout. I have beer and tequila.

He responds with nothing more than a thumbs up emoji, and I swear under my breath. Tonight is going to be a disaster.

MY ARM ACHES by the time I make it home. It usually does, even though the docs say I healed perfectly. A textbook case. Hell, they took enough photos and videos of me—and my arm— to fill a *dozen* textbooks.

The myoelectric prosthesis, liner, and sleeve I wear over what's left of my upper arm aren't *uncomfortable*. But after five months, even though I can use my left hand to operate my computer and mouse—slowly—lift weights, and carry a bag of groceries, there are days I still can't stand the damn thing.

Austin's leaning against the wall next to my door with a pizza box in his hands when I get off the elevator. Tapping the right side of my glasses, I clear my throat. Most days, I don't talk to a lot of people. My idiot coworkers seem to think since I can't hear, I can't speak either.

"Austin." His hazel eyes hold an odd mix of pain and... peace. "Well, come on in. That pizza better not be cold."

Unknown: "I'm not that much of an asshole."

Guess I should program Austin's voice into the speech-to-text software. Assuming this dinner doesn't go south in a hurry.

"Dax told you about the glasses?" I ask, glancing over my shoulder. "Since, in your words, you're 'not that much of an asshole.'"

"Mick and I went to Boston last weekend. He filled me in."

Dropping my keys onto the counter, I turn and stare at the man I almost died for. "Mick? Dax said you'd met someone in Mexico. He didn't say it was a dude."

Austin rolls his eyes, sets the pizza down, and pulls a pen from the inside pocket of his leather jacket to scribble on the box top. *M-i-k-a-y-l-a. Mik.*

Oh. With a sigh, I reach for my phone. "Get the beers out of the fridge. I need a minute to program this damn software. And you better have a picture of Mik."

The corners of Austin's lips twitch into a half smile as he heads to the kitchen. The man's gone and fallen in love. Wasn't sure he had it in him. This should be good. I need some good. Or...at least some normal.

Thank God for the invention of text messaging and swipe keyboards. Programming Austin's voiceprint and the proper spelling of Mik's name would be a lot harder if I weren't already an expert at typing one-handed.

A beer bottle *thunks* down on the table, the sound faint, but enough that I look up when Austin takes his seat across from me.

What the hell do I say to him now?

He looks as uncertain as I feel, and we pull slices from the box, stare at them, and start in on the beer. I can't—or won't—do this conversation watching Austin's words scroll across my lenses, so I take the glasses off, fold them carefully next to me, and lift my gaze.

"You disappeared on me, man. For five fucking months."

"I know." He doesn't look me in the eyes when he continues, "I thought I was helping. Keeping all of my bullshit far away from anyone it could hurt."

"Did you ever think maybe the rest of us had bullshit we were dealing with too?" The pizza tastes like cardboard, but I haven't eaten much today—or any day since the attack, so I down half a piece in two bites while I wait for Austin to get his head out of his ass and say something.

"I wasn't going to be any help to anyone. Not as low as I was."

My right hand curls into a fist, and I slam it down on the table before I realize what I'm doing. "As *low* as you were? I lost my goddamn arm, asshole. Most of my hearing. Want to know how I spend my days now? Chained to a desk while the other officers talk behind my back about how *helpless* I am."

Focusing on the bottle of beer, I raise my left arm and close the fingers around the neck. Austin watches, his shoulders relaxing when I manage a long swig.

"I'm not fucking helpless."

"Never said you were." He runs a hand through his hair, wincing slightly. "I screwed up. Epically. And I'm sorry."

Nodding, I kill the rest of the slice of pizza, then look up to find him staring at me.

"Well?"

"What? If you said something while I wasn't watching you...I missed it. And that's a shitty thing to do." This whole dinner was a mistake. Apology or not, there's too much distance between us.

"It's your turn," he says.

I almost choke on my sip of beer. "My turn?"

"To apologize."

He's serious. Staring right at me with an *I'm the boss and don't you forget it* look.

"Why the hell would I do that?"

Austin pulls out his phone, scrolls for a moment, and slides the device across the table. My last email to him glows on the screen.

I owe you an apology.

Son of a bitch.

"You're seriously going to hassle me about *that?*" Sending the phone back to him with a little more force than necessary, I shake my head. "Fine. I'm sorry I went off on you after you left me to deal with all this shit on my own. Happy now?"

Sadness lingers in his eyes. "I made a fuck-ton of mistakes this past year. Ignored Trevor, Dani, everyone at Second Sight and Hidden Agenda—"

I'm not sure I hear him correctly and hold up my hand while I steal a quick glance at my phone to check the transcript. "Hidden Agenda?"

"Dax has a brother. Well, no. They're not related. But the two of them...they're family. Ryker runs Hidden Agenda, a Kandahar firm out in Seattle," Austin explains.

Kandahar? What the hell? I'm tired of lipreading—it's like trying to make sense of a textbook you're staring at through a window screen—so I don the glasses and realize he's talking about a K&R—kidnap and ransom—firm. Dax's team really did program this software with everything I needed to know.

"Do I rate a spot on that list?" I ask.

"Fuck. Of course you do." Austin pushes to his feet and heads for the sliding glass door leading out to my balcony. "Those glasses have a hell of a range, right?"

"I can still see what you're saying. Go on." If the man needs his space, I'll give it to him. Even though I want to grab him and shake free whatever he's struggling to admit.

"When I came back from Mexico with Mik, I needed help. She almost died down there, Griff." His hands are clenched into fists at his sides, and though I can't hear the anguish in his voice, it's in his body language. The jerky movement of his back as he struggles to keep his breathing measured. "I love her." Turning, he meets my gaze. "She's my everything, and a group of asshole poachers *threw her off a mountain.*"

"Fuck. Austin, I didn't know…" Carefully gathering up both beers, I meet him at the door, and he accepts his bottle, then downs the whole thing in three gulps. The man's in pain, and right now, it doesn't matter that I am too.

"Because I didn't tell you. I didn't tell anyone until I had no choice. Until they blew up her trailer in Mexico, almost killed her grad students, and tried to murder both of us. I called Trev, and he told Dax, and when we got back to Edgewater, Dax gave me one of his guys on 24x7 surveillance. And they *still* came after Mik at the Smithsonian. If she wasn't the smartest woman I've ever met—she would have died with me twenty feet away from her."

His eyes shimmer, like he's barely keeping it together, and I sling my good arm around his shoulders. "We're going to need more beer. And I hope you told Mik you weren't driving home tonight."

The gratitude in his eyes makes me think perhaps, I'm not a total fuck-up. Even if I can't hear, can't shoot, can't do my job the way I used to, I'm alive, and maybe I matter to someone.

A LITTLE AFTER 10:00 p.m., I remove my prosthetic arm and sink into the recliner with Austin across from me. He tries not to stare at the end of my stump poking out from the sleeve of my Polo shirt, but after a few minutes, I lean forward. "My eyes are up here, asshole."

"I didn't mean…fuck."

Holding a straight face for even thirty seconds is damn near impossible, and I burst out laughing. A moment later, Austin joins in, though his expression is strained.

"You can look, man." Tugging my sleeve higher, I flex the remaining muscles. "Cutting edge shit you hooked me up with. I can even *feel* what I'm touching. Kind of. Hot, cold, hard, soft. That sort of thing."

"The Army, Navy, and Air Force all had an...uh...*hand* in the development of that tech," Austin says. "Made sense you should get the first commercially available model."

It takes me a minute to process his words. "The first...? Austin—"

He shrugs. "I couldn't help you through whatever shit you were dealing with. Turning you into the bionic man seemed like the next best thing."

His grin eases the lines of strain around his eyes. This might be the first time I've ever seen the guy truly relaxed.

Who am I kidding? Even relaxed, he hasn't taken off his shoes or loosened the top button on his Henley. "You do realize you're a civilian now, right?" I ask. "Has your back even touched the couch?"

"Once." Austin chuckles and drapes his arm over the rear cushion. "Twice, now. I'm not...good at relaxing."

"No shit. I thought *I* was bad."

"You were." His gaze shifts, focusing on his boots, and I sit up a little straighter. "I heard a little about it."

"From who?" I'm doing my best to sound as angry as I feel, but I have no fucking clue if I'm pulling it off. "You mean to tell me you *checked up on me* but couldn't be bothered to actually *contact* me?"

My bicep aches from the long day, and I head to the kitchen for an ice pack. Fuck. I wish I could drink myself into oblivion, but all that'll get me is a killer hangover and even more problems.

When I turn around, Austin's only inches away, his arm outstretched like he was about to clap me on the shoulder. I don't think. Instinct has me sweeping my leg out to catch him behind the ankles as I jab my right fist into his gut.

He goes down—hard enough I can hear the *thud*—before I realize what I've done. "For fuck's sake, Austin. Don't sneak up on a guy who *can't hear you coming.*"

"Learned...that lesson. Thanks." He coughs a couple of times, and apparently, I can still throw a punch under the right circumstances. "You should have Dax train you how to fight," he says as he grasps my offered hand and lets me pull him to his feet. "That jab has some serious promise."

Any *normal* person would laugh at the idea of a blind man teaching a one-armed mostly deaf man how to fight. But given what I've seen Dax do? He's probably got a couple MMA titles no one knows about.

Beeping.

The software programmed into my glasses doesn't just translate voices. It also alerts me to ambient sounds around me. Like the beeping of Austin's phone. He pulls it out of his pocket, and almost immediately, smiles and taps the screen. "Hey, sweetheart." There's a pause, and then he continues, "Yeah. I'll call a car. You go to bed. I'll be there before midnight. I love you."

"A car?" I ask.

"I was pretty sure this night was going to require alcohol. I have a car service on standby. Mik...she still has nightmares, and..."

"Call 'em. Go home to her. I get it."

All too well. I can go a week or two between my bad nights now, but when they hit? They're not pretty.

"Not yet." He leans against the kitchen wall across from me while I lay the ice pack over the scarred end of my arm. "Of course I checked up on you." At my raised brows, he blows out a breath. "Seriously, man. You had to know when the Johns Hopkins folks reached out."

"I knew you'd arranged things. Didn't know you kept tabs." Is this new bit of information supposed to make me feel better? Or worse?

"You got hurt because of me, Griff. Because of my fuckup with Clarke. Because I didn't overrule the Ambassador and insist we find another route. Because I didn't see that fucking wall about to collapse. So yeah. I checked up on you. Anything that I could do to help I was going to do."

"Except talk to me." The words sting my throat and eyes, and I'm so fucking done with feeling this way. Like I'm a broken tin soldier no one wants around anymore. Rusted and dented and missing some of its parts, but with enough battery life to run for years.

Austin's shoulders heave, and he stares down at me. He's got three inches on me, which wouldn't be much if I didn't feel about a foot tall at the moment. "That's why I came tonight. To try to atone for my mistakes. To let you know I'm back. Not just physically, but truly *back*. And...to offer you a job."

CHAPTER FIVE

Sloane

Just before dawn, when the air is fresh and clean and the city hasn't yet come to life, I slip out my door, pop a single earbud in, and launch my running playlist.

Half a mile later, the beach comes into view, and with the sun peeking over the mountains to the east, the water sparkles, golden ribbons interrupted up by glittering diamonds as the waves break offshore.

Surfers paddle out over the crest, and other runners pass me in both directions as I let the beat carry me through the five-mile loop. My left knee starts to throb a couple of blocks from home, and I shut off the music, cursing under my breath. I should know better. Running when I'm exhausted? That's how I got hurt last year.

"Sloane, you should stick to the elliptical from now on," the physical therapist tells me when I shuffle into his office barely able to put any pressure on my leg. "One more meniscus tear,

and you're talking surgery. Three months minimum recovery time, plus six months of PT."

A torn meniscus in April? Not a problem. May, June, and July shoots are all for winter campaigns. But November? That's when everyone wants you in a bathing suit or another skimpy summer outfit.

By the time I'm back inside, the joint is starting to swell, so I fish a bag of peas from the freezer, limp over to the recliner, and grab my laptop. Thank God for grocery delivery.

I didn't want to go the store anyway. *Beauty and Style's* winter campaign just started, and from now until Christmas, my face will be plastered on every end cap in every makeup aisle.

Hell, I'm on the grocery store's home page. The fake smile, the light in my blue eyes, the perfect skin... If people only knew how many hours it takes for me to look that...natural.

Once I place my order, shower, and mix up a green smoothie, I sink back down in the chair with my sketch pad and try to distract myself from the ache in my knee.

At thirty-five, keeping my body in a shape the modeling world considers *acceptable* takes hours a day. Elliptical, yoga, weights, not to mention the strictest of diets.

"Eight months," I whisper as I start with a simple sketch—all I remember of my childhood home. Four walls, a drafty old fireplace, piles of blankets in the corner...

A little over half a year, and my debt to Max and the Ulstrum Agency will be paid. Then, my life will be mine again. As long as I don't violate the myriad non-disclosure agreements I signed.

The lines on the page blur with each blink, and I rub at the contact lenses. Dammit, I can't take them out until the grocery delivery shows up, but some days, my eyes are so dry, the lenses burn non-stop.

The charcoal lines and curves on the page start to take shape, and with every tear in the wallpaper, each ripple in the worn-out curtains, my past bleeds through. It's been years since I've drawn that dilapidated shack in Penza.

Turning the page, I let my pencil drift across the paper like my hand has a mind of its own. A chipped pedestal sink, patterned linoleum, dents in the wall...and a crinkled candy wrapper poking out from behind the pipes.

Why did my thoughts have to go *there*? To that terrible hotel where so many men used me against my will? Of all the places I could have drawn...why that one? Why now?

I haven't had a Snickers bar since. I should have ordered one with my groceries. Though I'm on a strict regimen of green smoothies, veggies, chicken, and tofu for the next few weeks.

At least until the big press junket in Zurich. *Beauty and Style* throws a ritzy soiree every year when they debut their Christmas Book, and Max thinks I have a good chance of being included.

He's so confident, he's in Zurich now setting things up. *Beauty and Style* picks a dozen models each year for the catalogue and flies them all somewhere extravagant to mingle with their investors and the press.

The last time they chose me? Eight years ago. But Max is so certain, he told me to pack. If the call comes, I'll have to fly to Switzerland on Tuesday. Then, it's nothing but cocktail parties, pressers, and at least one—if not two—runway shows.

Pushing all thoughts of candy from my mind, I take a sip of tea and try to pretend it's hot chocolate. It doesn't work, but I'm not about to arrive in Zurich bloated and breaking out because I got low and deviated from my diet plan.

The dark image crumples as I crush the page in my hand and toss it into the fireplace. Maybe after another cup of chamomile, I'll be able to conjure a happier scene.

The doorbell helps me leave my little pity party behind, and I tip the kid with a face full of freckles and barely there stubble. "Thanks," he says, his voice cracking. If I had to guess, he's all of seventeen.

"Have a nice day...Kevin." His name tag is skewed so badly, I have a hard time reading it, but the smile he gives me? It's worth the struggle. Genuine, pure—the kind of smile you lose once you know how bad a place the world can be.

I pause, the bag balanced on my hip, as I gingerly scoop up the small pile of mail in my entryway. Junk, mostly, but one envelope catches my eye. The handwriting is vaguely familiar, but I can't place it and there's no return address.

After I put the groceries away—the spinach won't last on the counter for even an hour—I limp back to the recliner with a fresh cup of tea and the mystery envelope. Only a dozen people in my life know this address. All my official mail goes to a P.O. Box that one of Max's assistants checks for me once a month.

Tearing the letter open, I shake the contents into my lap, then freeze. The photograph is old. More than fifteen years old. My wide brown eyes, the lids puffy from crying, stare back at me. Frayed, red spaghetti straps hold up a dress that probably belonged to half a dozen girls before me. Fingertip bruises ring my throat.

Memories from that night come flooding back to me. The excitement of getting off the plane in New York City. Nerves as I handed the Customs agent my passport. *"Da. I am here for vacation. Seven days."*

Dimitri waiting for me, all smiles and a big hug. *"You made it, Sophiana! How was the flight? Did you get to watch a movie?"*

"Da! I watched The Fast and the Furious. *The second one too! The flight attendants were so nice."*

"I am glad. Let me carry your purse and your bag for you.

After such a long flight, you should not have to worry about anything."

And I didn't. Until he led me out to a van waiting by the curb. Inside? Six other girls. One from my flight—I remembered seeing her at the back of the plane when I got up to pee—and five others who'd landed an hour earlier. All frightened, some with bruises.

I asked him to explain. He answered with a slap to my face.

My lips press together over and over again, and my stomach protests even the simple smoothie I had after my shower. It takes me three tries to unfold the letter.

Tears fill my eyes the second I start to read.

Hello Sophiana,

No. Wait. It is Sloane now, yes? I see your pictures everywhere. Such a slut. Always selling your body for money. At least when you worked for me, you knew what you were. Now, you pretend to be someone better. Someone different. You will never be anything but the stupid shlyukha who thought coming to America would fix all her problems.

I know it was you who fucked that cop. You ruined my life, and now you owe me. So you will pay. Two thousand dollars every month or I will make sure the only pictures anyone sees of you are the ones I took. You know I have lots. The police never found my private stash.

Because I am a nice guy, you can pay every week. Your first payment of $500 is due on Wednesday, November 3rd. Do not be late, my little Sophiana, or I send a copy of your passport and this photo to Channel 5 News. Tell anyone about our new arrangement, and not only will I ruin your career, but you will never be pretty again.

Dimitri

At the bottom of the letter, he's scrawled bank account information. Along with a handful of Xs and Os.

Nausea crawls its way up from my stomach, and outside a car horn blares. With a yelp, I stumble to the front door, my fingers shaking as I double and triple check the locks, arm the security system, and cycle through the videos from every camera—all six of them—around my home.

The two panes of beveled glass on either side of my front door are no longer pretty. They're dangerous. Dimitri could be watching me right now. Choking back a sob, I head for my linen closet, and even though my heart is beating half out of my chest, I manage to tack up sheets to stop anyone from peering in.

I hate the darkness. Hate not being able to see the sky, the trees, the outdoors. But I close all the blinds, plunging my cheery bungalow into gloom.

Curling up on the couch, I wrap myself in my favorite blanket and stare at the letter, chewing on my lip, clenching and unclenching my fingers, even scrunching my toes to try to release an *ounce* of this terror.

Max. I have to tell Max.

Except, he's in Zurich. Where it's close to midnight. I don't care. He'll know what to do.

My phone slips out of my hands seconds after I pick it up, but I scrub my palms over my yoga pants and try again. As his voicemail greeting ends, I swallow hard.

"It's Sloane. I—there's a problem. From my...uh...past? Please call me back. It's important. I don't care what time it is. Just...call me."

I can't say anything more over the phone. His assistant screens his messages, and she's new. She knows nothing about what Max did for me all those years ago. Getting me fake papers that declare me an American citizen? A new name? A clean Social Security Number? He could go to jail.

I'm not naive enough to think I'm the only one he's helped.

Max has a good heart, but he's also a businessman, and I've made him a lot of money.

If I don't pay Dimitri and he follows through on his threats, *Beauty and Style* will drop me. They put a morality clause in my current contract. Not as strict as some, but I can't take illegal drugs, can't pose nude for any reason, and can't be charged with a crime or I'm in breach.

But that's only part of my problem. Admitting to the world that I lied about my name? That I was once forced to sell my body so men could do disgusting things to me? That I'm in this country illegally?

I'd never work again. Immigration would deport me—if they didn't arrest me and charge me with a crime first—and could I even access the money I've saved? All my accounts are under Sloane Sanders. If the world finds out that isn't who I am, I'll lose all of it, and I'll be penniless. Either in jail or back in Penza with Mama and Lana.

I ache to see them again, but I'd be trapped there for the rest of my life. My two older sisters married men they don't love just to have a roof over their heads. Food. Heat. And Lana? She'll have to do the same unless I can spare her that fate.

Do I even have a choice? Lana deserves a future. A *real* future. And Dimitri's final threat? That I'll never be pretty again? It was one of his favorites when he...*owned* me. He'll cut me. Scar me. If I cause trouble, he'll kill me.

The photo of me from all those years ago? It mocks me from the coffee table. Even though my knee is still tender, I rummage through my bathroom cabinet until I find a canister of hairspray, then kneel in front of the fireplace.

"I'm sorry," I whisper to nineteen-year-old me in the picture. The *hiss* of the spray is almost comforting. Tossing the old photo into the hearth next to the crumpled drawing from earlier in the day, I grab a matchbook and stare at the now shiny picture for several long minutes, the match clutched tightly in my fingers.

The flame sparks to life, almost blinding in the semi-darkness of my curtained living room. The second it touches the picture, the skinny, broken girl disappears—along with the drawing of that dingy bathroom—and I destroy one more sliver of the woman I used to be.

I'll survive this. I have to.

BY 11:00 P.M., I still haven't heard from Max. His assistant sent me a text assuring me he got my message and would be in touch soon, but that only made me more anxious. I've spent all afternoon and evening huddled under a blanket with my phone clutched in my hand. I didn't eat, just had cup after cup of green tea until I was so caffeinated, I could feel my body vibrating.

The crash hit hard, and now I'm struggling to stay awake, staring between my laptop and Dimitri's letter on the coffee table. Why didn't he leave a way to contact him?

Because this way, you can't beg for more time.

Swallowing my sob, I pick up the computer. I don't have a choice. But when I enter my password, the bank's website is down for maintenance.

Der'mo! Shit. Stop it, Sloane. You're not that girl anymore. No Russian!

The maintenance window ends in an hour. I'll be late with the payment, but only a few minutes. Taking the laptop with me, I trudge through the dark of my bungalow, the night light in my bathroom giving the hall and my room a subtle glow as I climb into bed and pull the covers up to my chest. Mama would be so ashamed of me for giving in, and when I can't stop my tears from falling, I bury my face in the pillow and let them come.

I'm so sorry, Mama.

A GUTTURAL SNARL pulls me from the comfort of sleep. My head is wrenched violently to one side as I'm yanked from my bed, then land on the floor with a yelp. Disoriented in the semi-darkness, I flail my arms out in front of me, blinking rapidly.

A dark shadow moves in my periphery. Heavy breathing. Not mine.

Shit!

My heels burn as I dig them into the carpet, trying to put some distance between me and my attacker. Why isn't my alarm going off?

A man's laugh sends ice settling in my belly, but another hard blink, and I can almost make out his silhouette towering over me.

I whimper, "Please—"

His hand flies, striking me hard across the cheek, and the stinging pain brings tears to my eyes. "Shut up. I don't want to hurt you. Not tonight. But I will if you scream." Grabbing my chin, he forces me to look up at him.

My vision wavers from the blow, but his dark eyes—all I can see of his face—hold a frigid glint, devoid of all emotion. He's big. Bigger than Max. And solid.

Pulling a copy of the latest *Beauty and Style* ad from his pocket, he holds it close to my face. "Sloane Sanders in the flesh. You're lucky my orders are just to scare you, hot stuff."

"Wh-what do you w-want?" I whisper, trying to inch back against my nightstand.

"Don't play innocent with me. You read his letter. The instructions were very clear. Five hundred dollars. Before midnight."

"The bank...I couldn't...maintenance," I force out before the man wraps his fingers around my throat and squeezes.

"Not interested in your excuses. Dimitri wants his money and he wants it right fucking now."

Struggling to suck in a breath, I claw and scratch at his arm, but he ignores my feeble attempts to hurt him and tosses me back onto the bed. My laptop bounces, and the motion wakes the machine. Five minutes after two. Oh, God. I fell asleep.

"Don't hurt me," I gasp. "I'll send it. I just need...a minute."

"I'm waiting." He stands over me, his arms loose at his sides, his gaze fixed on me. When I press my finger to the sensor to log in, the first thing that pops up is a half-composed message to Max.

Max,

I need to talk to you in person. This is too sensitive for the phone or email. It's about my past. About the man who trafficked me. Please tell me you have time for us to meet before the Beauty and Style junket.

-Sloane

The man grabs my braid and wrenches my head back with a snarl. "Do you know what will happen if you send that email?" He pulls a knife from his pocket and presses it to my temple. "I'll get to do much more than slap you around a little."

"I—I'll delete it. R-right n-now!" The tip of the knife pierces my skin, and a single drop of blood trails down my cheek to my jaw. "Please!"

He stares into my eyes, and his are so gleeful, so full of anticipation, I know without a doubt he'll kill me if I give him any excuse—but he won't do it quickly.

As soon as he releases his hold on my hair, I rush to delete the email. "See? Done. I won't talk to Max. Or anyone. Tell Dimitri. I promise. I wasn't thinking. I just...I was scared."

Why am I talking so much? Shut up, Sloane! Or you're going to say something that'll get you killed!

"I'll tell him. Whether he believes me or not—well, you'll find out soon enough. Now transfer the money."

Tabbing over to the bank's website, I do my best to hide at least some of my password from the hulking man standing next to my bed. He hasn't put the knife away and twirls it so the tip glints in the low light.

Once I'm logged in, I chance a quick peek up at him. "The letter. It's behind you. I need the account and routing numbers."

He doesn't move, just rattles off the codes, and two minutes later, the money's on its way and my heart is hammering so hard, I'm afraid I'm going to pass out. I can feel each beat in my rapidly swelling cheek. He could kill me right now. I'm still logged in; he could take the eight thousand I have in that account and disappear. But Dimitri would find him. Just like he found me.

"Don't be late next week, or we'll spend *a lot* more time together before I let you touch that computer." Flicking the knife, he cuts through the strap of my tank top. "And I'll get to see what all those surgeries bought you." His fingers dig into my jaw, and he leans in to sniff my hair. "If you tell anyone about me, I'll cut out your tongue before I have my way with you."

And then he lets me go. I'm shaking so badly, I don't trust myself to stand until I hear the front door click shut. Stumbling into the bathroom, I barely make it to the toilet before I vomit. I'm fucked. Dimitri will never let me go.

CHAPTER SIX

Sloane

As the plane starts its descent, I pull out my emergency makeup bag. The yellowing bruise spreads from my cheek all the way up to my right eye, and after a six-hour flight, I need a touch up.

Dotting the concealer wand over the slightly swollen skin, I grit my teeth so I don't wince. There's a bruise twice as big on my hip where my attacker slammed me to the ground, but that one I can explain away.

Oh, I'm just a klutz and fell on a run.

No one will doubt me. Marina will give her standard lecture about how I should be more careful, and then she'll cover it up with the same body paint she uses to hide tattoos. But my face? She can spot a makeup faux pax across a room in dim lighting. There's no way I'll be able to hide this from her.

Why couldn't *Beauty and Style* book me on a flight that *didn't* go through New York City? Because of the time change,

Max told them I'd need an overnight stay in the city before continuing to Zurich with Marina tomorrow evening.

She lives in New York, and when she found out they'd not only selected half a dozen of my photos for their Christmas Book but also gave me the *cover*, she screamed into the phone for a good five minutes.

What the hell am I going to do? I kept the attack a secret from everyone—even Max. The man who hurt me knew how to bypass my security system. What if Dimitri put a camera in my home? I lost all day Thursday searching bookshelves, every nook and cranny I hadn't dusted in way too long—even my nightstand and under my bed. But I found nothing.

Marina's going to notice the damage to my face. Layers of foundation and concealer, styling my hair to drape *just so*—that won't do shit in the face of Marina's trained eye.

With a sigh, I turn away from the window. Flying into New York City always triggers bad memories, and today is no different. I'd close the shade, but the teenage girl next to me—traveling with her mother—points excitedly at the Statue of Liberty.

I was like her when I came here from Russia. I just *knew* my life would be perfect. A fairy tale, even. And then it turned into a nightmare.

"Do you live in the city?" the mother asks. "We're staying in the Theater District, and I have no idea if we'll have time to get dinner before we see *Hamilton* tonight."

"I'm only here for work," I say softly, and the woman's face falls. Regret hunches my shoulders, and I glance down at my phone. Even though I don't live in the city, I've been here enough to answer her. Not everyone I meet is out to get me. I have to remember that. "Unless you can get a bite at the hotel, you won't have time. The drive from the airport takes over an hour this time of day."

"Oh, wow. I had no idea."

"If you can afford it, take a taxi, not one of the airport shuttles. It will cost a little more, but you'll save at least half an hour."

"Mom, I can just have a candy bar," the teen says. "I don't want to be late for the show."

"Emma, you are *not* having candy for dinner." Mom huffs out a breath, then relents. "Granola bar first. Then candy." She turns back to me and flashes me a smile. "She'd eat candy every meal if she could."

"I would have too at her age. Good luck with the traffic." Before the mom can say anything else or draw me deeper into conversation, I lean my head back and close my eyes.

Maybe when I wake up tomorrow morning, the bruise will be gone. But my problems won't fade that quickly. I have to send Dimitri his second payment before we board the plane for Zurich. If I wait until we land, I'll officially be *late* again, and even though I'm not at home for my attacker to break in, I have no doubt Dimitri will find another way to get to me.

* * *

"Over here!" Marina calls, jumping up and down, her black curls bouncing around her heart-shaped face. "Sloane!"

Adjusting my oversized purse to sit higher on my shoulder, I sidestep a large family and wrap my free arm around Marina. "Please tell me you didn't make plans for us tonight."

The look she shoots me is nothing short of pure disbelief. "I would *never*, sweetie. We're going straight to my place, where we'll feast on lean protein and fresh veggies, along with sparkling cider and chamomile tea. But in the morning, we're booked for mani/pedis, massages, and facials at the Equinox. By the time we get on that plane tomorrow night, we're going to be more relaxed than we've ever been."

Shit. Facials. Without makeup. I hope to all that's holy in

this world there's a scheduling mix-up and we won't be in the same room at the same time. But I know better. Marina loves "girl time" and, if I'm honest, so do I. As long as I'm not recovering from a black eye and a bruised hip.

Forcing a smile, I link my arm with hers. "You're the best. Come on. Let's get to baggage claim."

* * *

My makeup skills get me halfway through the evening, but after Marina brings out the fruit plate—and the dark chocolate sauce to drizzle on top—she parks herself next to me on the sofa. Before I reach for a strawberry, she draws in a sharp breath. "Sloane. What happened to your face?"

"Huh?" I ask like I don't know *exactly* what she's talking about.

"Come with me. And don't even think about playing dumb. I know what half a dozen layers of concealer look like." Taking my hand, she leads me into her bathroom and grabs a cotton pad and a bottle of mineral oil.

"Don't. Please?" I shrink back, and my lips press together of their own accord. Great. I'd managed to avoid chewing them most of the day by popping piece after piece of gum, but seeing the confusion and disappointment in Marina's eyes? I can't help myself.

"Sloane, I have to know what I'm working with when we get to Zurich. And I'm worried about you. Ever since we found out about this trip, you've been distracted. Like you're not even happy about it. This is going to make your whole career. The *cover* of the Christmas Book? That's freaking amazeballs. I don't care if you have a massive zit. We can deal with that."

If only it were that easy to explain away. Or cover up. Desperate for a shred of control, I take the round pad from her, soak it in mineral oil, and gingerly swipe at my cheek. Each pass makes me cringe. Not because it hurts. The physical pain is mostly gone. But because once I'm done, I have to make a choice.

Lie to my best and maybe only friend or tell her the truth and risk not only my own life, but hers as well.

"Who hit you?" she demands, hands on her hips as she stares at the bruise. Tears well in my eyes, irritating my contact lenses, and the dam I built around my heart fifteen years ago crumbles into dust.

I don't know how I end up on the floor, but Marina wraps her arms around me and holds me until I stop crying. "Back to the couch with you. I'm going to get us something stronger than sparkling cider for this conversation," she says as she helps me up.

"I can't."

"You're not going to get all puffy from one drink—"

"I'm an addict."

Oh, my God. What did I just do?

I haven't said those words aloud since I left the hospital where I got clean. Even though I never had a problem with alcohol—I've had all of three drinks in my entire life—my counselors told me it would be easy for me to regress if I ever touched the stuff. One addiction can easily lead to another, even if Dimitri was the one who forced the heroin on me in the first place. I didn't want it. Until it made the pain go away. Then I wanted it very much.

"Holy shit. Sloane, what else aren't you telling me?"

Oh, nothing major. My whole life is a lie. I'm being black-mailed by a Russian sex trafficker, I'm not an American citizen, and Sloane isn't my real name.

I shouldn't admit any of my secrets, but dammit. I need a friend now more than ever.

An hour later, she knows my truth. Much of it, anyway.

How I came to this country. How Max saved me. Gave me a new life. A career. Freedom. Of a sort.

"Why didn't you tell Max?" she asks. "He needs to know!"

Sniffling, I tip my head back against the couch cushions and pull the cool washcloth from my eyes. "Because I was all of two hours late with my first payment and Dimitri sent a man to break into my house and hurt me. Max didn't call me for two days. When he did, he was so excited about Zurich, what was I supposed to say? 'Great news about the Christmas Book. By the way, I'm being blackmailed, someone broke into my house and threatened my life, and if I don't pay them, you'll lose your career, your freedom, and probably everything you've ever loved. Oh, and I'll end up deported or murdered or in jail'? Not a conversation we should have over the phone. If at all. What if Dimitri bugged my house?"

"Sloane, he needs to know. You can't keep giving this asshole two thousand dollars every month. You'll be broke in no time." Marina squeezes my hand, sending another few tears burning my eyes until I drape the cool cloth over them once more.

I thank God I can't see her as I clear my throat. "I'll tell him in person. It'll be so much easier to sit down face to face. Somewhere I know we won't be overheard."

"What are you going to do? About the money, I mean?" Marina asks.

"Max knows I want to retire. I only have eight months left on my contract with Ulstrum. That's sixteen thousand dollars. If I take out a loan, I can pay Dimitri with that money and move my savings and investments somewhere they can't be linked to me. Overseas. As soon as I'm not obligated the agency or to Max, I can disappear."

Marina snatches the washcloth from my face. "Disappear? Like, what? Move to Costa Rica?"

Shrugging, I sit up. "I don't know. I haven't thought everything through yet. But I have to convince my mama and sisters to leave Penza so he can't find *them* either. Because he would. To get to me, he'd hurt them. But as long as they agree, it's the best solution..."

"Bullshit. You can't give up your whole life because some piece of garbage sex trafficker has naked photos of you. That's insane. *In-sane.*"

God, I wish it were as simple as Marina thinks it is. "It's not the photos. It's everything else. I'm here illegally. My papers are forged. It doesn't matter that I've been paying taxes for fifteen years, that I've never broken a single law since Max got me into rehab. The government would deport me and take everything. And what about Max? He knew exactly what to do when he saved me. What does that tell you?"

"That he's done the same thing for other women. Shit." Marina drains the last of her sparkling cider and flops down next to me. "Sloane, you trust me, right?"

"You have to ask after what I just told you? If any of that gets out..."

"I know, but this is different," she says, covering my hand with hers. "I know someone who might be able to help."

"No." I sit up and grab her shoulders. "You cannot tell anyone."

"It wouldn't be just *anyone*. My cousin works for a security firm in Boston. They help people in trouble. All kinds of trouble. No police, no government. Let me call Clive and ask him some hypothetical questions. Please. He'll know what to do."

"No. This is *my* life, and *my* decision. You have to let it go." Fresh tears tumble down my cheeks, and I'm so desperate, I'd shake Marina if I thought it would help. But whatever she sees in my eyes must convince her because she sighs.

"Fine. I won't say anything. For now. But...it's an option, okay?"

Wrapping my arms around her, I swallow hard over the lump in my throat. "You're the only person I've ever trusted with this. The only person I ever could. But I can't put anyone else at risk. I'm sorry."

<hr>

Griff

The buzzer affixed to my headboard vibrates insistently. Dax and his team have been an endless source of gadgets to make my life easier. This one syncs with my phone and vibrates the bed frame whenever I get a call or a text in the middle of the night. Since it's barely 6:00 a.m., the text can only be from a handful of people.

Snagging the phone, I blink hard until the screen comes into focus. Yep. Pritchard.

Using yet another piece of software I wouldn't have without Dax, I answer the call, then tap the screen so Austin's words appear as text, but I can still talk to him.

"You do realize what time it is, right?" I ask.

"Can you get to Montgomery County AirPark in two hours?" he asks.

"Are you even awake, man? It's all of fifteen minutes away. Of course I can *get* there. Want to give me a good reason why?"

Pushing to my feet with a groan, I trudge out to the kitchen to start a pot of coffee.

"Got a job for you."

"That's it. Just 'a job'? I told you last week, no one's going to want a bodyguard who can't hear shit and only has one arm."

Nothing appears on screen for several seconds, and I'm

about to ask him if he's still there when he starts to speak again. "You do know how Dax and Evianna met, right? He was *her* bodyguard, and that worked out just fine."

The coffee pot sputters to life, the muffled pops and sizzles as the first drops hit the glass settling me. "Dax had six years before that to learn how to function without his sight. I've had five months."

"You're the best guy for the job, Griff."

I snort. "Bullshit. More like I'm the *only* guy for the job. You decided to start this network two weeks ago. Tell me the truth. I'm the first guy who said 'maybe,' aren't I?"

"The first. Not the only. I could send someone else, but I don't want to. This is deep cover and needs someone with experience thinking on their feet. Someone like you. And it's for a friend of Clive's cousin."

Dammit. He's got me there. Clive is one of Dax's guys, and if I don't say yes, I'd lay odds both Austin *and* Dax will never let me forget it. With a sigh, I pull out a coffee mug. "Fine. But if this goes south..."

"It won't. Pack your passport, anything you need for five days in Switzerland, and your best suit. Everything else...well, you're flying to Boston first to meet with Dax and Clive, then you'll be on the 8:oo p.m. out of Logan to Zurich. I'll help run point from Edgewater. Clive's working on your cover story now, and once you get there, we'll adjust if necessary. "

"Austin?" I stop him before he can go any further, and shit. I may not be able to hear myself talk any more, but I can *feel* the uncertainty in my voice. "Are you sure this isn't a huge mistake?"

There's a pause, and for a few long moments, I steel myself for him to admit it's a terrible idea. "If all I needed was muscle —two good arms, two good ears—I could find that anywhere. This job needs more. It needs your instincts. Your training. I trusted you with my life in Pakistan, Griff, and I wasn't wrong then. I'm not wrong now either."

The words glowing on screen are too much for me to unpack now. Too much to respond to. But they mean more to me than Austin will ever know. So I opt for the simplest reply I can manage. "Okay. Two hours. I'll be there."

CHAPTER SEVEN

"Wake up, sleepy head." Marina leans over the partition between our first-class seats, a wide smile on her face. "We're landing in half an hour!"

I wince as the ice blue contacts stick to the insides of my eyelids. Digging into the little toiletry bag next to me, I blindly fish out a tiny bottle of eye drops. "I hate overnight flights."

"We're in *first class!*" Marina whispers, glancing around like she's not sure we're supposed to be here. In truth, despite all my success modeling, I've never been on a plane this nice. Ever.

As soon as I can *see* the tiny button on the divider between our seats, I tap it, and the narrow bed transforms back into a plush recliner. "It's not fair," I mutter, then turn to thank the flight attendant for the cup of strong tea and hot towel that magically appear in front of me. "You look like you just got out of the spa."

"Because I can sleep anywhere, any time. Seriously, Sloane.

You fly every month. And you never learned how to sleep on a plane?"

"No." I don't tell her that the reason I don't sleep on planes is because every time I'm on one, I remember my very first flight. The one that should have been the start of a new life, not the beginning of my own personal hell.

A sip of tea helps chase away the pounding headache from tossing and turning all night, and I pop one of my anxiety pills to prepare for landing.

Marina squeezes into the seat with me and touches up my makeup so no one will notice my bruise or the bags under my eyes. As she works, I stare out the window and almost stop breathing. It's so beautiful. Lake Zurich—our hotel is right on its shores—shimmers like liquid metal and snow dots the countryside. If I weren't so worried about Dimitri, I'd have my nose pressed to the glass.

"Promise me," Marina says when she finishes with the concealer and powder. "You'll talk to Max first thing."

"I promise. We're free until the cocktail party tonight, so there should be plenty of time. I sent the payment before we took off, so Dimitri will have no reason to worry for another week." Linking our fingers, I give her hand a gentle squeeze. "I can't believe you're not mad at me. For not telling you…"

"I am." She gives me an air kiss, and my stomach ties itself into a knot as she heads back to her own seat. But after she sinks down, she meets my gaze. "If I'd been in your shoes, Sloane, I don't know that I'd have survived at all. I wish you'd trusted me, but I understand why you couldn't."

"I don't deserve a friend like you," I whisper, blinking hard to stop the tears threatening to fall and ruin everything she just did to my face.

"Sure you do. Plus, you're going to get me into all those fancy parties this week—the ones only the models and patrons are allowed to go to. As long as you promise not to keep any more secrets, consider us even."

"I promise."

* * *

The Baur au Lac hotel shines in the mid-afternoon sun. It took almost three hours to get through customs, and by the time we were done, the town car sent for us had left, so we had to wait in a long line for a taxi.

It's well after two, and the first cocktail party begins at seven. I wanted a nap, but I'll have to settle for one of Marina's quick eye treatments and a lot of makeup instead.

"Max!" I call, raising my arm to flag him down from across the opulent lobby. He waves back, the light from the crystal chandelier glinting off his watch. Reception is mobbed, but Max weaves his way among the white and blue velvet sofas, and once he's at my side, guides me to the VIP counter.

"Layla, take care of Sloane for me, will you? She should be in one of the deluxe corner suites—along with Ms. Marsh." He nods toward Marina, who's so excited, she's practically bouncing on the balls of her feet.

"Of course, Mr. Snood." In seconds, our bags are whisked away and two keys—actual keys with heavy golden fobs—are pressed into my hand. "Take the elevator to the top floor. Last suite on the right."

"I'll see you at the Patron's Soiree tonight, Sloane. I have some calls to make now that it's a *reasonable* hour in New York."

"No, wait!" He's five steps away before Marina prods me in the back to free my feet—which feel like they're glued to the fine marble. "I need to talk to you."

"Tonight," he promises. "Meet me at the bar half an hour before the ballroom opens. Then, I'm all yours." He pats my back—an almost fatherly gesture—but before I can protest, his phone rings.

Max is addicted to his phone in ways that are truly unhealthy. There's no way he'll hang up that call for me unless I want to yell my secrets across the lobby.

"Max! Dimitri Volkov is blackmailing me and he'll kill me—and you—if you breathe one word of this to anyone!"

That little stunt would probably get me kicked off the cover—and out of the hotel. Not to mention get both of us killed. The press is everywhere. A dozen different paparazzi have already snapped photos of me and Marina. The hotel, to its credit, is keeping them behind velvet ropes, but they'd hear every word.

Linking my arm with Marina's, I plaster on a smile. "Come on. Let's go up to the room and relax. I'll talk to Max before the party."

The worry in Marina's eyes makes my heart ache, but until I can get Max alone to tell him how well and truly fucked I am, maybe I can have a small bit of fun with my friend.

* * *

"This suite is *huge!*" Marina says once we're safely inside. She's not wrong. My bedroom has its own lavish bathroom with a smaller half-bath off the sitting area. One corner holds a Murphy bed, and two sets of balcony doors offer views of the lake.

We spend the afternoon sitting out on the main patio, wrapped in blankets, with a platter of fresh fruit and a pot of herbal tea between us.

Beauty and Style sent a complete wardrobe for me—separate from the outfits I have to wear for the runway shows—all hanging from a garment rack in the suite's bedroom.

"Thank God tonight's dress isn't skin-tight," I say as I pop another strawberry. "Flying always makes me feel like I gained ten pounds."

"Oh, puh-leeze." Marina rolls her eyes. "You're the size of a pencil. Well, a pencil with perfect B-cups and an ass that's the envy of half the universe. You're going to look fabulous in that dress, and I'm going to be your frumpy older sister."

Flashing her a wicked grin, I take one last strawberry and practically skip into the bedroom. "No. You are not. Come see!"

When she joins me, I'm holding a green, strapless gown in one hand and a pair of wedge heels dangling from the other. "I may have needed something frivolous and fun to take my mind off of...well...everything that's happened the past week."

Marina's mouth forms a little *o*, and she cradles the dress in her arms like it's a newborn baby. "Sloane! You shouldn't have spent all that money—"

"Before you get too excited, it's off the rack and I just had it altered. Your afterparty dress...that one took a little negotiation with *Beauty and Style*. It'll be here on Friday along with a seamstress. There was no way I was going to come here and let you be trapped in the room the whole time I'm out there *mingling*. If I have to suffer, you're going to suffer with me."

"It won't be suffering if I'm wearing *this*." She twirls around, the flared skirt a green blur against the room's mostly white and beige interior. "It's about time to get you ready so you can meet Max before the party," she says with a pointed glance at the clock. "Hop in the shower and I'll unpack my box of makeup magic."

Griff

Zurich is equal parts big city and ritzy vacation getaway. Rather than rent a car at the airport, I found an eager taxi driver who was thrilled to take three hundred francs to give me a *very* thorough tour of the streets within ten kilometers of the Baur au Lac hotel.

Only takes me ten minutes to get him to understand I can't hear shit but have a speech-to-text program on my phone that works if he doesn't talk too quickly. Plus, I promise him another hundred if I don't have to ask him to repeat himself more than a couple times.

"Can you show me the fastest way to get from the hotel to the city center?" I ask after half an hour.

"Is there somewhere specific you want to go?" He looks over at me from the driver's seat, brows drawn together.

Checking the screen, I shake my head. "No. Somewhere crowded. Lots of people." When he doesn't move, I add, "If I'm in a big crowd, it doesn't matter that I can't hear. Because no one else can either."

The best lies have a kernel of truth to them. If I have to get the woman I'm protecting out of harm's way quickly, getting lost in a crowd is the easiest way to do it. But when I'm at my lowest, the dull hum of conversation—even without being able to understand the words—*is* actually comforting.

When it's not terrifying.

Get a grip and pay attention.

The assignment—pretending to be in a relationship with Sloane Sanders so no one questions my constant presence— should be low risk, but that doesn't mean I can walk into that hotel with my thumb up my ass. Even if said thumb is made of titanium.

"There is no fastest way to the Bahnhofstrasse," the driver says.

"Why? It's that far away?"

"No." My new best friend—his taxi license says his name is Elias—pulls the car over to the side of the road. Pointing only a couple hundred meters behind us, he says, "See? The hotel is there."

"Yeah. Kind of hard to miss." While the fancy resort is only four or five stories tall, it shines so brightly, all the other buildings around it are dingy in comparison. The thought is so ridiculous, it almost makes me laugh. All of Zurich—all I've seen today at least—is clean, safe, and orderly. Not surprising for one of the biggest financial centers in the world.

Elias gestures ahead. "The *Bahnhofstrasse* is only two blocks away. Turn right on Barengasse, left on Talaker, and right on St. Peterstrasse. But since the *Bahnhofstrasse* is closed to vehicles, you can walk there faster than you can drive."

"Noted. Thank you for the tour, Elias." Reaching into my jacket pocket, I pull out another hundred francs. Never hurts to make friends in a city where someone wants your protectee dead. "Do you have a card? Can I call you directly if I need assistance again?"

"Yes, of course, Mr. Griffin. You can call any time of day or night. I live twenty minutes away, but I will be there. No problem. To the hotel now?"

I accept Elias's card and shake his hand. "Nah. I'll walk from here. Long flight. Need to stretch my legs."

Slinging my bag over my right shoulder, I give him an awkward wave, and I'm almost surprised when he doesn't stare at my prosthetic hand. Instead, he waves back and speeds away.

CHAPTER EIGHT

Sloane

After an hour of Marina's fussing, I kiss her on the cheek before picking up the small evening bag in the same cobalt blue as my dress. "I'll be in the Lac bar until the party starts," I say, swallowing hard, then pressing my lips together so I don't—yet again—chew off all my lip dye.

She's still working on her hair, pinning the black curls away from her face, and meets my gaze in the mirror. "Are you sure you're going to be okay?"

"Talking to Max? No. But if he doesn't have a plan, he just needs to keep this all quiet and he'll be safe." I hate the tremble in my voice, but no matter how many internal pep talks I give myself, it's been there all afternoon. "Hopefully, everyone staying at the hotel is getting ready for the party and we'll have the bar to ourselves."

Marina arches a brow. "Or they're all pre-funking and it'll be packed."

Only one way to find out.

I grimace and my lower lip finds its way between my teeth until I catch sight of myself in the mirror. "Shit. Not helping. Think empty bar thoughts for me. I'm leaving before I lose my nerve."

She calls my name as my hand touches the door knob. "Sloane? You've got this, sweetie. If you need me to come down earlier, just call the room. No one's going to care if *my* makeup and hair aren't perfect."

Flashing her a tight smile, I nod, even though I have no intention of disrupting a second of her prep time. She deserves to feel like a princess—a hell of a lot more than I do—and she was so happy when she saw her dress for tonight, there's no way I'll take this away from her.

The elevator is just as posh as the rest of the hotel with gleaming mirrors, polished brass and silver everywhere.

The woman staring back at me is full of poise and confidence—to anyone not looking too closely. My fingers tremble as I clutch the evening bag, my nails making soft *ticking* sounds over the beads. A dull ache throbs in my temples from clenching my jaw.

The *ding* as the car slides to an otherwise silent stop makes me flinch, but I plaster a serene smile on my face and step out onto the polished marble. The bar is hidden at the back of the second floor, and thank God, it's almost completely empty. Quiet jazz plays in the background, and Max waits for me in one of the booths, a thin, frosty glass in front of him.

He stands as I approach, his hand going to the small of my back as he leans in to *almost* kiss my cheek. The scent of vodka clings to his breath, and for a split second, I'm not here. I'm somewhere dark and terrifying where everything hurts. Until I hear his voice. "You look stunning."

"Thank you." It's an automatic response, nothing more, and I ease myself carefully into the booth across from him. A uniformed server appears at my elbow almost immediately with an eager smile that fades slightly when I order nothing but spring water.

"I know the schedule's a bit grueling," Max says, "but you can opt out of the luncheons if you'd like."

"That's not why I needed to talk to you." As soon as the server delivers my water, I take a long sip, unable to look Max in the eyes. "There is no easy way to say this—" Across the room, a man ambles into the lounge, six feet of gorgeousness in a black tux, and I stop until he heads for the bar and starts chatting up the pretty blond mixologist.

"Sloane?" Max asks, leaning closer. "No easy way to say what?"

With a slight shake of my head, I force a deep breath, my hands wrapped around my water glass so tightly, my fingers start to ache. "The man who...who..."

Shit. Why is this so hard?

Because you and Max haven't spoken a word about this in fifteen years.

Max reaches across the table to touch my hand, and I jerk away. "Don't!"

My cheeks catch fire, and my gaze darts all around the Lac bar until it collides with the guy in the tux. "*Sorry,*" I mouth to him—not that I expect him to understand from twenty feet away—then turn back to Max. "Dimitri Volkov."

"Who?" Max's brows pinch together, and I don't think I've seen him this confused in years.

My voice drops to a whisper. "The man who...*owned* me. He's out of jail. And he...found me."

"How? What happened?" He's genuinely shocked now, leaning closer, his voice low and raspy.

Tears lend a shimmer to the room, and emotion tightens my

throat. Every time I played out this conversation in my head, Max's first question was always, *"Are you okay?"*

"He sent me a letter. I...I'm the reason he went to prison. Or I helped, at least. And he blames me for losing his...*empire*. If I don't pay him five hundred dollars every week, he'll send all the photos he has of me—" I swallow my sob, "—along with my passport, to the media."

"Fuck." Max pulls out his phone and starts typing furiously. "We have to get a handle on this." Taking the cocktail napkin from under my glass, I dab at the corners of my eyes as Max mutters to himself. "Harvey's taking a long weekend, but it's only 1:00 p.m. in New York..."

With a quick wave of his hand, he calls for the bill. "Once I figure a way out of this mess, I'll tell you what you need to do. Until then, go to the party. Mingle. Do the job *Beauty and Style* hired you for. If I don't have a solution tonight, at least I'll know how much trouble this is going to cause."

He doesn't wait for me to reply, meeting the server halfway to our table and showing his room key before he rushes out of the bar, leaving me all alone and fighting off tears.

How much trouble this is going to cause.

Mingle.

I'll tell you what you need to do.

He didn't even give me a chance to mention the man who broke into my house. Or the money I've already paid. Does he realize what will happen to me if this gets out?

"Breathe. Don't cry. Marina can't fix your face if you lose your shit." My little pep talk doesn't help, and I take a deep, shuddering breath.

"Are you all right?"

I sniffle and blink hard before I look into the deep blue eyes of the man from the bar. He offers me a handkerchief—such an old-fashioned gesture—and when I take it, our fingers brush. "Thank you. I'm...I'll be fine."

He watches me closely while I dry the tears balanced on my lashes. "Are you sure? You don't look fine." My fingers start dancing over my thigh under the table, my fear mixing with a hint of outrage that someone I've never met can judge me like this. Before I can form a reply, he rubs his left shoulder and shakes his head. "That came out wrong. You look perfect. To anyone who didn't see you five minutes ago."

A weak chuckle escapes through my tears. "Nice save."

"Just call me Captain Foot-In-Mouth. Seriously, though. Are you sure you're okay? Need me to go teach that guy some manners?"

"That guy is my manager," I admit. "He means well. I just surprised him with some bad news." After I whisk away one last tear, I fold the handkerchief carefully and hold it out to him. "I can send this to the hotel laundry if you're staying here—"

"This tux came with five of the damn things. Keep it. Just in case." His eyes darken and he takes a step back, his hands in his pockets. "Good intentions don't make up for leaving a woman in tears. You're worth more than that."

As he walks away, still with that slightly uneven gait, I realize I never asked him his name. Because Captain Foot-In-Mouth? That doesn't fit him at all.

***

Griff

What the fuck were you thinking?

I should have introduced myself. Or pretended to ignore

Sloane completely. Right before I walked into the bar, my watch buzzed with an incoming text.

Clive: Sloane doesn't know you're coming.

Griff: What? Don't tell me I flew to Zurich for nothing.

Clive: The threat's real. You read the file on Volkov. But Sloane made Marina promise not to call me until after she talked to her manager.

I'd intended to just keep an eye on her. Clenching my right hand hard enough two of my knuckles crack, I slip behind a pillar and wait for Sloane to emerge from the Lac bar. With how she was dressed, she's clearly on her way to the *Beauty and Style* welcome party, and I'm not letting her out of my sight for more than a few minutes until she's safely back in her room.

The room right next to mine.

With the adjoining door she probably hasn't even noticed.

She's going to be fucking pissed when she finds out Clive—with Wren's help—hacked the Baur au Lac's reservation system and bumped another model from the top floor to the smallest room in the entire hotel.

Retrieving my phone, I send Clive another message.

I need everything Wren can find out about Sloane's manager. He seems like a Grade A asshole, but she doesn't see it that way.

Wren—Second Sight's hacker and tech genius—moved out to Seattle with Dax's brother-in-arms, Ryker McCabe, more than a year ago, but since the two men merged their companies, she works almost non-stop. If Austin wants to make this international black ops *thing* he's running work long term, he's going to need to find his own tech resources. Pretty sure Wren's not going to be available this much once she has the baby.

From my position, I have a clear view of Sloane as she exits the bar. The photos Clive and Wren included in my intel packet didn't do her justice. They were mostly professional pics. The ad campaigns she's been a part of, the head shots on file with the Harvey Ulstrum agency, a handful of social media posts.

In person, she's every bit as beautiful, but a thousand percent more...*real*. And hiding a bruise on her cheek. The swelling is subtle—almost gone—but there's a lingering puffiness underneath her right eye that didn't come from her tears.

As she reaches the stairs to the third floor—and the cocktail party, she touches the corner of my handkerchief to her nose once before sliding it into her tiny purse.

Her lips are in almost constant motion, much like they were after Max-hole left her alone in that big booth in the corner of the bar. The fingers of her left hand too. Like an anxious tic. With one foot on the first step, she pauses, gripping the railing tightly and pressing her lips together.

"You can do this. Just like any other shoot."

I don't need my glasses when I'm this close. Sloane speaks with a precision I assume comes from learning English as a second language—and hiding that fact from the entire world.

Clive's cousin better tell her about me soon because she's spooked, and the longer I watch her, the stronger my need is to protect her.

Sloane

By the time I reach the Pavilion, my jaw is locked tight, my lips pulled firmly into a smile, and my breathing steady. Everything will be fine. Max has been protecting me for fifteen years. He won't stop now.

Then why didn't he listen?

Because the Ulstrum Agency has three other models here

and Max has been campaigning to get you on this cover for years. You're being ridiculous. He's busy and you surprised him. He'll fix it. Fix everything. Just like he always does.

If only the emotional side of my brain listened to the rational side more often. Or...ever.

The tuxedoed attendant stands up a little straighter when I approach. "Ms. Sanders! Welcome! Do you have a coat to check? Or your bag?"

"No, thank you. Is there a powder room inside or...?"

"Oh, yes. All the way to the back on the right. Enjoy the evening, Ms. Sanders."

"Sloane, please." I flash him a practiced smile, and he steps aside so I can enter the brightly lit space.

Through the windows lining every wall, garden lights twin-kle, and the white tulle-wrapped tables, the sparkling chande-liers, and the music lend an air of magic to the night. Maybe it'll be enough for me to forget my problems—at least for a few hours.

At the moment, all I want is five minutes to check my makeup and tell Marina to get down here so I don't have to socialize alone.

Even the bathrooms are over the top. Taking a seat on what looks like a literal *fainting couch* from the 18th century, I flick open my evening bag and retrieve a small tube of concealer and the pocket square from the handsome man at the bar.

In the fifteen years since Max saved me, I've had exactly zero romantic relationships. Real ones, anyway. When you have to hide everything about who you are, it's damn hard to trust anyone enough to get close to them.

Shit. The mirror behind the couch reveals a hint of the yellowing bruise just under my right eye. Carefully dabbing at the exposed skin, I do my best to cover the damage, then pull out my phone to text Marina.

Get down here! The party's started and I'm hiding in the bathroom.

After a minute, Marina's response pops up.

On my way, sweetie. I hope I don't break my neck in these heels.

As if. Marina's been in this business longer than I have, and though she's almost always behind the scenes, her stint at *Vogue* required her to schmooze at more than one party.

Taking a couple of deep breaths, I apply a fresh coat of lip dye, tuck everything back in my evening bag and try for another pep talk.

You can do this. Put on a show. Smile, laugh at every joke—good and bad—air kiss everyone. This trip, this cover? They're everything you ever wanted.

At least that's what I keep telling myself.

CHAPTER NINE

Griff

At the doors to the Baur au Lac Pavilion, two guys in tuxes try
—unsuccessfully—*not* to look like bodyguards. "Harry Griffin,"
I say, producing an embossed ticket from my jacket pocket.
"With *Beauty and Style Magazine.*"

One of them looks it over carefully, then checks his tablet.
"Welcome, Mr. Griffin. Coat check is right inside the doors.
Enjoy your evening."

I'd feel better if they'd asked to see my ID, but knowing
there's at least *some* security at this event is reassuring. The
crowd inside the room? That bothers me.

Four ways in and out. The main entrance, two sets of
French doors that lead to a covered patio, and one fire exit.

My glasses are largely useless with the crowd and the
music playing, so I tap the temple to turn the voice-to-text
functionality off. In this mode, it'll alert me if it hears any vari-
ations on my name as well as loud, recognizable sounds like
sirens, alarms, or shots, but I won't be bothered by endless

unintelligible banter that means nothing scrolling across the lenses.

I put the crowd at close to eighty people, and tonight's party is only for the VIPs and investors. Sloane's at the center of the room, surrounded by men in suits and tuxes. A petite, dark-haired woman stands at her side, and though I can't see the other woman's face, I think that's Clive's cousin, Marina.

Max is nowhere to be found, and I check my watch, hoping for a message from Clive.

Calm down, idiot. It's been all of ten minutes. Wren's amazing, but she's not a machine.

Staff circulate with plates of appetizers, and after I snag a small cheese-stuffed pastry on a toothpick, I weave through the crowd to reach one of the four bars in the room. "Club soda and lime," I say, hating that I have to take my eyes off of Sloane to hear the bartender's reply.

"Coming right up, sir. We also have a selection of mocktails for the evening if you'd care to peruse the menu."

"Maybe later."

The man's eyes widen at the overly generous tip I drop into the silver carafe on the corner of the bar. "Thank you, sir. If there's anything else I can do for you, please don't hesitate to ask."

"Much obliged." After raising the rocks glass in a quick air toast to him, I retreat to the side of the room, close to a long row of floor-to-ceiling windows. A post wrapped in fancy silver netting stands between me and Sloane, but it's narrow enough I can keep an eye on her without her noticing my stare.

If I still had my hearing, I'd have asked Dax for a parabolic mic—or gotten here early enough to bug the room. But as great as his software is, it maxes out at four voices.

Instead, I study body language. While I can't detect subtle changes in a person's voice any longer, the rest of my training—

micro-expressions, fidgeting, sweat and breathing patterns?—those I can still read.

By the time I've polished off the club soda, I've eliminated a third of the room as potential threats. Most are in the industry. They're easy to spot. They put on a show, strutting around like they own the room, but there's no deception beneath the surface.

Others? They're here to gawk. Stare. Ogle. Three different men have been hanging on Sloane's every word for half an hour, and while they seem harmless, she's not comfortable with the attention. If *someone* had told her why I was here, I'd have rescued her by now.

Marina gives Sloane's hand a squeeze, then heads for one of the bars, and I follow, keeping to the fringes of the room.

By the time I come up behind her, she's chatting up the bartender I overtipped. I can't see what she's saying, but his response is easy to read. "One glass of champagne, and one glass of sparkling water." Sparing me a quick glance as he sets the two drinks on the bar, he adds, "Another club soda and lime, sir?"

"Yes, please."

Marina reaches for the drinks, but I stop her by brushing my hand to her upper arm. "Clive sent me."

"Oh, thank God," she says once she turns around and gets a look at me, but her relief quickly turns to panic. "Crap. Sloane doesn't know... ... ... pissed."

"Slow down. I'm mostly deaf, Marina. I read lips. And I'm well aware Sloane doesn't know anything about me." Accepting the club soda from the young man behind the bar, I pop another ten franc bill in his tip jar before leaning closer to him. "Can you pour fresh drinks for this lovely woman when she returns in just a couple of minutes? I need to steal her away, and warm champagne is—"

"A travesty," the bartender says, then smiles. "Of course, sir."

Leading Marina just out of Sloane's eye line, I almost lose half my drink when she slaps my arm. But since she hit my left arm, she's the one flinching. "What the hell?"

Great. I wasn't planning to admit *all* my damage less than two minutes after introducing myself, but there's no way around it now. "Might not want to do that a second time. Titanium's nearly indestructible."

"Wait. Clive sent a deaf man with only *one arm* to protect Sloane? I'm going to murder him. Slowly. Or better yet, tell his mother what he did." The petite woman in front of me looks like she could go full nuclear any moment, and I freeze, torn between intense anger and shame. Until I remember Austin's words.

"If all I needed was muscle—two good arms, two good ears— I could find that anywhere. This job needs more. It needs your instincts. Your training."

"Go ahead. Call Clive. I don't give a shit. His boss and my boss sent me here because I know what the fuck I'm doing." Transferring my drink to my left hand, I take a sip, the fingers steady and smooth—like they always are when I'm angry. "I lost my hearing and my arm. Not my mind. Not my skills. See that guy standing at the windows directly across from us?"

Marina turns her head briefly, then meets my gaze again. "Yes."

"He's former military. Israeli if I had to guess. Loaded. Also, completely uninterested in the female models. The guys on the other hand... He'd like to bang at least two of them. The six-foot-four blond in the white suit and the even taller blond wearing a bowtie who hasn't stopped staring back at him all night."

Marina gapes at me.

"Should I go on? Sloane wants nothing more right now than for you to come back and find a way to get her the hell out of the conversation she's been having with those three assholes for a full—" I check my watch, "—thirty-seven minutes. The guys are harmless—*Beauty and Style* execs. I memorized their photos on the plane. I don't know why Sloane's uncomfortable, but she is. So get those fresh drinks and make excuses for her. She has to mingle, needs to use the powder room. Anything. And figure out how and when you're going to tell her about me so I can stop hiding in the fucking shadows and do my job."

I know I'm being harsh. Too harsh. But Marina knows what Clive and Second Sight do. And while I'd probably be just as concerned if our positions were reversed, I'm the guy who's here, and I'm not leaving until the threat against Sloane is neutralized.

"Meet us at our suite in an hour," Marina says, though she doesn't look me in the eyes. "I'll tell her as soon as we can make our excuses and leave the party."

Nodding, I watch the woman sashay back to the bar, wait for fresh drinks, and return to her friend's side. The relief on Sloane's face is almost immediate, and she links her arm with Marina's before the two make their way to another one of the cocktail tables across the room.

Sloane's tired. Her shoulders hunch inward for a quick moment until the mask of the woman of the hour slides back into place. Then, she laughs at something Marina says, and I start to relax. Time to find another shadowy hiding spot.

Sloane

"I hate this part of the job," I whisper, leaning down so I'm close to Marina's ear. "At least on the runway or during shoots, I get a few breaks from being 'always on.' Here? It's nonstop."

"I know, sweetie. But we can probably get away with leaving in half an hour or so. After all, we flew all night, and they certainly don't want you looking like a zombie for the press tomorrow." Marina smooths a lock of my hair, twirling it around her finger to reset the curl before she scans the room. "Who else do you *need* to talk to?"

"Besides Max?" I check my phone, trying to hide my disappointment that he *still* hasn't texted me. Or shown up here. "Just the *Beauty and Style* photo selection committee. I think I saw the chairwoman head for the patio."

"Then let's get some fresh air and find her." Marina takes a sip of her champagne, then sets the drink down before taking my hand. "Ugh. I remember why I so rarely have champagne. I can feel the headache starting already."

Searching her face, I'm shocked at the weariness in her eyes.

"If you want to go back to the room, I'll be fine alone. You should have eaten more earlier. Just because *I* have to watch my calories all weekend doesn't mean you can't have a little fun."

She clenches her jaw to fight off a yawn but isn't completely successful. "I've got another hour in me. And don't worry. When you're posing for the press tomorrow, I'm going to have the biggest Swiss breakfast womankind has ever seen. That's the plan, at least. Assuming a traditional breakfast here isn't something like blood sausage and haggis."

"Well, that would be Ireland and Scotland, I think, so you should be safe," I say, chuckling. "And I expect you to tell me all about it. Because the morning after the gala? I plan to eat everything in sight."

The crisp, autumn air sends goosebumps racing down my arms, but given how little I've slept in the past twenty-four hours, I'll suffer a little chill to stay awake.

"Sloane! Over here!" Donna Mills, one of the three women responsible for putting my photo on the Christmas Book cover stubs out her cigarette in a nearby ashtray and waves us over to one of the outdoor tables. Radiant heat warms us from above, and string lights woven around the greenery provide a romantic glow to the entire space.

"Donna, you remember Marina?" I step aside so the two women can embrace and set my half-full glass of sparkling water down on the far edge of the table. Within seconds, a uniformed server whisks it away. He's back inside before I can call out to him. It's a good thing I was only carrying it for show. Parties like this where everyone wants a piece of me? If I spend any time without a drink in my hand, someone will take it upon themselves to "fix" the situation. Or try to.

"I need to get some rest before tomorrow's press confer-ence," I say, a hint of contrition to my voice. "Long flight and all. But I couldn't let tonight go by without thanking you—and the rest of the committee—for selecting me as your cover model this year."

We embrace, air kisses all around, and Donna's laugh, despite being raspy from her cigarette, warms me with how very genuine it is. "My dear, Sloane, I have wanted you on our cover every year for the last five. But you know how things are. The politics of this industry. Sometimes...what we want and what we must do are very different things."

Her admission shocks me, though I catch the strong scent of scotch or bourbon on her breath. "That's...so nice of you to say."

"It's the truth. You're more than just your looks, Sloane." Donna reaches out and lightly skims her fingers along my jaw. "You have depth. Wisdom."

Whether she isn't fully aware of what she's saying or my poker face is failing me this late at night, she quickly claps her hand over her mouth, her cheeks darkening in the dim light.

"Oh, my God. I did *not* mean to imply that you look old. Not in the least. You could pass for twenty-five, twenty-seven easily! No. I meant that you're *real*. If we shot you with no makeup, wearing a pair of baggy yoga pants and a bulky sweat-shirt, you'd be every bit as beautiful. It's how you carry your-self. Your presence. *That's* what we want on our cover. That's what *I've* always wanted on our cover."

"Excuse me, Ms. Sanders?" A server appears just behind me, balancing a tray on his arm. "A gentleman sent this over for you."

I hold up my hand and offer the server a smile. "I'm sorry, I don't drink before runway shows. Please thank the gentleman for me, though."

"He was quite insistent." Angling the tray so it's closer to me, he adds, "The bartender had to call up to the Lac Bar for the ingredients. I believe this is called a Kvasya?"

My knees buckle, my heart skipping a beat—or two—and I shove at the tray as the cloying scents of cinnamon and yeast hit my nose. The drink tumbles to the ground, splashing my bare toes.

"Sloane!" Marina wraps her arm around my waist. "What is it?"

"Who...who sent that?" I ask, unable to force the words out much above a whisper.

The server peers through the windows into the ballroom. "He was standing just inside a few moments ago. But I do not see him now. Please, Ms. Sanders, wait right here and I'll return with a towel and some club soda."

"N-no. That's all right." Swallowing hard, I try for a smile, but I'm not sure I succeed since my lips have a mind of their own right now and my fingers are trembling and tapping against one another like I'm playing the piano. "My apologies. I overreacted. I'm tired and I should get up to my room."

Turning to Donna, who looks a bit shell-shocked, I lean in for another two air kisses. "We'll talk more tomorrow, yes?" I ask.

"Of course, dear. Get some rest."

I don't know how I'll be able to now, but I nod and pull Marina with me back into the ballroom. A flash of black tuxedo in the corner of my eye almost stops me. Was that the man from the bar? The one whose handkerchief I'm now clutching in case my impending tears spill over? But when I turn my head, he's gone.

Griff

Sloane and Marina flee the ballroom like someone lit their shoes on fire, and I start after them until Marina glances behind her and mouths, *"Patio."*

Though I had them in my sights most of the time they were out there, I missed whatever happened to put the fear of God into Sloane. The idea of leaving the two of them alone doesn't sit well, but as indecision freezes me in place, my watch buzzes.

Marina: Going back to our room. Find out who sent the drink.

Well, at least Sloane's friend can keep her cool—when she's not about to rip me a new asshole.

A server is crouched next to one of the tables piling pieces of broken glass onto his tray, and a group of women gather under one of the radiant heaters thirty feet away, smoking and paying no attention to the staff.

"Hey." I crouch down next to the guy, catching the heavy

scent of cinnamon along with something that is vaguely reminiscent of beer. "What happened?"

Without raising his head, the guy's lips start to move, and I tap the temple of my glasses.

"*...of the models was upset that a gentleman inside bought her a drink.*"

"Who?"

"Pardon me, sir?" Now he looks up, confusion pinching his brows.

"Who sent the drink? And what was it? Smells like a can of beer made out with a box of Red Hots."

"Red Hots, sir?"

"Sorry. American cinnamon candy. They're...strong."

"Ah. Here we have Zimtsterne. A cinnamon cookie we make for holidays." After wrinkling his nose, the server swipes a damp rag over the tile, then stands. "The bartender called the drink a Kvasya. I do not see the gentleman who ordered it."

"What did he look like?" As soon as I'm alone, I'll look up the drink name, or—if Marina finally tells Sloane about me—ask her why it made her freak the fuck out, but right now, finding the guy who sent it to her is a hell of a lot more important.

"Shorter than you, sir. Black hair. Wide nose. Brown eyes. He was in a suit that did not fit him well. Ask Bernard. He may know more." Pointing to the same bartender whose palm I greased earlier, he nods at the tray. "I must return this to the kitchen."

He's gone before I can thank him—not that I want him remembering my face—or that I asked so many questions.

Bernard doesn't have much more to offer besides one very telling bit of information. The man who ordered the drink—and told him how to make it—had a distinct Russian accent.

"And he did not tip," Bernard says, his mouth curving into a frown. "I provide my services to events like this every weekend. Most have two types of guests."

"Oh?" This should be interesting.

"Those who remember what it is to work hard for a living and those who prefer to forget."

Offering Bernard a weary smile as I tuck another ten franc note into his tip jar. "And which type am I?"

"You, my friend, are unique. A man used to hard work, but with the means to forget. Or to be forgotten."

"Forgotten, Bernard. Let's go with forgotten."

* * *

Sloane

The elevator ride up to our suite passes in a blur. The disgusting odor of the Kvasya fills the small space, and memories hit me from all sides. Dimitri's fetid breath after he had his third or fourth of the night. How once, when I angered him, he punched me hard enough to break my nose, then threw the drink in my face.

That night, I tried to sleep with toilet paper shoved up my nostrils, but that wasn't enough to dull the sweet, cinnamon stench.

"Sloane? Look at me, sweetie?" Marina cups the back of my neck, and I meet her gaze. "We're safe."

I blink hard and see the cream-colored walls of our suite. Shit. I didn't even realize we'd gotten off the elevator. My toes are sticky, and the brand new shoes *Beauty and Style* sent to go with my dress? They're ruined.

"I have to get out of these clothes." I don't give Marina a chance to say another word before I lock myself in the bathroom. Sinking down onto the edge of the tub, I unbuckle the strappy heels and dump them into the sink before spinning the hot water knob as far as it will go.

I'll have to pay for those. But I don't give a damn. Even if the brand new Louboutins likely retail for over $1000.

The dress is unscathed, thank God, and I reach under my arm to undo the hook and eye catch and lower the zipper. A few rational thoughts start to hammer away at my hysteria, and I shut off the water and open the door to a very worried Marina with her hand raised, ready to knock.

"Don't ask. Please," I whisper. "Just take care of the dress and get me something to change into?"

My best friend folds me into a gentle hug. "No more secrets, remember?"

"Marina—"

"Shhh. You don't need to explain right this minute. But don't think I'm going to be patient for much longer." Helping me out of the dress, she drapes it over her shoulder and arches her brows. "Arms up. You know that bra is a bitch to get out of."

She's not wrong. The strapless number relies on adhesive to hold it in place, and I *hate* peeling it off.

"Ouch! Dammit!" Between the lingering scent of cinnamon syrup in the air and the pain as Marina digs her nails under the edges of the sticky side panels, I struggle not to cry.

"One, two—" Ripping both sides off at the same time is one of Marina's many talents, and she *never* waits until three to do it. "There. All better. Put some aloe vera on those marks before you come out, and I'll order up a fresh tea service."

A velvet and silk bathrobe hangs on the back of the door, and I pull it on, retrieve the shoes from the sink and shove them into the plastic-lined trash can. Ten minutes later, my feet and ankles scrubbed within an inch of bloody, I slather on the aloe vera and tiptoe gingerly into the bedroom.

Instead of my sleep shirt and shorts laid out on the bed, I

find a pair of black yoga pants, a tank top, a soft blue sweater, and socks. I'm too tired to care, so I dress, but before I open the door to the main room, my phone buzzes in my evening bag.

Max: Need to talk to you. Come to Room 422. Alone.

It's about damn time. My lightweight, cushioned Sketchers feel like heaven after hours in heels. I don't bother swapping out my evening bag, just tuck it—complete with the heavy key inside—under my arm and rush into the main room.

Marina pauses, a bone china tea cup in her hand. "Sloane? Where are you going?" The cup rattles as she skirts the beige velvet sofa.

"Max texted. Finally. I have to go to his room so we can figure out what to do next. It's going to be okay, Marina. I promise." Waving the phone at her, I flash a tight smile. "Be back soon."

She calls after me, but the heavy door clicks shut, leaving the silence of the hall to envelop me.

The plush deep purple carpets are like walking on air, and I rush through the empty corridor, around the corner, and to the opposite side of the hotel. If Max *tried*, he couldn't have booked a room farther from mine.

The door to room 422 isn't locked—the swing bar latch flipped backwards to stop it from closing completely. "Max?"

Knocking quietly, I push on the door and peek my head inside. His room is the mirror image of mine. The same over-stuffed sofas, the same thick beige carpet over polished marble floors, the same heavy drapes—though his are drawn shut.

I can't see *anything*. The single lamp next to the desk is on its lowest setting, casting a pale, yellow circle that barely reaches the edge of the dark cherry wood.

"Max? I got your text." Two steps into the room, the door rattles against the slipped latch, and I stifle my yelp. But at least my eyes adjust. He's sitting in a chair in the corner, shadows hiding half his face, head tipped back like he's asleep. But the man has a strong, sharp nose, and I'd recognize it anywhere.

"This is ridiculous. Are you pretending to be *The Godfather* or something? After what I told you earlier? It's not funny. I'm turning on the lights."

Brushing the switch next to the door, I turn back to him.

He's not asleep. My purse hits the floor. I want to scream, but no sound comes out.

Crimson spills from a rough, ragged gash across his throat, soaking the front of his white dress shirt. There's so much. It's everywhere. I can't smell the Kvasya anymore. Only the thick, coppery stench of blood.

Falling to my knees, I cover my mouth as a wail builds in my chest.

No, no, no. Not Max. Not here.

"Sloane! Look at me!" The strong, deep voice carries weight, and I fall onto my ass trying to twist around.

It's the man from the bar. The one who was so nice. The one whose handkerchief is still tucked in my purse. Was he following me? Following Max? Oh, God. He could be the one who...shit. I have to get out of here.

My fingers curl around the strap of my evening bag, and I stagger to my feet. I have to get out of here. But he's between me and the door.

Think, Sloane. Distract him. Do something.

"Who are you?" I ask, adjusting my grip on my bag. It's heavy—the Baur au Lac's room key enough to do some serious damage.

"There's time for that later. Right now, you need to listen to me—"

I swing the purse with all my strength, and it collides with the man's jaw.

"Fuck," he groans, cupping his cheek and staggering a few steps to the right.

I take off at a run, the purple carpet nothing but a blur as I spring down the corridor toward my room.

Get inside. Just get inside and call the police.

The room key falls from my hand, and I scoop it up and slam it into the lock. With a quick twist, the door opens, and Marina's there, catching me so I don't fall. "Lock it. Now. Please," I beg.

Marina shuts the door firmly but doesn't flip the deadbolt. "Sloane—"

"Now! Max... Max is...shit. Call your cousin. I need...I need help."

Someone pounds on the suite's door, and I skirt the couch. Like that'll protect me. "Don't let anyone in!"

"Sweetie, look at me." Marina takes me by the shoulders and forces me to meet her gaze as the pounding continues. "That's what I was trying to tell you."

Keeping one hand held up in the universal gesture for *stand still*, she checks the peep hole, then opens the door.

"Stop!" I scream.

The man—the one I ran from only seconds ago—stalks into the room, slams the door, and fixes me with a cold stare. "Did you touch *anything* in that room?"

I jerk back, looking around wildly for anything I can use as a weapon, until Marina wraps her arm around me. "Sloane, I called Clive before we left New York. This is his guy," she says.

What? *This*...this man who followed me, who's glaring at me like he's ready to kill... Her cousin sent him?

She offers me a weak smile. "This is Griff."

CHAPTER ELEVEN

Griff

Wide blue eyes stare up at me, equal parts terrified and livid. After what she saw in that room, I'm amazed she's still standing.

But she hasn't answered my question, and before I do *anything* else, I need to know if her prints are anywhere in that room.

"Did you touch *anything* in your manager's room?" I ask again, using my foot to kick the door shut behind me so I don't have to tear my gaze from Sloane's face.

"What?" She blinks back tears as she stares at Marina, then me.

"Fingerprints. Are your fingerprints anywhere in his room?"

"N-no? I...the door wasn't locked. I pushed on it. The outside. And I turned on the light."

Shit. I'll have to call the guys, but I flipped the latch to rights and set out the *Do Not Disturb* sign, so I should have at least an hour.

"Good." Spotting a tea service on the table, I glance at Marina. "Pour her something and keep her calm. I need to call Clive and then we'll talk."

Sloane wriggles out from under Marina's arm and straightens her shoulders. Her lips are doing that thing again. The nervous pursing and mashing together until she clenches her jaw and the rapid movements transfer to her fingers tapping against her thighs.

"Wait. You knew who I was in the bar, didn't you? I thought I saw you at the cocktail party too. Were you following me?" After a beat, she shakes her head. "You were. You were following me."

Thank fuck she didn't destroy my glasses. She's talking too quickly for me to read her lips, and I suspect she's about to lose her shit all over the place once my presence stops distracting her from the memory of her manager's dead—and very bloody—body.

"Yes, I was following you. That's my job. And yes, I should have introduced myself, but then again, *someone* should have admitted she called me in before the party tonight so I could have been with you the whole damn time."

Sloane sinks down to the floor and covers her face with her hands. Her voice is so muffled, even the glasses can't pick up what she's saying, and Marina rushes over to her.

"Go. Make your call. I'll take care of her," she says, and I close myself in what appears to be Sloane's bedroom. It smells like her. Aloe, along with a hint of coconut and something decidedly tropical.

The space is pristine, except for a velvet and silk bathrobe draped over the end of the bed and several tubes and bottles— lotions and shit, I assume—lined up on the dresser.

Clive answers almost immediately, and his words scroll across the phone screen. "What's wrong?"

"Can you call Austin? Or Dax? Conference them in? Max is dead, and it's fucking obvious someone killed him to send Sloane a message."

"Shit. Yeah. Hang on a second."

While I wait, I check the balcony doors. Locked, but any idiot with a credit card or even a paperclip wouldn't need more than thirty seconds to break in. Pulling a thick rubber band from my pocket, I loop it twice around the door handles. It's not much, but given its strength, it'll at least cause a racket and wake her up if someone tries to break in.

"Got both Austin and Dax on the call," Clive says, his words switching to blue text on the screen.

"Max is dead? How?" Austin asks, the green type an homage to Mik's job as a botanist.

"Someone cut his throat. In his hotel room. I was only in there for a minute, tops. Sloane was the one who found him, and I didn't want to leave her alone. But no obvious signs of struggle or other injuries. Body was posed in a chair facing the door."

Dax—whose words appear in black, cuts in. "You secure the scene?"

"I'm not an idiot. Put out the *Do Not Disturb* sign, made sure the door was closed, and left. Her fingerprints will be on the light switch, but that's it. I'll go back after I've explained things to Sloane, but the way I see it, we've got three options." Taking a deep breath, I stare out over the serene water of Lake Zurich. "At the party tonight, someone tried to rattle Sloane by sending her a distinctively Russian drink. I have a vague description of the asshole, but nothing solid. And Marina told me Max texted Sloane and *asked* her to meet him in his room.

Given the condition of the body, there's no way he sent that message. The killer did."

"Fuck. And the options?" Dax asks.

I tick them off on my finger, "Dangerous, dumb, and risky. Dangerous is sending Sloane back there to *rediscover* the body and call the authorities. Dumb? Taking the sign off the door so housekeeping can find him in the morning. And then there's risky. Cover the whole thing up. But if we do that, and the killer saw me follow Sloane into that room, my cover's blown."

No one speaks for several long moments, until Austin's green text appears. "Wren managed to Photoshop you into a couple of Sloane's existing Instagram posts, and the hotel reservation system has you listed as the second guest on her suite with Marina staying next door. It's not that much of a stretch that her overprotective boyfriend wouldn't want her going to Max's room alone."

Dax adds, "Or that the two of you got distracted and didn't make it there at all."

When I first saw Sloane tonight at the bar, the one-shoulder number in midnight blue hugging her curves, she took my breath away. Finding myself distracted with her for a few hours? That's not my mission. But while I'm damaged goods, I'm not dead.

Clenching my right hand, I relish the pops of my knuckles. Even if I can't hear the sound, I can imagine it, and the sensation helps drive the inappropriate thoughts out of my mind. "It's not out of the question. But that may not be as easy to sell as we'd hoped. She's pretty pissed at me."

"Shit. I told Marina she couldn't keep this from Sloane," Clive says.

"Your cousin has a decent right hook. If she were any taller, she might have done some damage."

The word *laughter* flashes on the screen in Austin's green

text, and damn. There aren't many sounds I miss—at least not more than I miss simply being *able* to hear. But laughter? I blink hard against the burn of emotion rising from my throat to my cheeks to my eyes.

It hits me so hard, I sink down onto the bed, take off my glasses, and mutter, "Need a minute."

I need a hell of a lot more than that, but leaving Sloane and Marina alone for much longer? Not an option.

"Griff? Clive and Dax are on hold. It's just the two of us. You okay?" Austin asks.

"Fuck no, I'm not okay. This was a goddamn mistake, and you know it. Sloane doesn't know about my *limitations* yet, but when Marina found out? That was a shitshow." Shaking my head, I swallow my pride and clear my throat. "I'll keep Sloane safe. You know I will. But for the love of God, send someone else to take over for me tomorrow. Someone with two good arms who can hear more than thunder and semi trucks. Please."

My voice cracks on the final word, another thing I can feel but will never hear again.

"There's no one else to send. I just recruited a former FBI agent out of Texas, but he's recovering from a serious concussion and won't be mission ready for another month. They're doing a major remodel at Clive's mom's care home, and it was stressing her out to the point she was hospitalized. He can't leave her. Ronan's back in Ireland for his brother's wedding. Tank is in Seattle training with Hidden Agenda for a week. Vasquez is on another assignment, and Ella's on vacation. But dammit, Griff. I wouldn't have sent you if I didn't believe you were the best guy for the job."

Fuck. "Do what you can. Okay?"

"I will. Gonna bring the others back on now."

My phone announces the return of the other two guys, and Dax's name flashes on screen first.

"I talked with Clive, and we think the best move is something between risky and dumb. I'll send a cleaning crew in tomorrow morning posing as housekeeping. This shindig is a big fucking deal, and there's no way the hotel—or *Beauty and Style*—would want a murder made public. Wren's going to hack into the manager's email. We can analyze his writing patterns and communicate with the event's organizers so no one misses him. Family emergency, that sort of shit. Your cover story has you working for the Ulstrum Agency as a junior agent—that's how you and Sloane met in the first place—so you can take over any day-to-day management tasks and it'll give you an excuse to be with her 24x7."

They're not going to let me out of this. "Fine. Once I talk to Sloane, I'm going back to Max's room to record the scene."

Dax stops me, "Don't. My guys will take video and send it to you. Wren's scrubbing the security feeds so there's no footage of the two of you coming or going. Cleaner that way."

"Will do."

Call Disconnected.

Shit. I'm on my own. And if I fail? Sloane will pay the price.

Sloane

"Look, I'm sorry I didn't tell you, but if I'd waited until now, the closest help would still be eight hours away," Marina says as she drags me to the cream-colored couch facing the balcony. "Sit. I'm going to turn on the kettle for more hot water. You've had a day."

"You can say that again." My phone buzzes in my pocket, and I pull it out and peer at the screen.

Unknown Number: You were warned, Sophiana. His death is on you.

There's a photo of Max with the text, and there's so much blood, all I see is crimson—and his open, vacant eyes.

Oh, God. A sob sticks in my throat, and Marina takes one look at me, runs to my bedroom door, and starts pounding on it.

I can't form the words to tell her to stop. That man? Griff? He can't fix this, and if he tries, he's going to end up just like Max.

"What?" Griff says sharply. I don't hear Marina's reply, but it doesn't matter, because he's in front of me in only a couple of seconds, holding out his hand. "Phone."

"You know, barking orders isn't the best way to endear yourself to me," I choke out. "Neither is lying."

With a sigh, he sits next to me, takes off his glasses, and gently touches my jaw to get me to look at him. The intensity and pain in his blue eyes shock me. "Sloane, I didn't lie. Exactly. I didn't intend to disturb you at the bar. I was going to keep my distance, but you were upset and," he shrugs, "I couldn't just sit there."

"And at the party?"

"Standard surveillance." Griff rubs his right hand up and down his thigh, his left still tucked in his pocket. "Can I see your phone? Please?"

Tapping in the unlock code, I pass him the device, and he swears under his breath. "Fuck." Forwarding the message to a number in the States—Boston, I think—he adds his own text.

"Find out who sent Sloane this message and put a trace on the number - Griff"

"Who did you just send that to?" I ask, staring at my fingers —which are tapping on my thighs so fast they're practically a blur before looking back up at him—and he shakes his head.

Anger swallows my fear, and I give him a hard stare. "No? You won't tell me?"

Dropping the phone next to me, he sighs, the kind of deep, whole body sigh that hints at a lifetime of weariness. "Sloane, I can't hear. Much, anyway. If I'm not wearing my glasses, you have to look right at me if you expect me to read your lips."

"You're deaf?" I shoot Marina a glance. "Your cousin sent a deaf mercenary to protect me?"

"That's not all," Griff says, an edge to his tone. His shoulders slump unevenly until he grits his teeth and straightens.

"Oh, great. You can't be blind too. So what is it?" I know I'm not being rational. Or sensitive. Or even a halfway decent person. But I'm still too raw, too terrified to be myself.

Griff pulls his left hand from his pocket and rests it on his thigh. His fingers open and close slowly, and I stare until I figure out what's *different*. The words tumble free before I remember to turn to him, but I catch myself and start over.

"You have a prosthetic hand."

"Arm." He knocks on his elbow joint, and it's decidedly *not* flesh and bone. "Mid-humerus amputation. Five months ago. Same time I lost most of my hearing."

The change in his voice from earlier? It's like he's a totally different person. One who expects me to yell or cry or tell him to get his broken self out of my room.

"Sloane?" Marina asks, then clears her throat and jerks her head to indicate I should follow her into my bedroom. "Can I have a minute?"

It's obvious Griff didn't hear her, so I meet his gaze. "Marina wants a minute. Don't...leave?"

He huffs what might be a laugh. "I'm afraid you're stuck with me for at least the next twenty-four hours. Go talk about me. I'm used to it. But do *not* go out on the balcony or open the drapes and stay away from the windows whenever you can."

The idea that someone would try to hurt me *through* the french doors makes me shudder, but I follow Marina into my bedroom. "I don't think you need to shut the door," I offer.

"Oh, he can eavesdrop if he wants," Marina says. "Those glasses? Clive told me they were cutting edge tech."

"Like...they can what? Help him hear? Like a hearing aid?" Curiosity bleeds through the worst of the fear, and I cast a quick glance at the handsome bodyguard sitting on the sofa with his back to me.

He's texting, and mutters something to himself that sounds a little like, "I knew this was a bad idea."

Marina shrugs. "No clue. I didn't ask. I was ready to call Clive's mom and pitch a shit fit when he introduced himself to me at the party, but then he pointed around the room and picked out every single person in the industry, down to being able to tell who was there for the money, who was just interested in banging a model, and which models were into one another." She frowns, her sigh full of regret. "He also told me those three guys from *Beauty and Style's* accounting department were making you uncomfortable. Clive knows his stuff. He wouldn't have sent Griff if he didn't think he was the right man for the job." Marina won't let go of my hands, and now that we're *mostly* alone, her presence calms me enough to stare at the man in the main room.

He's on his feet now, closing every one of the drapes, checking the door twice, and then heading for the far wall, turning a knob on the Murphy bed Marina was going to use, then exposing a panel in the wall next to it.

What the hell is he doing? After he enters a code on a keypad, the bed doesn't pull down like it's supposed to, it *swings* outward. Revealing an adjoining room.

"Hey!" I shout, completely forgetting that he can't hear a word I'm saying. Stalking after him, I touch his arm, and he whirls around, the look on his face one of barely controlled rage.

It takes him a beat to get himself under control before he takes a deep breath. "Ground rules, Sloane. No sneaking up on me. If you need to get my attention and I'm not looking at you, stomp your foot. Clap. Slam a door. Something I can *feel*. Don't grab me from behind. Until my injuries, I was a CIA operations officer, and you don't want to know what I could do if I thought you were a threat. Even now."

Taking a step back, I nod. "Sorry. I'm not used to being around someone who can't hear."

"That makes two of us," he says with a half smile—one that transforms his face completely. *This* is the man from the bar. The one who gave me his handkerchief and tried to make me feel better. "I know it's late. And that picture couldn't have been easy to look at. But we need to talk while everything's still fresh in your mind."

The picture. Of Max's body. Max's dead *body.*

Whatever self-preservation mechanism allowed me to function the past fifteen minutes gives up, and my chest tightens, my breath catching in my throat. "Max...they...shit. I can't..."

Griff wraps an arm around my waist and presses his other hand—the real one based on how warm it is—just above my chest. "Count for me. Backwards from forty-seven."

"Forty-seven?" The odd number surprises me, but he repeats the order, this time with more force behind his words.

"Count. Now."

"F-forty-seven. Forty-s-six. Forty...shit. Forty-five. Forty-four. Forty-three. Wow. No one's ever been able to help me stop a panic attack this quickly before."

"Starting from a random number gives your brain something to focus on," he says quietly. "Take another couple of deep breaths for me."

I do, feeling his palm rise and fall with my chest, and it's so comforting, I don't want him to let me go. But if we're going to talk about everything, I have to take a Xanax or this is going to happen again and again. "I need a pill." Searching for my best friend, I meet her gaze, and she nods.

"On it."

"What do you take? How much, and when?" Griff hasn't released me yet, and I take comfort in his warmth and the solid feel of his body against mine, even if I do think he's being a little intrusive with all the questions.

"That's personal."

"Nothing's personal anymore. Not until we *know* you're safe." He shifts, taking my hand and leading me back to the couch. After I sink down onto the cushions, he snags a silky throw from the back of the sofa and drapes it around my shoulders. "Get comfortable, take your pill, and focus on your breathing. I need my tablet and a couple of ibuprofen, then I'll explain everything."

CHAPTER TWELVE

Griff

My shoulders ache, and my left arm—or what remains of it anyway—feels like I jammed it into a light socket. I'd kill to take my prosthetic off, but Sloane barely trusts me as it is. Seeing me even more damaged? Not happening. Not yet.

With my tablet tucked under my arm, I snag a bottle of water from the ice bucket on the bar. This hotel is the nicest I've *ever* stayed in. Despite what the recruitment brochures claim, the life of an undercover CIA agent is *not* glamorous. We spend more time trapped in dank, dark spaces staring at a computer or video surveillance screen, in hot, sweaty cramped rooms waiting for our informants to show up, and catching a few hours sleep sitting up in a vehicle than we do in swanky hotels—or our own beds.

Pausing at the open door between our two rooms, I study the woman I held in my arms just a few minutes ago. Marina hands her a small plastic case and then pats her shoulder. Meds. But Sloane barely acknowledges her best friend. Shock has set in, and dammit. I shouldn't have left her alone. She was still verbal when I left, and in the five minutes it took me to shed my tuxedo jacket and tie, she shut down.

"What does she take?" I ask Marina.

Clive's cousin leans in, apparently forgetting I don't care how loud her voice is. "Xanax for panic attacks. Zoloft daily. But she needs to eat something."

"Can you order room service? Whatever you think she'd be able to keep down."

"You want anything? I need a piece of cake the size of Manhattan."

My stomach rumbles—or feels like it does—and shit. I haven't eaten since the tiny breakfast plate SwissAir offered before we landed and a single puff pastry at the party. "I'd kill for a club sandwich or a burger. *Anything*, really."

"I'll take care of it. I don't need to...leave or anything, right?" Marina's lips curve into a frown. "I've never seen her like this."

"Emotional overload. And no. Don't leave. She needs you. But from now until this is over, I'm staying here with her. Wren hacked the hotel reservation system so I'm listed as the second guest in this room and you're staying next door."

"What?" Sloane asks.

I programmed her voice into my phone after I talked to her in the bar, and her question appears in red text across the lenses of my glasses.

Skirting the couch, I take a seat next to her and hold her watery gaze. With every blink, a hint of brown appears around her blue irises. "You wear contacts? Your file didn't mention corrective lenses."

She doesn't expect the question and shakes her head. "My file?"

"Sweetheart, I'm CIA. For a little longer anyway. And the

guys I work for? They don't take jobs unless they run a full background check on the client. I memorized just about everything in your file on the flight from Boston. And I know at least part of what's in there is a bald-faced lie."

Sloane jerks back, and if I could kick myself, I would. "I'm sorry. That came out wrong. I'm not accusing *you* of lying. I have a pretty good idea why your file's full of half-truths and fairy tales. But now that I'm here and we've seen how serious this is...I need you to tell me the truth. All of it."

A few tears escape her lower lids, and she swipes them away with my handkerchief. The sight of it, the dark blue stitching all around the edges, gives me a strange warm feeling deep inside.

Nodding at the pill case, I start with a simpler question. "Did you take what you needed?"

She flinches and whips her head around as the word *Knocking* flashes across my glasses.

"Don't answer it," I say sharply, stopping Marina in her tracks.

"But you told me to order room service—"

"I know. Doesn't mean you throw open the door for just anyone." What I wouldn't give for my Sig right now. Dax had a pistol, ammo, a shoulder harness, and various other tools and weapons waiting for me when I checked in, but the gun is a last resort. One-handed shooting isn't half as reliable as the movies and TV make it out to be.

Dipping my right hand into my pocket, I slide my fingers through a set of brass knuckles. My cross is pretty damn effective, but I'll take whatever extra power I can muster.

I can *feel* Sloane and Marina watching me as I check the peephole and close my prosthetic hand around the knob. "Who is it?" I call.

"Room service, Mr. Griffin."

Opening the door, I offer the uniformed bellhop a tight smile. "I've got it from here, thanks." He nods, and I ease the rolling cart into the room before shedding the brass knuckles and pulling a ten franc note from my pocket instead. "For your trouble, mate."

Marina takes over as soon as the door closes, setting a tall glass of thick green liquid in front of Sloane, my club sandwich and fries on the table next to it, and cradling her own plate like it's a slice of heaven rather than simply chocolate cake.

"Sloane, you need to eat," I say when I've double-checked the locks and joined her on the couch again. I didn't think it was possible for her to look any smaller, but somehow, she's managed to wedge her body into a ball in the corner of the sofa. She doesn't react, and I glance over at Marina for help.

"*You* try getting a model to eat when she doesn't want to."

Snagging a french fry, I offer it to her, and she shakes her head. "No salt before a press conference."

Is it my imagination? Or does she look at the fry like it's the *only* thing she wants in this entire world?

I touch her arm so she'll turn toward me. "The first time I saw a dead body out in the field, I puked on my SFO's shoes."

"SFO?" she asks.

"Senior Field Officer. My boss at the CIA. I was a junior officer, working in Afghanistan, and the Taliban killed one of our informants."

"How long were you CIA?" Sloane reaches for the smoothie and takes a single sip. It's a start.

"Almost ten years. Still am, technically. Though, I don't expect I will be for long after this op." A little wrinkle appears between her perfect blond brows, and I rush to explain, hoping she'll relax, at least a little. "This isn't exactly on the books. And what we're about to do? Very *not* legal."

"What are we about to do?"

"Cover up your manager's death. Or at least not report it for a while. Find the asshole who's stalking you. Make sure he never hurts you or anyone else ever again."

She sniffles—I think—and reaches for the small plastic case on the table before withdrawing a single white pill. "These are Xanax. I take one before a lot of my shoots, and whenever I feel a panic attack coming on. The blue ones on the other side are Zoloft, and I take one of those every night at bedtime."

I file that information away, hoping I won't need it, but I hate how defeated she looks. "Sloane, I don't care if you need meds to get you through some of this shit. Or even everyday life. There's no shame in it."

"You don't spend your time with photographers yelling at you and documenting your every move," she says, washing down the pill with a few sips of her smoothie. "And you haven't seen the worst of the side effects." Her lips roll together, she rubs her jaw absently, and her shoulders heave. "Shit. Until now."

"What? The nervous tics? Those are caused by your meds? I thought it was just stress."

"Oh, God. You noticed. When? At the bar?"

"Yeah. And before you went up to the party."

"Tardive dyskinesia." Sloane's fingers dance across her thighs until she shoves her hands under her legs. "I can control it for short periods of time. But stress makes it worse. I need to switch my meds, but I have to titrate down off of Zoloft, and when I do, I'll have vertigo and dizzy spells for a couple of weeks. Not something I can manage while working."

Shit. She's so matter-of-fact, so calm. I thought getting her to talk to me would help, but now, I'm not so sure.

"I don't know shit about your job, Sloane. But how much have you eaten today? Total. Be honest."

"A handful of strawberries. Iced tea. A banana. Coffee. I hate international travel."

"You're not the only one." I toss back half the bottle of water and a couple more fries, Sloane's gaze following my every movement. "You can have whatever you want off my plate. I won't tell anyone."

Sloane smiles, and though it's weak—weary even—the light it brings to her face is something I want to see more of.

But before that can happen, we have to get through the bad stuff first.

"One french fry. It's been months since I let myself have carbs."

SHE ATE THREE. And half the smoothie. No one said a word while we finished the food, and Marina used the suite's electric kettle to make a big pot of chamomile tea. She's perched in an armchair a few feet away, hovering like a mother hen. Her nervous energy isn't doing a damn thing for Sloane's peace of mind, but then again...after what she saw? Would anything?

"I need you to respond to that text message," I say after setting the room service cart back outside the door and returning to the couch.

"What?" Her shoulders hike halfway up to her ears, and she starts chewing on her lip again. "I can't."

Covering her hand with mine, I hold her gaze. "Yes. You can. You have to. Volkov—or whoever he's working with—wouldn't have sent the photo of Max if he'd been certain you'd seen the body. This is good news. It makes it a hell of a lot easier for us to keep Max's death quiet."

She jerks her hand away. "Keep it quiet? Why? He's dead! We have to call the police." A trio of fresh tears tumble from her eyes, and she reaches for the handkerchief again. I should have brought her a fresh one.

"No, we don't," I say with a shake of my head. "The call I made earlier? Clive's boss—Dax—is going to send a couple of cleaners posing as housekeeping to Max's room tomorrow. They'll get me video of the room so we can piece together what happened and when. But their main purpose? To make it look like housekeeping discovered the body in the morning, and the hotel covered it up to avoid any bad press for the event. A place this swanky? They're not going to want the news getting wind of a murder on the premises. I can't imagine *Beauty and Style* would be happy about that either."

"Dimitri knows I told Max about the blackmail. Max texted me. Why wouldn't I go to his room?"

"Because your boyfriend showed up and kept you thoroughly distracted."

Sloane sits up straight, her eyes narrowed. "Boyfriend? What are you talking about?"

"My cover story." With a quick tap to the tablet screen, I bring up the file Austin, Clive, and Wren created for me. "Officially, my name is Harry Griffin—nickname Griff—and I work for the Ulstrum Agency as a junior agent. That's how we met, a little over two months ago." Swiping to the next page, I click the link to her Instagram. "We altered two of the photos you posted over the past couple of weeks to show me in the background."

"Oh my God. How do you even know how to do this stuff?" She pulls out her phone and checks her account, zooming in on the most recent photo Wren swapped out—one of her on the beach in San Diego. Somehow, Austin's graphics guy managed to put me in a t-shirt and board shorts in the background, and even got the details of my prosthetic arm right. It's blurry, but it's most definitely me.

"Austin—my boss—has a kick ass designer on the payroll.

How do you think I got a fake passport, driver's license, and my own social media accounts in less than a day? I should be tagged in that photo of yours."

Hell, I haven't even browsed my own fake Instagram yet, so I peer over Sloane's shoulder while she scrolls through Harry's feed. Pictures from the Ulstrum Agency's New York City office, random dogs at Central Park, latte art, me smiling behind a couple different pairs of Dax's special glasses. And a shot I took from the window of the plane as we were about to touch down in Zurich.

Landing in one of the most beautiful cities in the world, about to meet up with my girl and see her dream come true. #blessed

"Your girl? I'm thirty-four years old. That is not a girl," Sloane says, her shoulders jerking in what I assume is a huff.

Oh, for fuck's sake. This would have gone so much better if she'd been in on the planning from the beginning. But no. Rather than glare at Marina, I take Sloane's hand in a futile attempt to calm her down. "Your brand new boyfriend of less than two months is gushing over you, and in order to keep you safe, he has to be possessive and overprotective."

She stiffens. "I'm in this mess because when I was eighteen, I made one mistake—one huge, awful mistake—and a possessive, evil *mudak* made me do things I never want to speak about again! I put all that behind me after another man took control of my entire life. This isn't the face I was born with. The eyes. The voice. What's in my file? Those lies? They are all I have in this world, and I will not let another man take them away from me!"

Marina gets to her feet, but I wave her off and scoot closer to Sloane, taking her hands in both of mine. I expect her to flinch at the feel of my prosthetic, but she doesn't, tightening her grip on my fingers like she's desperate for an anchor in this storm. What she doesn't know? Her touch is anchoring *me*.

"Listen to me, sweetheart. *No one* is going to take anything away from you. I won't let them. I can't promise you're going to like my plan, and despite how shitty this sounds, I don't care. This cover story is going to keep you safe because it means I'll be by your side until we know the threat's neutralized. And Volkov *will* be neutralized. But if you want, we can have a very public fight tomorrow where you tell me in no uncertain terms to never call you 'my girl' again."

"Promise?" she asks.

"You can even throw a glass of water in my face." I try for a smile, and she stifles a laugh. "Just make sure I take off my glasses first."

CHAPTER THIRTEEN

Sloane

By the time I stagger into the bedroom and close the door, it's after midnight. Griff—whose real name is Griffin Hargrove, not too far off from his cover identity—is hard to read.

He bounces between prickly and almost angry to understanding and caring in ways I desperately need. When he held my hands, I expected his prosthetic to be cold. Hard. But it wasn't. And when I squeezed his fingers, he squeezed back.

He kept rubbing his left shoulder, and I wish I knew him well enough to ask him if he's in pain. What did he say? He was injured less than a year ago? I can't remember. So much of tonight is a blur.

Changing into a t-shirt, I make sure the curtains are drawn before going through my nightly routine. Makeup removal, a steam treatment with a mint tea bag in a bowl of hot water, moisturizer, and finally, a cold water rinse to counteract all my tears and the salt from the french fries before I climb into bed.

The quiet knock makes my heart race, and I struggle to untangle my legs from the sheets. "Just a minute."

As I reach for the knob, Griff calls, "Sloane? I need you to open the door."

"What is it?" I ask when there's nothing but two feet of space between us. And, oh my. No more tuxedo, just a t-shirt that strains across his hard chest and a pair of loose shorts. Gray metal extends from the end of his sleeve to the hinge of his elbow and continues down his forearm to just above his wrist. His hand looks *almost* lifelike, though it's a little lighter than the rest of his skin.

Shit. I'm staring.

Forcing my gaze to meet his, I clear my throat. "Sorry. I didn't mean—"

Griff offers me a brief, wry smile. "You can look. We're supposed to be dating. Pretty sure if that were true, you'd have seen a lot more of me by now." He has all the right words, but his tone? The way he angles his body so the left side is farther away from me? He's uncomfortable with anyone seeing him like this.

"Does it hurt?"

"Sometimes." He shrugs, as if it's no big deal, but at the same time, his lips press together and his eyes crinkle slightly until he sighs. "Yes. It was a long day. Usually I don't wear the prosthetic more than eight hours at a time. I'm coming up on... nineteen at this point."

"Oh. You don't have to...for me." For a moment, neither of us speak, and Griff studies me like he can't figure me out. I rush to fill the awkward silence. "Everyone judges me for how I look. Three years ago, I came down with the flu when I was in Mexico for a swimsuit spread. For two straight days, I could *not* stop throwing up. A photographer caught me accepting a room service tray looking like death. The rumors were awful. 'Has

Sloane Sanders given up? Is she pregnant? Having weight loss surgery?' It was awful."

"No one should have to live like that," he says.

I run nervous fingers through my hair, suddenly realizing I'm only wearing a t-shirt and panties. "It's part of the life. And why I want out. I have eight months left on my contract. After that, I can disappear somewhere Dimitri can never find me. And start eating carbs again."

I try for a smile, but the sound Griff makes is almost a growl. Goosebumps flare along my arms, and the way he looks at me? I feel *seen* like I never have before. "My job is to make sure you don't have to disappear. Ever."

"You don't know Dimitri." I want to look away, but I can't. Not if I expect him to be able to understand me. A fresh tear balances on my lashes, and Griff reaches up and brushes it away.

"The brown suits you," he says quietly.

"What?"

"Your eyes." His hand is still cupping my cheek, and the touch sends sparks all the way down to my toes. "Any time you want to leave the blue behind..."

"I can't. My contract..."

Griff balls his hand into a fist and shoves it into his pocket. "If you want that contract terminated tomorrow, say the word. It's so far outside the mission parameters, it won't be easy, but dammit, Sloane. No one should have to hide who they are from the whole world."

"I do," I whisper and start to close the door. If we continue this conversation any longer, I'll say something I can't take back. Like admitting my real name.

"Wait." He blocks the door with his left arm, the metal making a solid *thunk* against the wood, and holds out his other hand, a small device no bigger than a quarter in his palm.

"Keep this with you at all times. It's linked to my watch, my phone, and a device I put under my pillow at night. If *anything* happens, if someone threatens you or tries to break in or if you're just alone in this room and need me, I can't hear you if you call my name. But if you press this, I'll come for you. Wherever you are."

It's solid and warm, and I run my fingers over the small depression in the center.

"Try it now." Griff's stare is so intense, I shift from foot to foot, but press down on the device. A second later, a subtle buzz comes from his wrist, and he shows me his watch face.

Sloane 911

"Get some sleep," he says. "Marina took the adjoining room, and she has her own panic button. I'll be on the couch."

"The couch? There's a perfectly good bed—"

"Can't use the Murphy bed without making it damn near impossible for me to get to Marina if anyone tries to break in. Just...don't lock this door, okay? I have to be able to get to you."

The idea that someone would break in while I sleep—here, so far from home—makes me shudder, and I glance at the curtained balcony doors.

"Hey." His warm fingers graze my elbow, and then I'm shaking against him, his arms around me. "I won't let anything happen to you, Sloane. I know I'm not...what you expected. The idea of a guy as messed up as I am keeping you safe is... ridiculous. I asked Austin to send someone else, and I still hope he will. But until then..."

"I don't want anyone else." The words escape before I can figure out why I feel this way, and since my chin is resting on his right shoulder, he can't hear me. But it's the truth.

"Get some sleep. We'll talk more in the morning." Griff smooths a hand over my hair, and the gesture is so tender, I can't manage a response until he's heading for the couch, and by then, it's too late.

Griff

I wait until Sloane shuts her door before closing myself in the second bathroom and pulling off my t-shirt. I wasn't thinking when I knocked. Hell, I'm not sure I've had a clear thought since seeing her manager's dead body—and her reaction to it. But I didn't remember the panic buttons until I told Marina to take the bed in the adjoining room. And then realized I couldn't hear either woman if they screamed.

Thank fuck Austin and Dax are used to this sort of shit.

But now that I'm alone, I can let my arm breathe and lessen the strain on my shoulder.

Rolling down the sleeve that runs from just above my elbow to my armpit, I blow out a breath. The cool air feels like heaven, even though I still have the arm and the liner in place.

"You're lucky, Griff. You have enough of your upper arm that you don't need to worry about a harness unless you're plan-ning on carrying heavy loads."

JoAnn's overly perky face flashes behind my eyelids with each blink. Going into an unknown situation, I couldn't be certain what I'd have to deal with, so I snapped the harness into place before I dressed for the party tonight. It's not all that different than the harness I wore for my Sig, except it attaches to my arm socket with industrial-strength snaps.

Suction and friction—along with the sleeve—keep the socket in place, and I tug on the liner to break the seal, then remove the damn thing and set it in its case.

My arm throbs, and I run the water as cold as it'll go before thrusting my residual limb under the faucet. Hissing out a breath as I let the icy flow soothe the aches and pains, I rest my head against the mirror and close my eyes.

Every time I get close to Sloane, there's a spark unlike any I've ever felt before. Does she feel it too? Or am I so desperate for human connection that I'm imagining the whole damn thing?

Jet lag—along with my racing mind—conspire against me when I lie down and try to sleep, so I prop my tablet on my bent knees and review her file yet again.

It's perfect. On paper. Elementary and high school records, a few community college classes, summer jobs at a beauty salon, then waiting tables. But one of the first lessons I learned at the Farm—a CIA training facility for elite undercover agents —is that anything that looks perfect is suspect.

She's so young in the first headshots and the press release the Ulstrum Agency sent out when they signed her. Twenty years old, thin as a rail. Only the barest hint of curves. Her eyes though...those deep blue eyes full of pain give her away.

Bringing up my email, I message the rest of the team back in the States hoping for some word on Dimitri Volkov's location.

Before I even think about putting the tablet away, a chat window pops up.

Wren: Got a couple of minutes?

Griff: Not sleeping. Got all the time in the world.

Wren: Volkov got out of prison six weeks ago. He made every single meeting with his parole officer until last Monday. Then he went dark. But get this—there are no warrants out for his arrest.

Griff: Someone in law enforcement is helping him. Any idea what he's been doing since he got out? Besides disappearing?

Wren: When he was arrested for procurement—that's a

terrible term for what he did, by the way—eight girls entered the system in Philadelphia. Sloane wasn't one of them. Four testified against Volkov in exchange for asylum; the other four were either underage or flat-out refused.

Griff: Not uncommon for trafficking victims. Worked a couple of cases in Afghanistan years ago. The assholes in control convince them if they say a single word, not only will they die, but their families will too.

Wren: Volkov is making good on those threats. One of the girls OD'd on heroin six months after the trial. But the other three? They died in the past month. All home invasions. One in Kansas, one in Spokane, and the last in Orlando.

Shit. This is a hell of a lot bigger than we thought. And Max wasn't this fucker's first kill.

CHAPTER FOURTEEN

I can't breathe. Sirens blare, getting closer every second, but Dimitri has his hands around my throat and he's smiling.

"Goodbye, little whore."

Sitting up with a gasp, I blink hard until the room comes into focus. Until my fingers register the fluffy down comforter clenched in my fists. Grabbing for my phone, I silence the alarm and force slow, deep breaths.

You're okay. It was just a dream.

Except Max is dead, and there's a man in the next room whose entire job is to stop Dimitri from making me his next victim.

It's still early—just after eight—and I don't know if Griff is awake, but I need some caffeine. The coffee pot is in the main room, so I tiptoe to the door and open it just an inch.

Peering at Lake Zurich through a small crack in the drapes, he takes a sip of coffee, and my God. The man really is nothing but muscle. If there's an ounce of fat on him, I'll eat a *pile* of french fries.

His left arm ends a couple of inches above where his elbow should be, and the scars on his shoulder and his waist are a testament to the violence of the attack that stole so much from him.

The rich scent of coffee temporarily distracts me, and I snatch the robe off the end of the bed. I will *not* be making last night's mistake again. No more parading around in just a t-shirt. Well, in front of Griff anyway. God knows what *Beauty and Style* has in store for me on the runway tomorrow.

I don't want to spook him, so I skirt the small table next to the couch, moving slowly to give him a chance to see me.

The second he knows I'm there, he stiffens. "Shit. Sloane." Coffee sloshes onto the marble in front of the balcony doors, and he forces out a breath. "I didn't know you were up. Give me a minute." Shoulders hunched, he sets the cup down and snags his t-shirt from the couch.

"Remember what I said last night?" The words escape before I realize he can't see my lips while he's struggling into the shirt, and I snap my mouth shut until his blue eyes are completely focused on me again. "You don't have to hide, you know."

"Hiding is kind of my thing these days." He shrugs, then nods toward the coffee pot. "Want some?"

"God, yes. But I'll get it."

"I can still pour coffee," he says, an edge to his voice.

"Fine." Rolling my eyes, I perch on the arm of the sofa while he fills one of the bone china cups for me and tops off his own.

"You take anything in it?" He glances over at me, and the intensity of his stare is both comforting and unnerving—he's giving me his full attention like I'm the most important person in his world, even though he's just trying to read my lips.

"Not unless it's the off season." I miss lattes. Hell, I'd kill for a bagel right now. "Black coffee, green tea, fruits and veggies, lean protein, and lots of water."

"That sounds boring as fuck."

It feels good to laugh, and when I accept the cup, his hand lingers on mine for an extra second. "It's easy. And mindless. But yes. Boring…'as fuck.'"

Griff sits stiffly, and I slide down across from him, tuck my legs under me, and turn so I'm facing him, the coffee cupped in my hands like it's the most valuable possession in this world. Which, after last night, it almost is.

"We need to talk about today. The schedule, how we're going to pull this off. What I need you to do to stay safe. How we communicate."

He keeps his tone gentle, like he's trying to ease me in to this whole idea of being in danger. If only he knew the truth. That I've feared for my life every day since I got off the plane in New York City more than fifteen years ago.

But if you tell him, he'll figure out how damaged you are.

"You need to see my lips. I remember. We need to be close for that, yes?"

Griff reaches for an eyeglass case on the table and flips it open. "Yes. But there's another option. Put these on."

"Your glasses?"

I'm confused, but he gives me an encouraging nod. "Now say something. Anything."

"Did you sleep—? Oh, my God." My words scroll across the lenses in a bright red. It's odd—staring at the text so close to my eyes and having Griff's face blur in the background.

"My eyesight is fine. Those glasses can pick up multiple voices at once. Each one gets its own color. They don't work in crowded or loud rooms, but lipreading is sometimes unreliable. Different accents, rapid speech, strong emotions... The glasses don't care."

My words faded in the middle of his explanation, and I frown. "Why didn't it pick up what you said?"

Griff chuckles as I set the glasses back in the case. "Because *I* know what I'm saying. It doesn't need to." Picking up his tablet, he taps the screen. My words appear there too, and he scrolls back to the previous night where everything Marina said appears in orange. "I can program the voices with names and colors, and any unknown voices will be assigned random numbers I can go back and categorize later."

"This is amazing. How far away does the microphone work?" Another sip of coffee, and I feel almost human.

"Thirty feet. Give or take. It depends how loud the person's voice is. The official story is that I wear them to look cool. Not because I need them."

"The official...*story*?" Everything I know about the CIA comes from TV, but that's another one of those pastimes I rarely get to engage in unless I have a long break from shoots.

Griff nods. "My boss and the rest of the team in Boston built a whole cover persona for me. Business major in college, bounced around three different agencies, then took a job with Ulstrum a year ago. That's where we met. You need to memorize as much of the file as you can before the press conference." Setting his cup on the table, he scoots closer to me. "Are you okay with me touching you?"

"What?" No one's ever asked me that question before. Not the doctor who examined me after the police raid, not the plastic surgeon or the counselors at rehab, not Max, Marina, or anyone I've worked with over the past fifteen years.

"We're supposed to be dating. People will expect us to be affectionate." Griff's entire body language screams how uncomfortable he is with this plan, and I wonder. Is he worried about touching me? Or the other way around?

"You don't know anything about modeling, do you?" I hold the coffee cup between us like a shield, hoping it will help him relax.

"Nope. Only how boring your diet is."

I laugh, and we both relax by degrees. "People touch me all the time. The Christmas Book *Beauty and Style* is releasing after tomorrow's runway show? Every one of the outfits I'm wearing in those shots required boob tape, butt tape, or nipple covers. Some of them needed all three."

Griff gapes at me, his cheeks taking on a ruddy tinge. "Oh. Well, that's…"

"Uncomfortable?" I drain the last of my coffee, then pick up his empty cup as well before refilling them both and returning to his side. "Humiliating? Degrading?" My voice cracks, and I'm relieved Griff can't hear it.

Keep it together. Smile. Change the subject. He doesn't need to know how hard it is to have someone pawing at your breasts to get them to spill just so or being stripped of your panties so wardrobe can thread the string of a thong up your ass instead.

"Sloane? Take a deep breath," Griff says, close enough now we're hip to hip. "The most important thing I need you to do over the next few days? Talk to me. Don't shut down like you were about to."

"I wasn't—" The words die in my throat. He saw right through the emotionless mask I slide into place when I'm scared.

"Hiding's my thing, remember?" He lifts his left arm slightly. "I know the signs." With his right hand, he cups my cheek and his thumb skates over the remains of the bruise I didn't even try to cover up this morning.

"You don't know what you're asking me to do." I'm dangerously close to letting my guard down, despite only meeting this man last night. "The file you have on me? The one filled with lies? I have to live those lies every single day. If I don't..."

"What? What's going to happen if you tell me the truth?" He's so earnest. Like he truly believes there are no secrets I could reveal that would send him running as far and as fast as he can.

My phone alarm—blaring from the nightstand—saves me from answering. "I have to start getting ready. Can you send me the file? Everything you want me to memorize? I can read it while I dry my hair." Without waiting for a reply, I hurry into my bedroom, scribble my email address on a piece of the hotel stationery, and turn around, only to find Griff standing just inside the door. "Here."

Defeat weighs on his shoulders as he tucks the note into the pocket of his shorts. "There's still a lot we need to talk about."

"In an hour. We have time. Just...not right now."

With a nod, he backs out of the room and shuts the door with enough extra force, it shatters the small bit of peace I found sitting with him, pretending we were two *normal* people getting to know one another.

This is why I can't get close to anyone. Why Marina is my only friend. Because eventually, no matter how hard I try, my secrets always get in the way.

Griff

Fuck.

Why did I have to push her? Our conversation felt almost *easy* in parts, and then she shut down like a switch.

Rubbing the end of my left arm, I head for the bathroom.

Marina hasn't opened her door yet, but she moved all her stuff from this suite into the adjoining room, so I don't expect her until close to ten—the time she said she needed to start on Sloane's makeup.

This is the fanciest bathroom I've ever seen. Six knobs and three separate shower heads let the hot water hit me from all angles, easing some of the tension in my shoulders. For a brief second, I wonder if Sloane would be open to booking a couples massage at the hotel spa, but then I'd have to take my prosthetic off in front of a stranger. Not to mention, it'd be an hour I wouldn't be able to defend her properly.

The idea of jumping off a massage table, naked, to fight a killer is enough to make me smile and shudder at the same time.

You're already at a disadvantage. Stay focused.

Water sluices down my back, and I brace myself with my right arm against the shower wall. Every time I see the end of my residual limb—or say the *words* residual limb—I wonder how Austin can trust me to protect *anyone*. What the hell am I going to do if someone comes after us? Sure, the prosthetic is the most advanced on the market. But it still has a fuckton of limitations.

I run my hand over my scarred shoulder. I'm lucky to have full sensation—luckier still that Austin had contacts at Johns Hopkins who rerouted my nerves so I can feel whatever I touch with the prosthesis. But no amount of luck will make me whole again. Or free me from this quiet, lonely prison of near deafness.

"You don't have to hide, you know."

God, how I wish that were true.

Dumbass, get over yourself.

Sloane didn't run away when she saw me without my shirt. Didn't look disgusted. Or horrified. Maybe she'll understand.

Maybe she's the only one who can. She has her own past, and it's not a pretty one.

Fuck it. This *relationship* may be all an act, but I can try to let her in. Maybe it won't all blow up in my face.

CHAPTER FIFTEEN

Griff

If I stop to think about this, I'll lose my nerve. As soon as I dry off and pull on a pair of boxer briefs and dark gray slacks, I grab the case for my prosthetic arm and knock on Sloane's bedroom door.

A full three minutes pass before she answers, and I walked away twice, only to turn around and knock again.

"Griff. What...?" She pulls the plush, hotel bathrobe tightly around her, and a thick white cream covers her face.

"We're dating. Remember?" I nod toward my left arm. "You need to know how this all works."

"Let me rinse this mask off. I can't stand the smell of tea tree oil. Plus, if I leave it on too long, my entire face will be red for the next eighteen hours and Marina will kill both of us."

That's it? She doesn't protest, doesn't stare at the ugly scars on my upper arm, just disappears into the bathroom while I set the case on her dresser and pop it open.

I can't read her, and that bothers me more than I want to

admit. One minute, she's running away from me. The next, she's an open book. Or...at least comfortable with *me* being one.

When she returns, her face clean, skin perfect, hair shining in the sunlight streaming through the french doors, I don't know what to say. How to begin. Or why I'm here.

Yes, we're supposed to be dating. But no one's going to ask her how I put my arm on in the morning.

"Our first date was at a Mets game? Really?" she asks. "I don't know anything about baseball."

She read the file.

"You don't have to. I only brought you there because the Ulstrum Agency has a luxury box at Citi Field and I wanted to impress you. It worked, too. Because even though the Mets lost—"

"*I agreed to a second date.*" She smiles, and fuck. The light it brings to her face? It's like she's a different woman. One whose past doesn't define her—or haunt her. "I'm assuming we had the box to ourselves and made out. A lot. Because otherwise, there's no way I'd sit through an entire game."

"We did. Until one of the staff walked in on us. Then you refused to let me do more than hold your hand until the seventh inning stretch."

What am I doing? This is more than assuming a cover identity. Those details weren't in the file. She's flirting—and so am I.

"I got you back on the second date, though." Mischief sparkles in her eyes. "Took you to one of my drawing classes where you had to watch me sketch a very naked, very fit male model for two hours and not say a word."

"That wasn't in the file."

She blushes and closes the distance between us. Her fingers skim the prosthetic, tracing its contours and hard lines before she meets my gaze again. "Because no one knows about those classes. They're just for me."

"Then why did you bring me?" Every little thing I learn about her makes me want more. I'm in too deep, and it's been less than a day.

"I was tired of hiding who I really am." Her sigh is utterly silent to my ears, but I feel it deep in my chest. "You should know…I've never had a normal relationship. Max—" she swallows hard, "—he set me up a few times. Photo ops only. An actor, another model on his way up, one 'everyman' he found at a local improv group." The roll of her eyes and her air quotes tell me exactly what she thought about these fix-ups.

"You can't tell me you *never* dated."

"When your entire life is a lie, you don't get close to people, Griff. It's too dangerous." That sadness is back in her gaze, and I'll do anything to chase it away.

Offering her a wry smile, I hold out my hand. When she drapes her fingers over mine, I guide them to my left shoulder. "I'll make you two promises, Sloane. First? As long as you trust me, I'll keep you safe."

"And second?" Her touch is warm and gentle, and an emotion that might just be hope brightens her expression.

"I won't hide from you. Don't hide from me."

"You don't know what you're asking." Her fingers squeeze my bicep and find the spot where the nerve is mapped to my thumb. It's the weirdest sensation, and it must show on my face, because she freezes. "What did I do?"

"Nothing, sweetheart." I cover her hand with mine, and she relaxes slightly. "I was part of a medical trial at Johns Hopkins. The nerves responsible for sensation in your fingers? They run down the arm. Most of the time when a person loses a limb, the nerves…? They freak the fuck out. The body doesn't understand the hand is gone, and the brain continues to try to send signals through the nerves. You've heard of phantom pain?"

Sloane nods.

"That's where it comes from. But there's a new procedure called Targeted Sensory Reinnervation that deadens the nerves to specific areas of the upper arm, then remaps the finger and hand nerves to those areas. Your index finger? Just touched what feels like my thumb."

"Seriously?"

I chuckle and pick up my prosthesis. "Yep. See the contacts in the socket? They send signals to the different locations on my arm when I use my hand."

"So, last night, I wasn't imagining it. I squeezed your hand, and you squeezed back."

"Because I felt it."

TEN MINUTES LATER, I roll the sleeve from the socket up my arm. "This is enough for most days. The sleeve, the socket, and the liner all work together to keep the prosthetic in place. But if I'm worried about lifting anything heavy or I know it's going to be a long day, I can reduce the strain on my shoulder by using a harness, too."

Sloane helps me with the snaps, and despite this being the weirdest interaction I've ever had with someone I'm protecting, the intimate contact, having her so close her scent invades my nose, and her hands on my skin are the keys to selling this "relationship."

She's relaxed now in a way she wasn't before. Asked all the right questions. Didn't shy away from touching me.

"And taking it off? Is it harder?"

"Just reverse the steps. If my arm swells—heat, overuse, exhaustion—it'll hurt. Or the socket won't want to come free of the liner. But a couple of gentle tugs will do it."

Sloane takes my hand—the artificial one—and lightly touches each finger. "You can feel all of this?"

Fuck. I didn't know how much I missed being touched by someone outside of the medical field. Even JoAnn, who has a wicked sense of humor when she's not mad at me, never touched my hand or arm with anything but clinical precision.

Sloane touches me like I'm real. Like *all* of me is real.

I move each finger in turn, and when she traces a line across my palm, I gently close the hand so I can capture hers.

"I didn't expect...I thought it would be cold." She doesn't pull away, and shit. The urge to do more than hold her hand? I don't know how much longer I can resist it.

"The titanium conducts heat from my arm. It's not magic. Or intentional. Helps me feel a little less like a robot, though." I force a chuckle as I turn away and lock the case, then catch sight of movement in my periphery. Dammit. I should have put on my glasses.

Marina stands in the doorway, her mouth hanging half open. Great. Why didn't I bring a shirt with me?

Because you wanted Sloane to see you.

Hunching my shoulders, I pick up the case, hoping it doesn't *look* like I'm fleeing the room—even though that's exactly what I plan on doing—until Sloane touches my right arm. She's laughing, and suddenly, I don't feel quite as small. "You didn't hear her. Marina just said, 'Hello, muscles.'"

When I turn back around, the raven-haired stylist levels me with a stern gaze. "Do I have to chaperone the two of you?"

"We're dating. Cover story, remember? Let it slip to *someone* today that you walked in on us kissing or half naked and Sloane threw a pillow at you or something. It'll help sell the act."

"Um, sure. Sloane? I need to be downstairs in an hour to

handle the makeup for the other models. I need you ready for me in fifteen minutes, okay?"

She must agree, because Marina grins. "Perfect. We'll do it in the main room. Better light out there."

"Wait." Relinquishing my hold on the case, I take a couple of steps back so both women are more or less within my line of sight. "Marina, anyone at the party last night is going to know you and Sloane are close. When you go *anywhere*, you take your panic button with you. I don't care if you're in the middle of a hundred other people. That button stays hidden somewhere you can get to it."

The color drains from Marina's cheeks, and Sloane brushes past me to take her friend by the shoulders. At the last minute she angles them both so I can see her lips. "Griff's right. If they got to Max, they could get to you, and I can't lose you." Turning back to me, she chews on her lip for a moment, and her anxiety bleeds through her normally serene expression. "I don't suppose you have a brother who could pretend to be *Marina's* fake boyfriend?"

"No. But I can call my boss and see if they can find someone local. Even a rent-a-cop would be better than no protection."

"Please?"

There are moments Sloane looks so vulnerable. So desperate. If I could give her the world, I would. In a heartbeat. Just to see her relaxed and happy again. Because right now? She's wound so tight, one more turn and she'll snap like a guitar string. "I need to call in before we leave for the press conference. We'll get someone."

Sloane's chest heaves as she blows out a breath and drapes her arm around Marina's shoulders. "Until then, you have to be careful. Okay?"

Marina nods, then ducks out of Sloane's grip. Picking up

the case, I head for the door so I can give Sloane space to finish getting ready, but she stops me, her hand flat over my heart. "Stay for a minute?"

"Sure." I don't expect her to close the door, or how intimate it feels to be alone with her after what we just shared. "What do you need?"

Her fingers tremble against my skin, and this close, I can *feel* her breath catch in her throat. "If we're dating, we'll need to kiss. Right?"

"Yeah." Half the blood in my body heads south, and my mouth goes dry. "Why?"

"I haven't kissed anyone in...a long time. I don't want our first kiss to be in public." Her cheeks are on fire now, and she won't meet my gaze. The case hits the floor with a *thud* I can feel through the soles of my feet, and I slide my left arm around her back.

My other hand, the one that's still flesh and bone, tangles in her silky blond hair. If I'm not careful, I'll fall for this woman, and that *cannot* happen. But fuck. She smells like the tropics, and her gentle curves mold to my body in a way I haven't felt in a very long time.

"Is this okay?" I whisper.

Her lips brush mine. Soft. Hesitant. She's about to pull away when I kiss her back. The slight rumble in my chest surprises me, but damn. She tastes like fresh mint, and when I trace the seam of her lips with my tongue, she gasps, opening for me.

If there were an ounce of blood left north of my waist, I'd stop. Let her go. But I can't, and when she figures out how to tangle her tongue with mine, white hot need shoots through me.

I'm hard as a rock in seconds, and though I could kiss this woman for days, I force myself to let her go and pull away.

Her brown eyes are dazed, unfocused, and she grabs my arm to steady herself, keeping me close enough she's going to notice my dick straining against the gray linen any minute now. "You okay, sweetheart?"

"Wow."

"Is that a yes?" Ducking my head slightly so I can meet her gaze, I offer her an encouraging smile. "I know this isn't real, Sloane. But I don't think anyone in the press will suspect a thing. Not if we kiss like that every time."

A flicker of...*something*...ignites in her eyes. Passion, if I'm not mistaken. But why? Does she feel this—whatever this is—between us as strongly as I do?

Her fingers are warm on my prosthetic hand, and she squeezes gently. "I don't think that'll be a problem."

CHAPTER SIXTEEN

Sloane

Alone, I brush my fingers over my tingling lips. Oh, my God. That was so much more than just a kiss. It was my *first* kiss. Something Griff can *never* find out. He wouldn't believe me. And then he'd ask questions. Questions I don't want to answer.

All the men who used me? They did not treat me like a person. I was nothing to them. Sometimes, one would slobber over my neck, but there was no true intimacy. No tenderness.

With Griff, I felt both.

"I know this isn't real, Sloane."

So do I. But that doesn't stop me from wishing it were. He believes he's too damaged, but all I see is a man who survived. Who's stronger than he knows, and more understanding than I deserve.

The rest of my beauty routine passes in a blur. Memories of that kiss—that perfect, all-consuming kiss—distract me, and when I'm done, I have no idea how much serum, moisturizer, or eye cream actually made it onto my face.

At least I'd finished drying my hair before he'd knocked, determination in the set of his jaw and the intensity of his gaze.

Shit. Contacts! I almost forgot them. Popping open the case, I stare down at the blue monstrosities. I hate them. Despise them, even. They're the one material *thing* that represents every sacrifice I made, every bad decision that brought me to this moment.

My vision blurs, and I blink hard until the lenses settle, my memories carrying me back to the moment I signed fifteen years of my life away.

"We have to change as much of you as possible," Max says. "Lighten your hair, give you a new nose, a smaller chin, higher cheekbones. And your eyes. What do you think about blue?"

"I like blue." I'm so out of it. Shaking, my t-shirt and fleece pants drenched with sweat, throwing up every few hours. It's been a week since my last fix. A week since Max checked me into this expensive rehab facility. A week since I feared for my life. But it's also been a week since I've been outside. A week since I made any of my own decisions. A week since I gave up my name. A week of wondering if I did the right thing.

"Stop it," I tell my reflection in the mirror over the marble sink. "You made your choices, and now you have to live with them."

Wishing my life were different? It's no use. So often, I wonder what I'd look like now if I'd turned Max down. Would I still be alive?

Doubtful. Heroin doesn't promise it will grow old with you. It just takes away the pain until it sucks out every ounce of your life that's left.

Would Max still be alive?

Yes. Most definitely.

My eyes start to burn, and I paw through the bag of toiletries until I find my eye drops.

You cannot cry, Sloane. The press will eat you alive if they suspect you're on the edge.

Desperate for a distraction, I lick my lips, tasting Griff. The only question running through my mind now?

Did he enjoy that kiss as much as I did?

Every moment I spend with him, I want more. He hasn't pushed me to tell him everything, even though I think he wants to. He's smart. He's probably figured it all out anyway. But if he's put all the puzzle pieces of my past together, he hasn't let it show. Not once.

The doctors at rehab? They knew. And though they were all nice, I could see the pity in their eyes every time they looked at me.

Finding a pair of luxurious slippers in the closet, I let the cushioned memory foam soles carry me to the main room. Marina pushed the desk in front of the balcony doors, set up her makeup mirror, and spread out her tools—brushes, sponges, tissues, and Q-tips—in precise order. She's tapping her foot, waiting for me.

"I was about ready to come get you," she says, glancing at her phone. "You are *always* my priority sweetie, but I have three other models to take care of for this presser."

"I'm sorry. Really. I had problems with my contact lenses." With a sigh, I perch on the edge of the chair and let Marina snap a hairdresser's drape around my neck, then tuck oil-absorbing tissue paper between the collar and my skin.

Griff, who's sitting on the couch a few feet away, meets my gaze in the mirror. "I'll miss the brown. It suits you."

Before I can reply, Marina dots concealer under my eyes, then picks up a makeup sponge. But a subtle buzzing startles me just as she starts to blot, and I end up with a streak of concealer along my temple. "Stay still," she hisses. "Or this is going to take forever!"

"Austin, I'm going to put you on speaker," Griff says. "Sloane and Marina are in the room with me."

"Won't that make it harder for you—?" I ask.

"The software still picks up everything." He shows me his tablet, where Austin's greeting appears in bright green text. "Don't worry about me, sweetheart."

"Sweetheart?" Marina laughs, blotting away the smear of concealer. "You're really trying to sell it, aren't you?"

Griff shoots her a look I can't read, and over the speaker, Austin clears his throat. "If he doesn't 'sell it,' he's not doing his job and you and Sloane are in a hell of a lot more danger."

"Sorry," Marina says, turning her focus to the various shades of foundation in her kit. "This is just weird for me."

And it's not for me?

As much as I want to snap at Marina, she starts dabbing foundation along my chin—probably on purpose. But I lock eyes with Griff, and there's that understanding again. Along with the promise that everything's going to be okay.

"Where's the video from Max's room?" Griff asks. "You arranged things with housekeeping, right?"

"Civilian life hasn't made me *that* sloppy," Austin mutters. "But I had to pay off half a dozen local officials to get Max's body to the morgue without raising any red flags. Sending the footage to your tablet now. I scanned it, and there's not much to see. No obvious defensive wounds, not a single piece of furniture out of place. Autopsy results will take at least twenty-four hours."

The details—or lack of them—about Max's death make my stomach churn, and I drum my fingers along my thighs while chewing on my lower lip. Marina shoots me a pointed glance, and I nod. I will *definitely* need a Xanax before the press conference.

"Shit. Fibers? Prints? Anything?" Griff runs his right hand through his brown hair, and the tousled strands fall across his forehead in a way that makes me want to touch them—and him.

"Nope. This guy's a pro. But his tech skills are nothing compared to Wren's. He erased any footage of him entering and existing Max's room, but Wren found the splices."

Griff lowers his voice, but if he thinks I can't hear him, he's very wrong. "Time of death?"

"Sometime between 19:33 and 19:49," Austin replies.

I jerk away from Marina's touch and twist so I'm facing Griff. I don't care that his glasses or tablet will pick up my words. I need to see him—without a mirror between us. Or maybe...I need him to see me. "He died less than fifteen minutes after he left the bar. That means—"

He nods. "The killer was probably watching you the whole time."

Griff

The look on Sloane's face? Shit. Why didn't I keep my mouth shut? Or take the call from Austin in another room?

Marina spins Sloane's chair back around, and fuck. All I want to do is take her in my arms and tell her everything will be okay. Instead, I can't touch her, can't reassure her, and have to watch her eyes fill with tears and Marina chastise her and then wick them away with a tissue.

"Griff? Are you still there?" Austin asks.

"Yeah. Listen, Marina is responsible for three other models during this junket. She's going to be out of pocket for at least a couple of hours every day, and I can't be in two places at once.

Can you check with Dax and see if he knows anyone local who could provide some backup?"

"I'll make some calls."

Sloane mouths, *"Thank you,"* in the mirror, and even Marina looks relieved.

"Appreciate it. I don't suppose Wren's had any luck with facial recognition?" Second Sight's hacker is a fucking genius from what I've seen so far, and supposedly another one of Dax's Special Forces buddies out in Seattle is just as good as she is.

The speech to text software displays the words *heavy sigh* on the screen. "Not yet. Whoever this guy is, she can't match him to any of Dimitri Volkov's known associates."

"Try searching for Rodney Carriger," Sloane says. She spells his last name but won't meet my gaze in the mirror.

"Who is he, Sloane?" With my tablet in my hand, I push to my feet and skirt the makeup table.

"Excuse me? Working here," Marina says, but I ignore her. From Sloane's body language, this wasn't an easy admission for her, and that name definitely was *not* in her file.

"Can you give us a minute?" she asks Marina. "Please?"

Her friend huffs—I think—and jams her hands on her hips. "Fine. I can give you three. No more. Either that or you can finish up your own damn makeup."

As soon as Marina slams the door to her room—a sound even I can hear—Sloane peers up at me, shame hooding her gaze.

"Austin, I'm going to put you on hold. Or...fuck it. I'll call you back." Jabbing the tablet screen to sever the connection, I set the device down and lean my hip against the desk. "Who's Rodney Carriger?"

Sloane stares down at her hands clasped in her lap, and I lay my fingers over hers.

"Talk to me, sweetheart. Whatever it is, we'll get through it." God, I wish I believed that. I want to. I'd give this woman anything. But this is all make believe, and even if it weren't, I can't possibly be enough for her. Not as damaged as I am.

"It's not a nice story. Marina doesn't even know." Tears brim in her eyes, and shit. If the makeup artist finds out I made her cry, she'll kick my ass into next week. Pulling one of the tissues from the box, I touch it gently to the corners of her eyes. The intimacy in that gesture is almost too much for my heart to bear without taking her into my arms and carrying her somewhere no one can hurt her again.

Her cool fingers brush mine. "Rodney worked for the Philadelphia police department. He was part of the team who arrested Dimitri."

"Sloane? I have to ask. Assumptions in this business? They get people killed. But how do you know that?" Deep in my soul, I have no doubts as to what happened all those years ago. She was one of Dimitri's victims.

Trafficked.

Sold.

Broken.

But she survived. Flourished, even, judging by all her accomplishments. They're not enough, though. No professional accolade or award can make up for months or years of hell. Of torture. Of pain. My file has more commendations than most of the men and women I trained with, and they don't mean a damn thing to me now.

"Please don't ask me that."

With the drape covering her upper body, she looks so slight. A stiff wind would blow her over, and she's convinced she's somehow to blame for Max's death. For the man who broke into her home. For me being here in the first place.

"I have to. No secrets, remember? No shutting down?"

Curling the fingers of my left hand around the arm of the chair, I pull the rolling monstrosity toward the couch, then sit so we're face to face. "Do you really think I'm going to judge you for anything that happened fifteen years ago? For things that weren't your fault? That you had no control over?"

"You should." Sloane pulls a piece of fabric from the pocket of her bathrobe. My handkerchief. She kept it close.

"Fuck that. Never was much for following the rules." Cracking a smile, I try to set her at ease, but it's no use. What I'm about to say? It's a risk. But Sloane needs to hear it. "I didn't tell you how I lost my arm. And my hearing. Not the real story, anyway."

She sniffles and dabs at her nose with the silky square, waiting for me to continue. The last thing I want to do is go back there, but if it'll help her? No hesitation.

"Ambush in Pakistan. Middle of the city. The bombs were so close, they blew out my ear drums and damaged a whole lot of things inside my ear that couldn't be fixed. My arm? A concrete wall collapsed. I pushed Austin out of the way, but I wasn't fast enough to save myself."

"Oh, God. I'm sorry," she says, her lower lip wobbling slightly until she starts chewing on it, then goes through the now-familiar pattern of unconscious movements that mark her stress levels rising.

"You could say everything that happened was my fault. I know that's what I think. Doesn't make it true, though." My mouth is dry as fuck, and I reach for the bottle of water on the side table, draining half of it in a couple of swallows and trying not to let Sloane see my hand shake.

"You didn't set the bombs." Her words scroll across my glasses, and I look up at her.

"Exactly. And you didn't turn Volkov into the worst excuse for a human being I've seen in a long damn time. I know he was charged and convicted for trafficking young women from Russia. The police report says he beat them, kept them locked in a basement in south Philly, and forced them to do unspeakable things. Your name isn't listed among the victims, but..."

There isn't a handkerchief on this earth that could dry Sloane's tears now. Her foundation streaks, and she buries her face in her hands. Across my lenses, a single word flashes.

Crying.

"Sloane, you have *nothing* to be ashamed of. Nothing. If you were one of his—"

Her head snaps up, and though her tears are falling faster and harder than ever, there's a fire in her eyes that wasn't there before. "If? Why do you think he's blackmailing me? I know the men he worked with. Both in Philadelphia and in Russia. I was not a dumb, naive child when I came to America, Griff. I was good with numbers. And art. But my family was starving. Mama worked fifteen hours a day to put food on the table. So when I found a man who promised to take me to America for twenty-five thousand rubles, I jumped at the chance. I was stupid. Desperate. And that choice took *everything* from me!"

Halfway through her admission, I tapped the temple of my glasses so I could focus completely on Sloane. And now? I'm in awe of her. Strong, ashamed—scared too, but not of me—yet desperate to stop hiding. To be seen.

"Listen to me, sweetheart," I say, setting my glasses aside and linking our fingers. Feeling her warmth against my prosthetic hand? It grounds me. "You may be the bravest person I've ever known. Don't think for a single second that what you went through changes how I see you."

For several long moments, she stares at me, a few errant tears dripping from her jaw onto the gown. "Do you mean that?"

Easiest question to answer in the whole goddamned world.

"Yes." In case she has any doubt I'm sincere, I cup the back of her neck and pull her in for a hard kiss.

Putting on an act, my ass. I don't have to pretend to care about Sloane Sanders. The challenge now? Pretending I'm not halfway to falling in love with her.

CHAPTER SEVENTEEN

Griff

The look Marina shot me when she came back out of her room? I'm interfering in her precisely organized day, and she hates it. Rather than continue to be a distraction, I left Sloane with a gentle squeeze to her shoulder and hid in her bedroom.

Sitting at the desk, I prop the tablet up in front of me. The left side of the screen shows the video from Max's room, and on the right, I have Austin on FaceTime with the speech-to-text program transcribing his words.

"The killer had to be right in front of him," I say, zooming in on the body and the carpet surrounding the chair. "What do you think? Wearing protective gear? Arterial spray would have soaked the guy."

"That's my guess. Otherwise, he would have tracked blood out of the room and down the hall. The techs found nothing outside of that five foot area other than some odd smears of blood along the perimeter."

"No defensive wounds either. Not obvious ones. Tell the coroner to run a full tox screen."

"This isn't the first investigation I've run, you know." The former JSOC commander rolls his eyes and moves off screen. "Need more coffee. I thought civilian life would let me pretend 4:00 a.m. didn't exist anymore."

Laughing feels good, despite the seriousness of our conversation. Like I'm part of a team again. Part of something bigger than just me and my fucked up life. "You're not the only one who wishes we could have done all of this in New York City. Or Boston. Or...anywhere in the States."

He settles back down, cupping his mug like it's the Holy Grail. "Dax just texted me. He'll have a retired SAS guy at the hotel in time for dinner tonight. I'll send his contact info and picture to you when we're done here."

"Good. That'll take a load off of Sloane and Marina. I should probably apologize to Dax for the early hour too, huh?"

"Nah. He's used to it. How's Sloane doing with everything?" Austin leans closer and takes a sip of coffee. "Her manager's death, getting a fake boyfriend, having to put on a show?"

I cast a glance at the door, wishing I could be out there with Sloane right now. "Not bad. She's a model," I say, shrugging my right shoulder. After yesterday, my prosthetic feels like it weighs a fucking ton, and though it's not painful at the moment, the less I move my left arm, the better. "She's used to faking it for the cameras. Said Max set her up with a couple of guys over the years for show. Keep the press from hounding her about her lack of a serious relationship."

Austin's eyes crinkle at the edges. "You have to kiss her yet?"

"You expect me to answer that? I protect my client's privacy."

He wants to play that game? He's going up against an expert. Staring right at his face on the screen, I arch a brow. "You still haven't told me how you and Mik got together. Not in any detail."

"That's a story best told in person. With alcohol." Austin rubs the back of his neck, then stifles a yawn. "I'm going to catch another couple of hours. Sent Carriger's name to Wren and Ripper, and they'll get on it as soon as it's not the middle of the fucking night in Seattle. Stay safe, man."

"As safe as I can." Ending the call, I switch the video to full screen and go through it another half dozen times. Later tonight, I'll have to show it to Sloane, even if all my instincts scream at me to protect her from the horrors documented in full color. Maybe by then, she'll trust me enough to tell me everything. Like why her name isn't on any of the police reports and what her relationship was with Rodney Carriger.

━━━

Sloane

"Look, he obviously knows what he's doing," Marina says as she brushes a light coat of setting powder over my entire face. "But that doesn't mean I have to like it when he throws me off schedule."

I roll my eyes. "Of course you don't. But you do have to be *nice.* Now turn the iPad back on so I can keep going over our cover story."

"So now it's 'our' cover story?" she asks.

"Until this whole thing is over? Yes. And you better pay attention too. Some of those reporters know we're friends. What if they ask you about me and Griff?" Frustration bleeds through my tone, and when Marina runs a brush through my hair a little more aggressively than necessary, I hiss out a breath. "Careful!"

"I'm running late. You're lucky I have time for this at all. Go on. Tell me what I need to know while I finish this."

Long, steady strokes of the boar bristle brush strain my neck, but it's worth it when Marina spills a dropper of argan oil mixed with a touch of my favorite perfume—a special blend of ylang-ylang, white musk, sandalwood, and pomegranate—into her hands and smooths the mixture over my locks.

"The official story is that Griff was injured in a car accident in Dallas last year. A semi-truck blew a tire and t-boned his sedan. He was pinned in the car for several hours before fire and rescue could cut him free."

"Shit. Okay. And you met because he works at the agency?" Pulling most of my hair up into a high ponytail, she secures it with a glittering silvery elastic, then adds a second, decorative tie of luminescent pearls.

"Yes. He's a junior agent with five years of experience." Swallowing hard, I tap my fingers against my thighs under the drape, struggling not to let my emotions show in the mirror. Once Marina's done, I can take a Xanax, but she's so late already, I can't make her stop now. "The hotel and the Ulstrum Agency agreed to keep Max's death quiet to avoid any bad press."

Marina stops with the curling iron poised a few inches away from my temple. "Wait, do *we* know?"

"I do. Whoever killed him might have seen me go into his room. And if not, they sent that text message last night. But you don't. Neither does Griff."

Wrapping a thick lock of hair around the hot iron, Marina arches a brow. "There's no way you'd keep that from me."

"Of course I would!" She flinches at the desperation in my tone and lets the hair release in a perfectly curled tendril.

"Don't look at me like that. You fell asleep in the chair last night, but that text message? Dimitri basically threatened to kill anyone I told. Said Max's death was all my fault because I couldn't keep my mouth shut. There's no fucking way I'd ever put you in danger like that. Not on purpose."

Don't cry. No tears. Not now.

I squeeze my eyes so hard, spots float behind my lids. If only I'd been able to hide that bruise. If only I'd paid Dimitri the moment I opened that letter.

"Stop it, sweetie." Marina rests a hand on my shoulder and squeezes gently. "Whatever you're stewing over? Regretting? It doesn't matter now. We're here, and we can't change the past."

It takes a few seconds for my vision to clear, and when I do, Marina's standing behind me. My hair looks amazing, as does my makeup, and once I take a deep breath, my reflection in the mirror reveals nothing but a calm, confident Sloane ready to take on the world. Or at least the press.

"You can't let on to *anyone* that you know what really happened. Max has the flu. You never talk to him anyway outside of hello and goodbye, so while you heard about his illness, you're just glad Griff is here to handle all of the agency shit so I can focus on everything else."

Talking about the man who saved my life—or at least changed it—like he's a character in a book? It feels too casual. Almost...disrespectful. He's so much more than that. But I refuse to let it show. This is the most important performance of my entire life, and I have to play my part perfectly. Otherwise, more people will die, and I won't be able to live with myself.

AT A QUARTER TO TWELVE, I emerge from my bedroom, praying I used enough tape to keep everything in place for the next few hours. The sweater dips low between my breasts, exposing more skin than I'd like, but I twisted, bent, and stretched over and over again in front of the mirror without a mishap. Dotted with tiny pearls, the silver cashmere is unbelievably soft, with long sleeves that flare at the wrists. Paired with black, stovepipe pants and silver heels, the entire outfit is simple, even understated—except for the sheer amount of my skin on display.

Griff stands when he sees me, and his jaw drops. The feeling's mutual. The man cleans up *very* well.

"Holy shit," he says softly. "You look amazing."

The sincerity in his voice brings a smile, and I glide over to him, tug on his gray suit jacket to straighten it, and reach up to skim my fingers over his cheek. He shaved, and he sucks in an unsteady breath as our gazes collide. "So do you."

"These might be the nicest clothes I've ever worn."

"Men's fashion is so much simpler. Except, you're not supposed to use all those buttons on your shirt." Flicking open the top three, I soften the lines on the crisp white shirt and expose a sexy glimpse of his chest. "That's better."

Griff moves to run his hand through his hair, but I stop him. "It's perfect the way it is. Don't touch it."

"Marina gave me a few tips as she was rushing out the door. Organized chaos, I think she called it?"

"Her specialty." Griff even *smells* good. Like bergamot, and something oaky and mossy. "So...you don't normally dress this well?" Thank God he can't hear the change in my voice—the huskiness, the desire. Because what I'm feeling? It's definitely desire. I may not have much experience in that department, but the butterflies fluttering in my stomach, the way my heart beats faster the longer I'm close to him, how I wish I'd skipped the shimmering lip dye? Definitely desire.

His laugh relaxes me by a fraction. "Hell, no. The CIA

does have a dress code, though it's pretty lax. Jeans or khakis. Polo shirts, Henleys, the occasional button-down for meetings with the higher ups. Deputy directors on up wear suits."

"And that's not you? I'm not sure you ever told me what your job really is there." I have to put some distance between us, so I snag the silver leather clutch that goes with this outfit and add my room key, meds case, lip dye, cell phone, and a tiny mirror.

"I'm a Senior Operations Officer. Before..." he gestures to his left arm, "I ran ops all over the world. My last one was with Austin in Pakistan. Can't really talk about the details beyond what I told you this morning, but..."

"It ended badly." Turning to face him again, I square my shoulders. "Are you going to go back? When you're done protecting me?"

He shrugs, an emotion I can't read in his deep blue eyes. "I don't know. I wasn't made to ride a desk." Clearing his throat, he picks up his phone and slides it into his pocket. "Where's your panic button?"

"Taped to the bottom of my left breast."

My matter-of-fact delivery combined with the intimate location throws him. Griff's eyebrows shoot up. "That's...uh... really smart."

"It was the only place I thought would be easy to reach and not totally obvious. This sweater doesn't leave much to the imagination."

That's the understatement of the year.

"It leaves enough that I *probably* won't have to punch any of the reporters today," Griff says with a smile. "But if any of them step one foot out of line, you just say the word, sweetheart. And I'll take care of it."

The conviction in his voice? It's reassuring in a way I desperately need.

"Then let's go. If I keep the wolves waiting much longer, they'll be out for blood." I hate press conferences. They're the worst part of this job. I'd let a wardrobe person lift and tuck and tape me all day, every day, if it meant I never had to face the press again. But at least I can take comfort in one thing.

This will be the last one I'll have to do. Whatever happens with Dimitri, I'm out after this trip. Even if that means I have to disappear without saying goodbye to Marina—or Griff.

CHAPTER EIGHTEEN

Griff

"Stay on my left side, sweetheart."

Sloane stumbles as she tries to change direction mid-step, and I steady her with my palm at the small of her back. "Your left side?"

"If I need to protect you, my right arm is a hell of a lot stronger than my left. Even if the prosthetic is practically indestructible. I can still feel you holding my hand, remember?"

She nods, and her lips purse and clench rapidly until I cup her cheek. "Relax. You'll be fine. Wren hacked into the hotel's security system last night and sent me a layout of the room we'll be in. I'll be standing against the wall to your right, less than thirty feet from you. If *anything* happens, you drop to the floor, cover your head, and wait for me to get to you."

Shit. She wasn't ready for that, asshole.

"Do you think..."

"No. Volkov and anyone he's working with would be fools to try something in front of all of those cameras. But it's my job to be prepared at all times. I'm sorry. I didn't mean to scare you like that."

Sloane's gripping my hand so tightly, the remapped nerves in my arm almost register pain.

"Breathe for me, okay? In and out. You took your meds, right?"

"Yes. Trust me, if I hadn't, you'd know." She laughs—or so the text on my lenses tells me—and continues. "When my anxiety started to get really bad...I refused to take anything. Until I had a giant meltdown at an evening gown shoot. I was in this huge dress with a dozen layers to the skirt and a full corset, and I just sat down on the floor and sobbed for a full ten minutes until the photographer called off the whole thing." She stares down at her shoes as we traverse the long hallway toward the elevator, her cheeks flushed a bright shade of pink.

We're alone in the elevator, and I press the button for the second floor. The rumbling of the doors calms me—one little spark of normalcy in my otherwise silent world. "You have nothing to be ashamed of, sweetheart. We all need help some-times. Asking for it—that's what takes true strength."

Sloane doesn't reply, but the weak smile touching her lips? It's everything. Relief, connection, a moment between us that's *real.* Her death grip on my hand eases slightly, though the way she keeps fluttering her fingers is a clear sign she's barely holding on.

"What do you want to do after this?" Distraction might help. "Lunch? There's this open air market half a mile away. The *Bahnhofstrasse.* Supposed to be great for walking and window shopping."

Hope brightens her eyes for a brief moment, but it's quickly snuffed out as she frowns and chews on her lower lip again. "Is it safe?"

"We'll be in public. In broad daylight. Besides," I nudge her shoulder with mine, "it'll help sell the whole relationship angle."

This time, the color in her cheeks has nothing to do with shame, and I will my body to calm the fuck down before Sloane —or someone else—notices how my zipper is straining against my erection. These pants are *not* loose by any stretch of the imagination.

Seconds after stepping off the elevator on the second floor, the words *Crowd noise* scroll across my lenses. Shit. Touching the temple a couple of times, I set the glasses to tune into Sloane's voice exclusively and shift so my arm is around her waist.

Flashbulbs go off at regular intervals, and her little flinches against my side worry me. Yet, she's plastered on a bright smile. Two uniformed security guards stand in front of a velvet rope barrier. Paparazzi line one wall, occasionally elbowing one another as the other models and the *Beauty and Style* executives walk a red carpet leading to the press room.

"Harry Griffin," I say to the men, flipping open my wallet to show them my ID. "With the Harvey Ulstrum Agency. I'm representing Ms. Sanders."

The taller one scrolls through a long list of names on an iPad. "I see a Max Snood as Ms. Sanders' representative."

Sloane tenses, and I tighten my hand on her waist. God, I hope it's as comforting as I intend it to be. "Mr. Snood came down with the flu. Check the morning update sheet. You'll see me listed as his stand-in."

If Wren didn't work her magic, we're fucked.

The two guards confer, one of them tapping his ear piece before speaking into the mic poking out of his sleeve. "We have a Mr. Griffin here who says he's taking Mr. Snood's place as the rep from the Ulstrum Agency."

Skimming my lips over Sloane's ear, I whisper, "Look impatient. You're the star here and they know it."

After a single, deep breath, Sloane extricates herself from my arm and places both hands flat on the table in front of us. "The press conference starts in less than ten minutes. How do you think the *Beauty and Style* execs are going to feel about their cover model not being there? I hardly think that's going to end very well for you."

The one with the mic clears his throat. "Apologies for the delay, Mr. Griffin. The notice came in overnight. The system has been properly updated now. You and Ms. Sanders can go in."

I nod my thanks, gesturing for Sloane to precede me down the runner of plush red carpet. "They're here for *you*, sweetheart. I'll be right behind you."

She closes her eyes for a beat, and when she opens them again, I see nothing but control in the blue depths. Passing me her clutch, she glides slowly down the hall, pausing every few steps to flash a smile or turn so the cameras can capture every angle.

I keep my gaze trained on the crowd, scanning each face, looking for anyone out of place, anyone *not* interested in snapping as many pictures as possible. Tapping the left temple of the glasses, I take advantage of the *other* feature Dax's team built into these damn things. A camera.

Wren—or someone on her team—will analyze the footage later, and I'll be able to review it before the runway show tomorrow.

I'm not sure if I'm happy or frustrated that everyone here looks like they belong. Not being able to hear a damn thing other than a low, dull hum of noise isn't helping my mood.

Sloane's warm fingers grip my left hand, and she squeezes to get me to look at her. "They're asking about you."

Shit. Get yourself together, idiot.

Stepping even closer to her, I smile, letting the paparazzi get their fill. This is uncomfortable as fuck, and thank God no one suggested I play some kind of diversity model for the week, because there's no way in hell I'd pull that off.

Sloane's talking—answering questions, I think—but from my position at her side, it's too hard to read her lips, and even the glasses are having issues. I catch maybe one word every ten until she releases my hand and *signs*.

This is my boyfriend. H-a-r-r-y-G-r-i-f-f-i-n.

It takes everything in me not to let my jaw hang open. She learned a few signs? Why? To be able to communicate with me?

Draping her arms around my neck, she tips her head back slightly, her lips parted, and I take the hint. With my left arm tight around her waist, I dip her and kiss the hell out of her.

The flutter of her tongue against my lips has a low growl vibrating in my throat, and I open for her, letting *her* take control this time, and hoping all the photos don't capture me with a massive hard on.

Sloane's kiss is *anything* but fake, and when she pulls back, we're both breathless. "They're asking if you're deaf, why you're here..."

Keeping a hold of her, I scan the photographers and clear my throat. "Sloane is the star here, folks. I work for the Ulstrum Agency, and I'm filling in for her agent who came down with the flu this morning. If you want my bio, it's listed on Ulstrum's website. Yes, I'm mostly deaf, so shouting at me isn't going to help anyone. Email me, and I'll do my best to answer any questions you have. Right now, the lovely woman I'm lucky enough to have on my arm needs to get inside."

We each give a small wave—Sloane's practiced and professional, mine much less so—and cover the last fifty feet to the conference room as quickly as we can.

"Is it quieter in here?" I ask.

"Much. Why?" She peers up at me, worry creating the barest hint of a furrow between her brows.

"Glasses didn't work out there." With a tap, I turn them on again, and thank God the noise level doesn't immediately overwhelm the system. Under the guise of kissing her neck, I whisper, "In case it gets loud and I have to turn them off again, I need you to pick a signal—something you do with your hands maybe?—that will let me know you're in trouble or need me to get you out of here."

She takes a shuddering breath and her fingers skim over the back of my head. No one's touched me like that in...well, a long damn time, and I want more. So much more.

"I'll play with one of my earrings. Did you...um...did the glasses work just now?"

We're still locked together, my lips trailing along her neck, and I press a kiss right behind her ear. "Clear as day. Now go kick some ass up there."

With a shaky smile, she releases me, and watching her walk away? Up onto a raised platform where she takes the center seat with six other models flanking her? I don't know how I'm supposed to keep things professional between us much longer.

I genuinely *like* Sloane Sanders. But if I can't shut it down and focus on the job? I could lose her. And then where would I be?

Fucked. A useless, damaged, relic with no hope of working ever again. And alone. Completely and totally alone.

Sloane

The young woman next to me—she can't be more than twenty-four—flashes me a million-watt smile. "Oh, God. Sloane Sanders. Excuse me while I fangirl all over the place. You're the reason I wanted to be a model in the first place! I saw you at Fashion Week ten years ago. My aunt works for *Yves Saint Laurent* and snuck me in with her, and you were just...radiant. I'm Jill, by the way."

"It's nice to meet you." We air kiss, the habit ingrained in me from early days in this industry. Impersonal, perfunctory, even, yet to anyone watching, we probably look like we've known one another for years. "What agency are you with?"

"Thompson and Taylor." Jill's bright red hair and wide green eyes give her a Red Riding Hood look, considering she's wearing a sheer black cloak over her skin-tight bodysuit. "They've been so awesome. I didn't think I'd make the cut this year, but when the call came...I screamed so loud!"

Her energy does nothing for my nerves, but she's so sincere, I can't be rude to her. Members of the press file in, taking their assigned seats, and the photographers adjust their lenses for some candid shots.

My gaze pings between Griff and the clock on the back wall. Thirty minutes. I can do this. Half an hour and I can change into something more comfortable—and much less revealing—and let Griff whisk me away from here like a knight on a white horse.

"Is this your first presser?" I ask Jill, not taking my eyes off my protector. His intense stare grounds me. Despite breaking eye contact to study each person in the room, he returns his gaze to mine every thirty seconds or so, and I don't know if I could do this without him.

"Yes. My agent prepped me a little, but I had so much

caffeine this morning, I'm sure I'm going to make a complete fool of myself." Coiling a lock of hair tightly around her finger, she tugs sharply before releasing it. Lowering her voice, she adds, "Do the caffeine pills upset your stomach too?"

Oh, no. This one is going to crash and burn if she's not careful. Turning my head so none of the press can read my lips, I whisper, "This industry has many dirty secrets. That's one of them. Never let the press hear you mention that again."

Jill recoils like I just slapped her hand, but she's still grinning—training trumps everything else—even for the inexperienced. "Uh...th-thanks."

Patting her thigh under the table, I offer her a practiced smile. "Your agent should have told you. Don't stress about it."

Gratitude shines in her green eyes, and she nods once before returning her attention to the full rows of seats.

"Ladies and gentlemen!" *Beauty and Style's* Vice President of Print Media bounds up onto the raised platform holding a microphone in her hand. "Welcome to the Christmas Book Debut weekend! My name is Nan Roberra, and I'm so pleased to introduce you to some of the models we've chosen to feature prominently in this year's catalog. As you know, this is the tenth anniversary of the Christmas Book, and I'm proud to announce we've expanded our distribution to twenty-three countries and nineteen different languages."

Under the table, my hands won't stay still, clenching and unclenching, fingers drumming against my thighs. If there weren't microphones all around me, I'd be cracking my knuckles one after another.

Nan's words fade into the background, almost like I'm listening to her underwater. Shit. I'm edging towards a panic attack, and if I can't calm down, this is going to be a disaster.

Finding Griff, I pray he understands how close to the edge I am. He's leaning against the wall, but after a beat, stands up straight, and rests his hand on his chest, all five fingers splayed. Then he tucks one under his palm. Followed by another. And another.

"Count for me. Backwards from forty-seven."

Was that only last night? With a small nod, I try. *Forty-seven. Forty-six. Forty-five.*

"...finally, I'll introduce you to our star, the woman you'll see on the covers of Christmas Books all around the world, Sloane Sanders!" Nan gestures to me, and I give the press a winning smile and a little wave. "And with that, let's get to your questions."

The first reporter to ask about Griff waits a full fifteen minutes to do so, which almost surprises me. Usually they're all over the relationship angle. But apparently Jill made a bit of a scene last night after the cocktail party making out with one of the other models, so that was priority number one.

"Ms. Sanders, Nigel Rathmore with the BBC. Your entrance was, shall I say, titillating? Who's the new man in your life?"

I don't need to fake my blush. Thinking about the kiss we shared in front of all those cameras? Warmth floods my core, and I struggle not to squirm in my seat. "His name is Harry Griffin, Mr. Rathmore. We met after he joined the Ulstrum Agency, and we've been together for almost two months now. He's a wonderful man, and I'm so glad he was able to accompany me to Zurich."

"Are there wedding bells in your future?" Rathmore asks.

"Nigel, you don't expect me to kiss and tell, do you?" Out of the corner of my eye, I see Griff smile, and I turn and blow him a quick kiss.

Another reporter immediately jumps to his feet, but half the room is clamoring to ask the next question, and I don't catch his name. "Mr. Griffin is deaf, is he not? His bio says he's also an amputee. How has that been a challenge for you?"

A muscle in Griff's jaw starts to tick, and I pin the reporter with a stare I hope can melt glass. "Is there some reason you feel that's an appropriate question? Millions of people around the world have some form of hearing loss or are missing a limb. I care much more about Mr. Griffin's heart and mind than I ever will about his arm or what he can or cannot hear."

The jerk sinks back into his chair, and I think I hear a muttered apology. Thankfully, someone from *USA Today* changes the subject to ask one of the male models what it's like to be one of the first transgender men to be featured in the Christmas Book.

I can't stop stealing glances at Griff. His face is still impassive, but the tension in his shoulders wasn't there before, and I wish I could find a way to ease his discomfort.

"One final question!" Nan announces, and in the last row, a man with messy black hair and a full beard stands and holds up his hand. There's something about him that's vaguely off-putting, but then again, I feel that way about a lot of the press.

"Ms. *Sanders?* I am Nikolai Lebedev with *Argumenty i Fakty* out of Moscow."

Lebedev. Moscow. No. No, no, no.

I can't breathe. Can't hear the man's question. My fingers find their way to the gray pearl hanging from a long strand of silver at my ear. If I thought my legs would hold me, I'd run. He knows who I am. Dimitri's sending me a message, and oh, God.

Griff. Please. Help me.

A flash of movement to my right, and then his warm hand cups the back of my neck as he leans close to the microphone and addresses the man. "Ms. Sanders' travel schedule for next year hasn't been determined yet. Rest assured, as soon as it is, our agency will release further details. If you'll excuse us, we have another event to attend shortly." A flurry of shutter clicks follow, but he slides his hand down to my elbow and squeezes gently. "Sloane? Sweetheart? We should go or we'll be late."

I can only nod as I let him help me to my feet and take his hand. The latex covering his prosthetic feels so real, so warm and natural, it helps steady me, and we escape out a back door into what appears to be a service corridor.

"Sloane? Look at me." Griff strokes my cheek, but I'm still numb. Still too shocked to speak. "Sloane!" It's not until his lips press to mine that I can move, but instead of enjoying what I'm sure would be another spectacular kiss if I gave in, I pull back. "That man...he knows. Whoever he was. He knows who I am. It was a message. A warning. From Dimitri."

Griff wraps his left arm around me, the hard metal oddly reassuring, so he can pull his phone from his right pocket. A few taps, and the name *Wren* scrolls across the screen.

A woman answers, her voice tired and a little raspy, and the speech recognition software fills the screen. "It's early, Griff. What do you need?"

"Facial recognition for one of the reporters in the press room. Last row, fourth seat from the left. Black hair, black beard, brown eyes. Six-two, maybe two-eighty. He claimed to be from a Russian newspaper. The glasses butchered the name."

"Argumenty i Fakty," I say. "They're one of the biggest newspapers in Moscow."

"He said his name was—"

"That is not his name. I'm sure of it. Griff, please." If Wren searches for the name Nikolai Lebedev, she'll find a dead man —my father—and it won't take her long to connect Nikolai to me.

Griff could easily tell her the man's name, but instead, he gives me a terse nod. "Get us his *real* name, Wren. And let me know if he's still anywhere on the hotel grounds. We're going back up to the room."

"Will do," she says and hangs up.

Anger and frustration stiffen his shoulders, but Griff keeps his arm around me all the way to the service elevator and back to my—our—room. But once we're inside with the door locked, he loses his patience.

"This only works if you're honest with me, Sloane. I need you to tell me right fucking now. Who is Nikolai Lebedev and why are you terrified of him?"

Sniffling, I dig in my clutch for Griff's handkerchief. I feel better with the soft cloth in my hand. "I have never been terrified of Nikolai Lebedev. He was my father, and I loved him." Taking a risk, I lock eyes with my protector. "My name...I wasn't born Sloane Sanders."

If Griff is surprised, he doesn't show it. Or perhaps he's too angry to display any other emotion. I wish he'd say something. *Anything.* But after another few seconds, I know he won't. Not until I tell him everything.

"I was born in a small town in Russia. Penza. When I came to this country, I was eighteen. A naive child who thought she would find a better life here. Maybe even a way to help her starving family. Instead, I found only pain." The barest hint of an accent tinges my tone, but I'm the only one who notices. "My given name is Sophiana Lebedev, and that is how Dimitri knows me."

CHAPTER NINETEEN

Griff

The name—Sloane's *real name*—fades away from my lenses, and I can't decide if I'm angry with her, with the asshole who used the name of her dead father, or with all the people who failed her in her life.

"Sophiana?" I ask.

"Yes." Tears brim in her eyes, and she won't look directly at me. "I came to the United States almost seventeen years ago, and for two years, Dimitri owned me. He took my passport at the airport, and I never saw it again. Not even after he went to jail."

"Sit. Please?" I can't stand to see her trembling, her arms wrapped tightly around her waist. The sweater leaves little to the imagination, and while sex should be the *last* thing on my mind, I'm still a guy. Still alive. She needs me present. Not distracted by so much perfect, creamy skin or the way her breasts heave as she tries not to cry. "Sloane? Or...do you want me to call you Sophiana when we're alone?"

"I can never be Sophiana again."

Not being able to hear a person's voice? Most of the time, it doesn't make much of a difference. I read lips well enough, can understand ASL if the person signs slowly, and with the glasses, texting, email? The only problems I have communicating are when my coworkers want to be assholes or when I'm in a crowd or a dimly lit room. But right now, I'm desperate to hear this woman in front of me. If for no other reason than she needs to know she isn't alone.

We're close enough, I can reach out and snag her cashmere-covered wrist, holding on until she huffs and drops her arms. "You're shaking. Sit down. I can put on a fresh pot of coffee. Or tea."

"Nothing will fix this."

"I'm not trying to fix anything. Not right this minute. I'm trying to take care of you." Tea seems like a better choice than coffee, so I fill the electric kettle with hot water and drop a bag of chamomile into one of the delicate china cups.

I'm half-tempted to crack open a bottle of bourbon from the mini-bar, but I need to stay sharp. By the time the water comes up to temperature and I fill her cup, Sloane has the blanket I used last night wrapped around her like a shield and her legs curled up under her.

It's her eyes that worry me the most. She stares out the french doors at the lake, but I don't think she's seeing anything. The tea will give her something to focus on. I hope.

"Here you go, sweetheart."

Her shoulders jerk, but she accepts the cup and saucer, though they rattle a little as she straightens. I slide my fingers over hers, and though these pants are ridiculously too tight for this move, lower myself to one knee in front of her. "Sloane, you need to tell me all of it."

"I know." After a sip of tea, she clenches her jaw so hard, the veins in her temples throb. "Doesn't make it any easier."

"Would it help if I asked the questions?" I'll do anything she wants. Anything she needs.

A single tear spills onto her cheek, and she dashes it away. "Maybe."

I take a seat beside her and drape my left arm over the back of the plush sofa. The motion takes some of the strain and weight off my shoulder, and I blow out a breath. "When Dimitri was arrested, something happened with Rodney Carriger, didn't it? The background check showed he was a cop. Retired now."

"Rodney was in on the raid of the house where Dimitri kept us. For a couple of weeks, he had been one of my regulars. He liked to talk. Always asking questions. I didn't know until the raid that he was trying to figure out where Dimitri kept us, how many girls were in the house, how many enforcers." Sloane takes another sip of tea, and her lips twitch slightly. "In Russia, we have mostly black tea. I hated it growing up. The first time I ever had chamomile was at the hospital in New York."

It takes me a beat to process her words, and a cold knot twists in my gut. "What hospital?"

Setting the cup down, she turns to face me, emotionless, her face—even her eyes—completely blank. "When your entire existence is nothing but fear and pain, you lose hope quickly. No one can live for long without hope. Not unless you have... help." Her fingers press to the crook of her left elbow, and for a second, shame flickers in her eyes. "Dimitri's *help*? Came from a needle."

Fuck. I should have known. "Heroin?" Sloane nods, still rubbing her elbow until I stop her. "So, the hospital? That's where you got clean?"

Another nod. "That's why I never take anything stronger than aspirin. Except for my anxiety meds. I don't even drink. Max...he set it up. All of it. He gave me a new life. And in exchange, I signed a contract. Sophiana *died*, and I became Sloane."

She's close to breaking down completely, and I can't push her for more. Not right now. Instead, I gently ease her against me until she relaxes. "How much sleep did you get last night?"

"A couple of hours."

The red text scrolls across my lenses, and I start rubbing her back. "We'll head to the *Bahnhofstrasse* this evening. After we figure out who that asshole is and how he knows Volkov. Until then, why don't you lie down?"

"I..." she shakes her head and pulls away, giving me a single, desperate look before turning toward her bedroom. "Okay."

Shit. My inner voice screams at me to stop her, and I catch up to her at the bedroom door. "Wait. What were you going to say?"

Sloane's lips press together, pursing and flattening like she's a fish struggling to breathe out of water. It isn't until I rest my hand at the small of her back that her chest stops stuttering and she tips her head up to meet my gaze.

"I'm terrified, Griff. For fifteen years, I thought I was safe. And that made it okay to be alone. But now?"

Whatever she wants, I'll give. Even if it scares the fuck out of me. "You're not alone. Not anymore."

FOR TWO HOURS, Sloane sleeps, curled against my left side, her head resting on my chest. I wanted to hold her properly, but Wren messaged me just as we tried to get comfortable. A few minutes later, with the help of a couple of pillows, we found a compromise that lets me use my right arm to carry on a painfully slow text conversation with Second Sight's hacker and still give Sloane what she needs most—a semblance of safety.

The "reporter"? A Russian thug who did time at the same prison as Volkov. Wren didn't find any evidence he was involved in sex trafficking, but though his only conviction was for assault, the police tried—and failed—to pin three separate murders on him ten years ago.

The phone slips out of my hand, and instinct kicks in. I try to stop it from hitting the bed, but my sudden movement wakes Sloane, and her entire body tenses.

"Shhh. You're okay, sweetheart. I'm right here."

"Oh, God. How long did I sleep?" She wriggles up, and I wince as blood rushes back into my mangled left arm. "Griff? What is it?"

Rubbing my shoulder, I force a smile. "Nothing a few minutes won't cure. Pins and needles."

Sloane frowns, then reaches up and trails her fingers over the tingling muscles. "Can I...?"

"Only a fool would refuse a massage from a smart, gorgeous, and brave model sleeping in his bed." With a grin, I put my glasses on and turn so my back is to her.

"Technically, this is my bed." Sloane starts slowly, feeling for the straps that stretch across my upper back. "Are you sensitive anywhere? Will I hurt you?"

"No. My shoulder is all good, so's my back. The wall—big cement block monstrosity—only crushed my arm." I unbuttoned my shirt before we lay down, and Sloane tugs it off me—mostly. The cufflinks were a bitch to fasten.

With one of her hands flat against my chest, she uses the other on my back—wait, are those her knuckles? Yep. Digging in along my shoulder blade.

Oh, fuck. Her touch is better than any massage I ever got in physical therapy. Probably because she's not *trying* to drive me to the breaking point.

"You slept for two hours," I say on a groan. "Marina's back in her room, safe, and the SAS guy is due here in thirty."

"Thank God. I'll feel better when she has protection." After a few seconds, she adds, "Your shoulder's hard as a rock. This might hurt a little."

Before I can tell her not to worry, that I doubt she weighs more than a buck twenty, even at five-foot-seven with perfectly balanced curves, she rises up on her knees and starts searching for my trigger points with her elbow. "Holy shit." She freezes, and I hiss out a breath. "Don't stop, sweetheart. I can take a little pain. Greater good and all that."

"Griff..."

"I promise. I'm okay." As she continues to work on my back, I fill her in on everything I learned.

"So this man—Pavel Andrei—you said? Is he still at the hotel?"

"Not that we can find. But I have a dozen photos of him from the cocktail party and the lobby security cameras the day you arrived. Before we go *anywhere,* you need to memorize them."

"We could order room service." Sloane stops with the magic fingers and scoots to the edge of the bed until she's right next to me. "If it's too dangerous to leave the hotel—"

"It's not."

"Don't lie to me, Griff." Her eyes narrow, and she studies me. "You promised."

Scooting back, I take her hands. "I'm not lying. Not exactly. You're in danger until we find any and all the men working for Volkov and figure out his end game. This is more than black-mail, Sloane. He's doing whatever he can to keep you scared.

Off balance. If we don't sell this relationship—really sell it—he's going to come after you again."

Sloane yanks her hands away, shoving them into the pockets of the well-worn hoodie she put on after a full fifteen minutes in the bathroom removing the low-cut cashmere. "He's going to come after me anyway. His operation was so much bigger than just the dozen girls at one Philly house. He ran houses all over the city and the east coast. I don't know where they were, and when I tried to tell Rodney about them, he refused to listen. All he cared about was keeping me to himself." She shudders, and I try to touch her, but she slides off the bed and stands just out of reach. "When Max saved me, I couldn't read or write English very well, though I could speak it. I had tutors, classes every day once I was clean, and after six months or so, I wrote down everything I could remember and sent a letter—no return address—to the District Attorney in Philadelphia. But even though I checked the news every day for months...there was nothing."

My watch buzzes, and I take a quick glance at the screen. "Marina's bodyguard is here. Once I vet him, we're going out to dinner." Sloane starts to protest, but I hold up my hand. "Dimitri's not going to come after us in the middle of the city. You—we—need a little fun. Plus, this is a chance for you to prove you're doing exactly what he wants. Keeping secrets from me."

CHAPTER TWENTY

Sloane

The hot former-SAS captain blocks the door, stopping Marina from leaving for the *Beauty and Style* staff party. "If anyone asks, we met at breakfast this morning and hit it off."

"Oh, puh-leeze." Marina rolls her eyes. "No one is going to believe *we* are hooking up."

"We're not." Jacob—all six feet of him dressed in a dark blue suit—stares down at my best friend with an amused half-smile. "But with your former plus-one 'hooking up' with Griff, you were not keen on attending this party alone, and asked me to accompany you. We're friends, nothing more."

Marina huffs, and some of her anger fades. "Fine. But can we go now? The appetizers are always the best part, and you wouldn't believe how much the gaffers eat." Draping her evening bag over her shoulder, she turns to me. "Be careful, okay? I don't like the idea of you leaving the hotel."

Honestly? Neither do I. But Griff insists we need this—that

I need this—and that we won't be in any danger. "We'll be fine. Go. Have fun."

Jacob holds the door open for her, and Marina ducks by him, the ruffled skirt on her bright red dress brushing his thigh.

"I told her all those ruffles would be annoying," I say. "But she fell in love with that dress the moment she saw it at Saks."

"It's...interesting." Griff unlocks the hotel safe, and my stomach twists into knots as he withdraws a gun, a very lethal-looking knife, and a second mobile phone.

My palms go damp, and I rub them on my thighs. Since this isn't an official event, I don't have to wear anything *Beauty and Style* provided. As soon as I put on a *normal* bra and paired a soft green sweater with flowing black pants and my Sketchers, I felt like me again.

Or, at least some version of me. After telling Griff about my past, I don't have a clue who I am anymore. Or who I want to be.

Griff drops to one knee and pulls up the right leg of his jeans. The knife—all five inches of it in a black sheath—straps to his calf, and I can't look away. "Do you really think you'll need that?" I'm not proud of the tremble in my voice, but at least he can't hear it.

Glancing up at me, his entire demeanor changes. The shift from all-business Griff to this-man-could-actually-be-my-boyfriend Griff is like a switch, and his blue eyes soften. "I didn't mean to scare you. But I'm not taking any chances with your safety, Sloane. None."

After he smooths the denim back down and stamps his foot a couple of times, he holds out his hand for mine.

"Have you ever shot a gun before?" he asks, squeezing my fingers lightly.

"N-no. Please don't ask me to." Every man in my life who

ever held a gun in my presence hurt me. Dimitri, all his men, Rodney...

"Look at me, sweetheart." His voice carries a rough edge, and I snap my gaze back to his and try to ignore the weapon on the table in front of us. "You shouldn't have to touch it. Hell, it's a last resort for me too." He closes the fingers of his left hand around the holster and pulls the gun with his right. "I got top marks on the range for years before I lost my arm, but I'll never be weapons certified again. Not by the CIA. Still, even with one hand, I'm better than most. So when we leave the hotel, I'll be armed. Every time."

He shows me where the safety is, how to flip it on and off, and the special pocket in his jacket where he clips the holster.

"You have your panic button?"

I run my fingers over the inside of my right breast, the small, thin button taped to the bra cup. "It's here. But you're not going to leave me alone, right?"

When he smiles at me, I want to believe everything's going to be okay. That he won't leave my side. That we'll have a nice, maybe even *normal* night out. "Unless you want me following you into the bathroom—or you like hanging out in the men's room—we might be apart at least once tonight. But otherwise, I'll be with you the entire time. I promise."

Draping a plaid tartan around my shoulders, I take a deep breath. I can do this. Go on a date with a handsome man at my side, and maybe...have a nice evening.

THE *BAHNHOFSTRASSE* IS COVERED in a canopy of tiny lights, lending a warm glow to the shops lining both sides of the street. We left the cars behind two blocks ago, passing under a massive arch to a large pedestrian-only boulevard.

Hand in hand, we take our time walking among dozens of tourists window shopping, taking photos, and milling around the various bars and restaurants.

"Still breathing?" Griff asks. Despite the people all around us, it's quiet, and so I don't worry about looking up at him to answer.

"Mostly. It's beautiful here." With a sigh, I press closer to him. "I wish we were on a real vacation."

He squeezes my hand, and though I know his fingers are made of silicone and titanium and various electronic sensors, there's something so *real* about the gesture. "We are."

"Do most of *your* vacations involve someone dying? If so, you need a new travel agent."

His laugh is the most comforting sound. Rich and strong and one hundred percent genuine. "I don't take vacations. Or, I haven't. Not for a long time." Guiding me over to an artist offering sketches for ten francs, Griff gestures to a stool positioned opposite the white-haired man.

"You don't have to—" He silences me with a tender kiss, and I melt against him. Every time I convince myself this isn't real, that we're only pretending, he does something like *that* and I think...maybe one day I could be happy. Not with him. This is nothing more than a job for Griff, and no matter how good he is at it, or what I might feel, that's all I'll ever be to him.

But with someone?

Is there another man in this world who wouldn't immediately see my damage? Who'd want me even though I'm not sure I'll be able to have sex ever again?

"Sloane?" His warm hand cups my cheek, and he's staring into my eyes like he can't find me anywhere. "What's wrong?"

"Nothing. I'm sorry. Just...thinking." Before we left the hotel, Griff explained the plan. Ninety percent happy couple, completely in love, ten percent secrets, lies, and distance.

Anyone watching us has to believe I'm terrified but keeping it to myself.

The first part is a breeze to sell. The second? Griff is easy to talk to. And now that he knows everything? I don't want to hide from him.

Giving his fingers a final squeeze, I sink down onto the stool, cross my legs at the ankles, and fold my hands on my thigh. One of the first lessons I learned. How to sit. Chin level, a gentle smile, head angled slightly to one side. I can hold this for hours if I have to.

"No good," the artist says, his German accent thick. "Together." He turns the page to start fresh, and Griff offers me his hand. The stool is only big enough for one of us, and I'm not sure what he's planning, but let him pull me to my feet.

Before I get my bearings, he's perched on the stool, an arm around my waist, and my ass resting against his thigh. Now it's my turn to laugh, and dammit. I *want* this. A life. Fun. With someone who understands me.

"Tell me something no one else knows about you," Griff says, his lips close to my ear.

"When I was eight, I won an art contest in school." It's so easy to be myself with this man. He doesn't judge me, doesn't doubt me, even now. "Where I grew up? It was such a small town. I think there were only twenty kids at my school. But the teacher entered one of my drawings in a contest..." Shit. I can't tell him where. Not in public. "It went all the way to the capitol. I didn't win the big prize. That would have been enough money for my family to eat for a month. But for a few weeks, my little picture of a mama duck and her babies was on display for thousands to see."

Griff gives me a gentle squeeze and brushes his lips to my cheek. "That's impressive. I can barely draw stick people."

"Anyone can learn to draw. I...could show you later." What

am I doing? This is real *relationship* talk. He won't be interested in learning how to sketch a tennis ball.

"I'd love that." The warmth in his voice makes me actually believe him. "Want to know mine? The thing no one knows?"

"Very much." Staring back at him, I find comfort in his easy, calm smile. "It's only fair."

"I can't sing. Well, that's probably a given now. But even before, I couldn't carry a tune to save my life. Not even *Happy Birthday*."

His eyes dart left and right, checking out the passersby, yet he still makes me feel like I'm the most important person in his world.

Sell it, Sloane. And maybe...enjoy yourself a little.

Dipping my head, I press my lips to his. In a single day, I've gone from having my very first kiss to craving them like they're my oxygen.

"Beautiful," the old man says with a chuckle. "New love, yes?"

"Two months," Griff replies. "Our first vacation together."

With a flourish of his green pen, he colors in my sweater, then nods at us. "Names?"

I spell them for him, then notice he's left our faces for last. "Griff? Is it okay if—" *Stop it. This isn't real.*

But I can't help myself. Right now, sitting on Griff's lap in the middle of one of the most iconic streets in Zurich, our connection is very much real, and I don't want the illusion to end. Not yet.

"*Your glasses,*" I mouth. "*Off.*"

The look in his eyes when he removes the black frames and tucks them into his pocket? If I didn't know better, I'd call it love.

Griff

The little cafe at the end of the *Bahnhofstrasse* is quiet, and I pull out Sloane's chair for her. The artist's sketch of the two of us is tucked safely in a plastic sleeve in her purse, and despite my protests, he refused the twenty-five francs I offered him.

Between his accent and his very bushy mustache, his words were mostly unintelligible, but Sloane thought he said something about "true love being so rare."

My seat—against the wall and facing the door—allows me to keep an eye on everyone coming in or out, and that calms me enough to take my glasses off while we eat. I don't want anything between us. It kills me to read her words on my lenses when she's at her most vulnerable, and for the first time since I woke up in the hospital at Bagram, I wonder if I should start practicing my ASL in earnest.

After the server brings our drinks—herbal tea for Sloane and a local non-alcoholic pear cider for me—I take a moment to study her. Cheeks flushed from the chill in the air, no makeup, her long blond locks tumbling over her shoulders, she looks free in a way I haven't seen her before.

"On the red carpet today, when you introduced me?" Concentrating on the movements of my left hand, I switch to ASL, *"You know sign language?"*

"I know a little bit." Her signs are slow—not that mine are much better—and she drops her hands before she continues. "I worked with a deaf photographer on a series of shoots five or six years ago. She was brilliant and patient and taught me a few sentences every time we took a break. I looked up the alphabet last night to learn how to spell your name."

"No one's ever done that for me before."

The flush to Sloane's cheeks deepens. "You said you don't sign much. But...isn't it easier sometimes?"

"To understand? Yeah. I do pretty well if someone's signing to me. But as great as my hand is, I can't move my fingers fast enough or with enough control to carry on a conversation for long. I can sign one-handed, but every time I tried to learn, it just reminded me of what else I'd lost—besides my hearing." Admitting my failings to this woman I genuinely *like?* Every word makes me feel less qualified to protect her. To keep her safe. "Lipreading was easy. I wasn't half bad at it before the attack. After, I had a full week in the hospital with nothing to do but watch closed-captioned YouTube videos. By the time they transferred me to McLean, I could *mostly* carry on a conversation as long as the person I was talking to kept things slow."

We stick to lighter topics while we eat—Sloane's favorite jobs, the worst outfit she ever had to wear, books and movies we've enjoyed. She's easy to talk to, and I continually remind myself why I'm here. To keep her safe. I don't want to tear my gaze away from her to check our surroundings. Or look up every time someone opens the door. But if I don't, she'll pay the price, and that's a risk I'm not willing to take.

The walk back to the arched entrance of the *Bahnhofstrasse* takes us twice as long because we stop often along the way, Sloane window shopping while I use the reflections in the glass to check out our surroundings. More than once I spot a shadow ducking into an alley, but unless I want to blow my cover, I can't investigate any further. All I can do is text Austin and Wren and ask them if there are any security cameras in this area.

With my arm around her, Sloane's bag rests against my hip, and her phone vibrates. "Let me check and make sure it's not Marina."

With a nod, I pull out my own phone and snap a couple of pictures of the street—like any good tourist would—and then take a candid shot of Sloane. She's beautiful with her head bent forward, her hair tucked behind one ear. Until her hands start to shake and the phone falls back into her purse.

"What is it?" I'm at her side in two steps, both hands on her shoulders.

All she can do is shake her head and whisper one word.

"Him."

The red text scrolls away. I tip her chin up so she has to look at me and keep my voice low. "Listen to me, sweetheart. I'm going to ask you what's wrong. Tell me it's nothing. Get mad at me. Yell if you want. Sell it. Right now." After a beat, I straighten. "Sloane, what's wrong?"

"It's nothing. Really, Griff. I'm fine." She's anything but, and there isn't a person alive that would believe her. But this is the act.

"You're *not* fine. We were having a great night. I *know* there's something you're not telling me. And I'm sick of it." Stepping back, I shove my hands into my pockets. "You say you love me, but you clearly don't trust me."

"I do!" Tears gather in her eyes, and she swipes them away. "This is a vacation for you, but it's work for me. I have to be *on* all the time, and right now, I'm tired and cold and one of my friends back home is going through a bad patch. I'm not hiding anything from you. I just don't tell you every single thing that happens in my life."

I reach for her hand, but she refuses to budge. Her TD is back, and she's going to chew right through her lip if I can't calm her down. But damn. She pulled off the act perfectly.

"Sweetheart? I'm sorry. It's been a long day. Forgive me?" A handful of tourists have stopped to watch our fight, and that's when the truth hits me square in the gut.

She's so fucking good at acting because she's been acting for fifteen years. Every single day. "Sloane, please. Come here."

Wrapping my arm around her waist, I brush a kiss to her cheek. "I've got you. You're safe, and we're going back to the hotel right now."

And once we're behind closed doors, she's going to show me her phone so I can protect her from whatever that asshole is threatening her with now.

CHAPTER TWENTY-ONE

Sloane

Marina isn't back yet, but the *Beauty and Style* staff parties are notorious for going late into the night, and Jacob responds to Griff's text in under two minutes with some code the two of them established before we left that means everything's fine.

While he puts his knife and gun back in the safe, I kick off my shoes, fish the panic button out of my bra, and set it on the nightstand. The last thing I want to do is pull out my phone, but Griff isn't going to let me avoid it much longer.

The whole way back to the hotel, he supported me, talked to me, tried to keep me calm. But he hasn't seen the picture. He doesn't know Dimitri.

"Do not be stupid, shlyukha." He punches me in the stomach, and I fall to my knees, vomiting all over the dingy bathroom floor. "Take off your clothes. Now. I want to see what I purchased."

"Sloane?" Griff shuts the bedroom door behind him, and now that we're alone, maybe I don't have to be so strong.

Nudging my purse toward him, I wait for him to fish out my phone, then give him the security code and hold my breath.

"'The price just went up, Sophiana. One thousand dollars each week. Don't make the same mistake you did with Max. If you say anything to your new lover, you will have more blood on your hands. Pay me $500 by the end of the night or you will regret it.'" With each word, the edge to Griff's voice hardens, and when he scrolls down to the photo, something inside him snaps. We look so happy. Laughing, his arm around me, my head bent toward his.

Seconds later, he'd kissed me, and I'd filed the moment away as one of those perfect, pure memories I'd hold on to forever. But now, it's tainted.

Griff forwards the message to his team, then deletes it, and, despite my fear, I'm almost sad the photo's gone. And that we didn't take one of our own.

Stop it, Sloane. There is no us. He's your bodyguard and he's playing a part. Just like you're supposed to be doing.

But when he sits next to me on the bed and wraps his arms around me, it doesn't feel like we're pretending. "I won't let him hurt you. You were spectacular tonight. Our fight? I know senior officers with a dozen years of experience who can't improv that well on a dime, and you didn't miss a beat."

The pride in his voice is hard to ignore, and it calms me as much as his warmth and the sculpted muscles of his chest.

"What do we do now?" I don't want to know the answer. I'd much rather fall asleep in his arms and pretend the rest of the world doesn't exist. Even if just for tonight. But I can't.

Tomorrow's runway show has to be flawless, and after that, we have the unveiling of the Christmas Book at yet another cocktail party. At least with so much going on, I won't have time to dwell on the danger I'm putting Griff and Marina in. But Saturday? I'm free all day until the gala celebration—a six-hour lavish party where I'll be expected to dance and mingle and pose for the press, no matter how terrified I am.

"I have to call Austin and Wren. See if they've managed to track down Volkov. Or the asshole who faked his way into the press briefing. You should relax."

"Relax?" I shove at him, scooting back until I hit the headboard. "How am I supposed to relax? Someone was following us all night! What if they'd hurt you?"

"They didn't." He sits up straighter and rubs his left shoulder. "I saw the tail. Four, five times. Whoever he is, he's good. Couldn't get a solid look at him. But I knew he was there."

"And you didn't tell me?" My eyes burn, the pain of his betrayal so much worse than my own fear. "I'm not that fragile, Griff."

"I didn't say you were." His gaze is so expressive when we're alone, and the regret in them now? It's enough for me to listen. "You were having fun." After a beat, he adds, "So was I."

This strange and wonderful connection we've forged? It's growing stronger every moment we spend together, and he feels it too. I'd bet on it.

Reaching into my purse, I snag the drawing of the two of us. We look so happy. Staring at one another, looking like we really are in love. There's only one problem.

"I wish this was me," I whisper.

"Unless I spent the night with your twin sister, and she's currently hiding under the bed..." Griff smiles until he realizes I'm not joking. "How is this not you?"

"In the picture, my eyes are blue."

Understanding dawns, and he swears under his breath. "Fuck. I'm such an idiot. But, Sloane..." He balls his right hand into a fist, his knuckles cracking, then eases the drawing from my fingers and traces the lines of his arm wrapped around my waist. "This *is* you. The woman I spent the evening with? She wasn't someone's creation. Her laugh wasn't for show. Her smile wasn't forced."

He's right. I hate having to hide my eyes. Not being able to speak the language Mama taught me. But even though this isn't the life I wanted, it *is* a life.

"What can I do?" he asks. "Tell me what you need right now."

You.

To know when this is all over, you'll still look at me the way you do now.

To be seen.

But I don't say any of those things. I can't. Because if I do and he rejects me? I won't be able to pretend any more.

Griff

I ordered a fresh tea tray from room service and set it on the corner of the jetted tub while Sloane removes her contact lenses. She asked for time alone to take a long, hot bath, and that'll give me a chance to talk to Austin.

"Promise me one thing," I say from the bathroom doorway.

"What?" She doesn't look directly at me, and there's nothing I want more than to hold her.

"Put your phone on do not disturb. Don't look at your messages or your email. None of it. That asshole doesn't deserve any more of your energy tonight."

"I have to pay him first." She fiddles with the hem of her sweater, and dammit. I want to punch something.

"Sloane, I don't think that's a good idea. Let me talk to Austin."

A tear tumbles down her cheek, but she doesn't seem to

notice—or care. "I was two hours late with the first payment, and he sent someone to break into my house and hurt me. What if tonight, he comes after Marina? Or you? Let me do this. Then I'll turn my phone off completely. Okay?"

Agreeing goes against my every instinct, but Volkov's willingness to hurt Sloane—and anyone she cares for—without a second thought is too dangerous until we know more about his whereabouts. "Okay. But this is the last time. We're going to find him."

She nods, and I shut both the bathroom and bedroom doors. If our evening together showed me anything, it's that my feelings for Sloane have gone beyond the casual. It's easy to care about her. Easy to...

Stop. She's too scared right now for anything to happen. Even if you both want it to.

Austin picks up seconds after I finish dialing. "We got a lead on Volkov."

"Thank fuck. You got the text? From Sloane's number?"

"Ripper's on it. He's going to send Sloane some link that'll open a program to clone her cell. I don't know how it works, but it'll let us see any messages she gets simultaneously. Whoever's on the ground there is smart. The threats each came from a different number, and neither of those SIMs are in use now. But Volkov left the U.S. the same day Sloane did, only his flight took him from Philly to Germany. He traveled under a fake name—Donny Vance—so he's obviously got contacts. And money."

"And the guy at the presser?" I can still see the glee on that asshole's face as Sloane fought against her panic.

"The cameras around the *Bahnhofstrasse* didn't get a single clear shot of your tail. There aren't many of them, and they need to be cleaned. But facial recognition between those shots and the footage from the press conference? A seventy-five percent match. The man following you was Pavel Andrei."

"I'm assuming Wren—and Ripper?—are tapped into the hotel's security system now?"

"If Andrei gets within a hundred meters of the hotel, we'll see him. You get a 911 from anyone on the team, you get Sloane somewhere safe. Immediately. We'll take care of the rest." On screen, Austin runs a hand through his hair, the exhaustion evident on his face. He and Ripper have been working Zurich time. Wren's pregnant—three or four months, I think—and her husband, Ryker McCabe, called in Ripper for backup.

"Fuck, Austin. You look like death. What does Mik think about you being up at all hours. Have you slept at all?"

"You've been rubbing that shoulder the whole damn phone call. That and looking over at Sloane's bedroom door." He stares directly into the camera, frowns, and leans closer. "Fuck me."

"What?" The impulse to turn off FaceTime and switch to a text only convo hits me like a sledgehammer, but that'll earn me more shit than taking whatever lumps he's about to give me.

"You do realize the assignment was to *pretend* to be her boyfriend, right? Not actually fall for her?" When I can't figure out what to say to him after a very tense few seconds, he starts laughing. "Guess I'm going to have to put that in the recruitment packets from now on."

"I'm keeping it professional. You know I'd never fuck up a job."

Not on purpose, anyway. Because this one? Totally fucked. Up, back, and sideways.

"Listen, Griff. This business? The stress, the emotional toll it takes on the protector and the target? It cuts through a hell of a lot of the crap you deal with in a 'normal' relationship. Forces you to zero in on what's really important. If you feel something for Sloane—something real—don't fuck it up. Her safety's your top priority. Absolutely. That's the job. But I'd be a Grade A hypocrite if I told you *not* to fall for the woman. That's not my call. You're the only one who can decide if she's worth forever."

With a quick glance behind him, Austin's whole demeanor changes. The stress leaves his shoulders, and a smile tugs at his lips.

"Mik's home, and I only have two hours with her if I want to stay on Zurich time. Keep your girl safe."

"Not a girl," I add, but Pritchard's already ended the call.

Keeping her safe, I can do. Making her whole again? Not sure I have a chance in hell at that. But I'm going to try.

BY THE TIME I remove the prosthetic, wash the liners, and hang them up to dry, the hour I promised Sloane is just about over.

I swap out my phone for its backup—keeping a phone charged in the field is damn near impossible, so I carry a couple of clones—and check in with Jacob. He sends me a picture of Marina dancing with some balding executive, having the time of her life.

Jacob: She is not sober.

As long as she's not careless, Marina can drink as much as she wants. I snag a couple of the bottles of water from the large, silver ice bucket on the bar and tuck them under my arm before knocking on Sloane's door.

The scents of honey and coconut rush over me when she answers, and her skin is practically glowing. The red rimming her eyes, though, worries me. "Can I come in?"

I left my glasses charging next to the spare phone, and her

lips tremble before she steps back. "Did you find the guy? The one following us?"

"Pavel Andrei. The 'reporter' from earlier. Austin's certain of it. Didn't get a full facial recognition match, but close enough."

The velvet bathrobe is already tied tightly around Sloane's waist, but she double and triple checks the belt before sinking down onto the edge of the bed. "So he's the one Dimitri is paying to threaten me?"

"He's involved. Still don't know who's sending the messages, but they're using burners, and Andrei, at least, hasn't stepped foot into the hotel since the press conference. If he does, I'll get an alert, and Austin will have this place locked down in under five minutes." Offering her one of the bottles of water, I use what's left of my arm to hold the second bottle so I can twist off the cap.

Sloane stares at me for a moment, then shakes her head. "I didn't realize you'd taken off your prosthetic. I would have opened that for you."

"You...didn't realize? It's pretty obvious. Big void on the left side of my body?"

She's so honest, so matter-of-fact sometimes, it's almost unnerving. But also comforting.

Frowning, she shoots me a look that says, *"Well, duh,"* before taking a long drink from her bottle. "I was looking at your face, Captain Foot-In-Mouth."

Fuck me. Even after tonight's stress, after another threat from the man who made her life hell for—God, I don't even know how long—she hasn't shut down completely.

"You remember that?" I ask, leaning against the door jamb.

"I remember everything about last night in the bar." Setting the bottle of water down, she nods at the bed next to her. "You can sit."

There's nothing I want more than to be close to her, but that's the problem. I want it too much. "I should let you get some sleep."

Her brown eyes cloud over. "It's a big bed. I was hoping...I don't want to be alone tonight."

Fuck. This is a bad idea. I don't care what Austin says. I'm falling for Sloane, have been since I first laid eyes on her. But that doesn't mean she feels the same. Or that she's ready for anything more than what we've shared so far. A few hot-as-fuck kisses and comfort.

"Do you have a side?" I ask as I shut the door. In less than twenty-four hours, we've gone from strangers to something *more*. Something real. I could screw it all up by staying in her bed tonight, but I want this—need this—as much as she does.

Sloane fiddles with the belt on her robe. "I like being able to see the sky. Even if it's just through a crack in the drapes." Before I can grab the duvet, she reaches for my arm. "I don't like the dark. There's...um...a nightlight next to the dresser. Is that...okay?"

I wish I could hear her voice. Because her expression? It's like she's expecting me to say no. Or to call her a coward. Or weak. "I'll turn it on."

By the time I flip the switch, she's shed the robe, only a soft t-shirt and pair of barely there shorts covering her body. I don't know how I'm supposed to sleep next to her all night without a massive hard-on. Distraction? There aren't enough baseball stats in the world to keep me from thinking about how good it feels to have her pressed against me. Kissing me. Smiling at me. I'm so far gone for this woman, it's ridiculous, and we only just met.

But Austin's right. Protecting her? It cuts through so much of the standard relationship crap—all the shit that gets in the way of falling in love. We're together twenty-four-seven, and that makes it impossible to hide so much. Like my arm. Her nervous tics.

Before I get into bed, I slide the small vibrating button under the pillow, but when I reach for the light, the truth of what's about to happen hits me like a sledgehammer, and I drop my hand, staring at the lamp like it's my worst enemy. Until Sloane skims her hand down my arm.

Turn around, idiot. Talk to her.

But I can't. Not even after she scoots closer and tugs on my right sleeve. But then she places her palm over my heart and moves it in a circle. The ASL sign for *please*.

"What's wrong?" she asks when I face her.

Taking a deep breath is harder than it should be. Like my next words are tying themselves around my chest and squeezing the life out of me. "Once I turn off the light, we can't *talk* anymore."

"Oh." After a long moment, she presses a small button right next to the headboard, and tiny lights flicker on, set into the wood. "One advantage of fancy hotels. Reading lights."

The simple gesture makes my eyes burn. It's nothing. Less than nothing. All she did was flip a fucking switch. But the idea of being able to lie down next to her and carry on a conversation? It makes me feel like I'm not so broken.

But when we face one another? A dozen questions battle it out in my head, all scrambling to break free until Sloane silences them by leaning in and kissing me.

"I'm sorry," she says as soon as she pulls back enough for me to see her lips. "I know this is just pretend. But you were right. I did have fun tonight. With you. And it wasn't just because you make me feel safe."

Reaching out to cup the back of her neck, I pull her half on top of me and claim her lips with all the passion I've been holding back since this morning. No one has ever affected me like Sloane Sanders, and I'm starting to think no one ever will.

One of her legs drapes over mine, and our position allows me to feel the vibration in her chest as she moans—at least I hope that's the sound she's making. She fists my t-shirt, and if I had the full use of both arms, I'd wrap them around her and hold her close all fucking night.

Instead, I let my hand trail down her back until I reach her ass. Her entire body goes rigid, and she jerks, breaking off the kiss, and sits up.

"Sloane? What did I do?"

She won't answer me, just covers her face with her hands as her entire torso shakes with the force of her sobs. Her fear and shame fill the room, and, by God, I'd do anything just to get her to smile again. Or even look at me.

"Sweetheart, talk to me. Please."

Shaking her head, she swipes at her cheeks and turns away, burrowing under the covers with her back to me. Is she purposely trying to shut me out? Or is this just a defense mechanism?

With no other option, I get to my feet, skirt the bed, and kneel in front of her. The pain etched on her face is enough to send me back onto my ass, and the puzzle pieces fall into place.

"I haven't kissed anyone in...a long time."

"I've never had a normal relationship."

"Have you ever had sex?" The question is blunt as fuck, but it gets her to look at me.

Her eyes hold none of their usual warmth. "You know what happened to me when I came to this country."

"That wasn't sex. That was rape." She flinches at the word, and I want to apologize, but I don't know how else to get through to her. "I won't pressure you, sweetheart. Nothing has to happen you're not ready for. But, I need you to trust me. Trust *one thing*."

"What?" Sloane's gaze darts to the night stand where I placed the last four handkerchiefs that came with the tux. All with the same dark blue stitching. Her eyes well with more tears until she uses a fresh one to dash them away.

I don't dare move. The last thing I want to do is spook her. But eventually, she locks eyes with me, and I can tell her the one thing I've wanted to say since we had our first kiss in this room a little over twelve hours ago.

"This isn't just pretend for me. I care about you, Sloane. I don't get *involved* on mission. It goes against everything I've ever been taught. But you're special. You're smart, incredibly strong, and brave as fuck. You learned how to sign my name. And you don't care that I'm half the man I used to be."

"You're not." Sloane sits up, and her nipples strain against the thin t-shirt. "Griff, you're amazing. I'm a coward who's scared of *everything*. I have the best security system on the market, and the man Dimitri sent to hurt me back in San Diego? He disabled it like it was a child's toy. I've been used by *hundreds* of men, and yet...our kiss this morning?" Fresh tears spill down her cheeks, and she wipes them away with a hatred I save for scorpions and spilled scotch. "I lied to you. That wasn't my first kiss in a long time. It was my *first kiss ever*."

Holy shit. I can't continue having this conversation from the floor. I need Sloane in my arms. Or at least close enough to touch. If she'll let me. Rising to my knees, I hold out my hand and wait for her to take it. Her warmth grounds me in a way I didn't know I needed. "Sweetheart, this is going to sound like a line. But I swear on my right arm, it's not. I want you. In every way. But if this is all we ever have? If we can't go any further than whatever-the-fuck base we just slid into? I don't care. This assignment was the best damn thing to ever happen to me, and

I'm not giving up on you—or us—unless you tell me to walk away."

For several long moments, neither of us move. I'm about to give her space and tell her I'll sleep on the couch when she sniffles and peers down at me with swollen, red-rimmed eyes. "Will you just hold me tonight? Please?"

"I'll hold you every night, sweetheart."

Sloane settles against me, and when I drape my damaged arm over her, she settles with a deep sigh.

My brain and my heart are waging a battle neither can win, and if I'm not careful, they'll both die trying.

CHAPTER TWENTY-TWO

Sloane

With Griff at my back, curled around me protectively, I slept until 5:00 a.m., but something woke me, and I can't stop my mind from racing. Last night's kiss, my panic, his understanding, Dimitri, today's runway show, Marina's safety. The last words I spoke to Max.

An inch at a time, I ease myself out of bed and tiptoe to my suitcase. Between the moon reflecting off the placid lake and the reading lights we never turned off before falling asleep, I can see well enough to pull out my sketchbook and calm myself by drawing.

For a moment, I think the lake would make a good subject, but then I focus on the man in my bed. At some point overnight, he took off his shirt, and he's a study in opposites. Hard muscles, relaxed in sleep, his face peaceful in a way I haven't seen before.

The lines and curves take shape on the page. His hair—long on top, shaved close on the sides—lips relaxed, stubble darkening his jaw. A tattoo arcing from just over his heart to his left shoulder is marred by several thick lines of scar tissue, but it's still gorgeous. Lightning and sparks, pure and raw power.

I don't gloss over his injuries, adding the surgical scars on what remains of his left arm, what looks like it might be a long-healed bullet wound just above the waistband of his shorts. The sheet pooled around his hips, the way he sleeps with his bent right arm under the pillow.

Drawing has always been my escape. When I pick up a charcoal pencil, I can pretend I'm anywhere. Times Square. Niagara Falls. On the beach in Mexico. Rarely do I choose to draw what's right in front of me.

Dawn breaks while I add the finishing touches. A small scar next to his right eyebrow. A hint of freckles sprinkled over his shoulders. Shading under each abdominal muscle—all eight of them. The *v* of muscle leading into his shorts.

"That wasn't sex."

"This isn't just pretend for me."

Could this be something real?

"Sloane?" Griff's voice, rough with sleep, startles me, and the pencil hits the plush carpet without a sound. "Are you okay?"

With a groan, he sits up and rubs his left shoulder, then squints at the sketchpad in my hand. My first instinct is to hide the drawing, but if I want this to be anything other than fake, I can't keep hiding.

"I couldn't get back to sleep," I say, but he shakes his head.

"I can't see your lips, sweetheart. The sun's about to rise over the lake and you're backlit. Can you come closer?" Griff holds out his hand, and though a part of me is terrified he'll ask me questions I can't—or don't want to—answer, I'm not that much of a jerk that I'll use his deafness to my advantage.

Setting the drawing on the nightstand, I flip on the lamp

and climb back into bed with him. "I woke up a little over an hour ago. Couldn't get back to sleep."

"Any reason?" He's not touching me, holding himself stiffly, his deep blue eyes searching my face for answers he's afraid I won't give him.

I shrug. "All of them?" His chuckle makes me smile, and it's easier to continue than I thought. "I worry about everything, Griff. The runway show today. What Dimitri is going to do next. You."

He arches a brow—just one—and it's both cocky and funny at the same time.

"Yes, you. What happens if Dimitri didn't believe our act last night? Or if he saw you go into Max's room with me? What if he's just toying with me? That was always his thing. String us along with promises of McDonald's or hot showers or a fix..." I swallow the sob desperate to escape. "If he wasn't beating us or letting his men have their way with us."

Griff slides a little closer. "I'd ask if I could hold you, but my glasses are charging in the other room and I don't want to read your words on my phone. I can't stand not being able to touch you right now." He's not the only one, so I link our fingers. His strong grip grounds me, and I take a deep, almost steady, breath as he continues. "I was awake for at least an hour last night, wondering if I needed to know the details. What happened to you all those years ago. I'll listen if you ever want to tell me, but Sloane, you aren't that scared eighteen-year-old kid anymore. That asshole doesn't own you. Not your body, your mind, or your heart. *You* get to decide what happens now. With your career, with your life... and with us."

"I want to be...normal," I whisper. "I shouldn't panic if you touch my ass. I walk into a shoot, strip down to almost nothing, and let strangers lift and tape my breasts, spray me with bronzer, and even *sew me into* skin-tight dresses on occasion. But last night—"

"It wasn't my hand on your ass. I know, sweetheart." There's so much understanding in his voice, it threatens to break me, and I hold my breath. "You were scared what would happen next."

I nod. Somewhere in the middle of sketching him this morning, I came to the same conclusion.

"I don't break promises." Griff holds my gaze, the intensity of his stare impressing on me just how serious he is. "Which is why I don't make many of them. You do what I do for long enough, you realize pretty damn quick that tomorrow isn't guaranteed. Not for anyone. But I can promise you one thing. If you want to try again—at any time—and it gets too much? Just say the word and we'll stop. I won't be angry, I won't pressure you for anything you're not ready for. I might ask you to talk to me, but hell, I won't force you to do that either. On my life, you're safe with me."

Tears threaten, but I can't let myself cry. Not if I expect to walk the runway in six hours. Instead, I wrap my arms around his waist and rest my cheek against his chest. His heartbeat comforts me, steady and strong, and I think maybe I just might be falling in love with him.

Griff

I feel it the second Sloane's breathing steadies and slows. It's barely 7:30. With her runway show call at fourteen hundred, we have a little time, so I let her sleep, relishing in her trust, her strength, her honesty. Hell, I haven't really opened up to anyone since the attack. Not even my CIA-mandated shrink. Not any more than I had to.

Sloane's been so honest—even through her fear—that anything she asks me? I'll tell her. Shifting slightly to lessen some of the pressure on my left arm, I catch a glimpse of her sketchpad.

For a full minute, I don't think I can breathe. She said she'd won an art contest in school, told me about the private classes she takes, but I never imagined... This is how she sees me? Carefully, trying not to wake her, I reach for the book. There's nothing broken about the man in the drawing. Nothing angry or frustrated or lonely—all the emotions I struggle with every day. He's completely at peace, and though he's definitely me, definitely missing most of his left arm, Sloane captured my bulked-up shoulder muscle, the surgical scars, and my tattoo with all its imperfections from the attack and the subsequent surgeries.

Setting the book back on the nightstand, I press a gentle kiss to the top of her head. "You're fucking amazing, sweetheart. I hope someday, you believe that as much as I do."

⁂

WHEN THE ALARM GOES OFF, Sloane jerks up, and her cheeks flush a bright red. "Oh, God. I didn't mean to fall asleep."

"You needed the rest. Don't apologize." When her gaze lands on the sketchbook, she covers her mouth with her hand and stares between me and the drawing. We're close enough, I can *almost* hear her mumbling, and I reach out and touch her arm. "Are you saying something, sweetheart? Because I can't see your lips."

Sloane picks up the book and clutches it to her chest. "I'm

sorry. I didn't mean to...I was going to draw the lake, but you just looked so..."

"Asleep?" Cracking a smile, I expect her to laugh with me, but she levels a serious gaze at me.

"Strong. And...content." Her shoulders heave with what I think is a sigh, and she frowns. "I couldn't stop myself."

The sketch is exactly what she just described—and the complete opposite of how I'd describe myself. "Sloane, is this really how you see me?"

The question surprises her, and her brown eyes widen. "Yes. Of course. You don't? See yourself that way?"

The lump in my throat makes it hard to reply, so I shake my head. "Not anymore."

Subtle vibrations echo in the room, and Sloane rolls her eyes. "Marina. She says the coffee's hot and she's ordered breakfast. So if you don't want her opening the door alone, you'll 'get your ass out there.'" She exaggerates the air quotes then reaches for her robe. "We're not done with this conversation." Leaning in, Sloane cups my cheek, her thumb rasping over my stubble. "Your injuries aren't what I see when I look at you, Griff. They're part of you, but they don't define you."

The brief touch of her lips to mine settles me in a way I didn't know I needed.

Until she gets to her feet and shrugs into the robe with a sad smile. "I should warn you. Given the tone of Marina's voice? She probably assumes we had sex last night. I hope you're prepared for an interrogation."

"Wait." Rolling out of bed, I find my t-shirt and struggle into it. "Marina doesn't know? About everything you told me?" Marina is Sloane's best friend. Don't women talk about these things?

Sloane doesn't meet my gaze, and her fingers clench and unclench rapidly at her sides. "No one knows." Sadness etches small lines of stress around her lips and eyes, and I wrap my arm around her waist. "When your whole life is a lie, it's easier to keep everything *real* hidden deep down inside."

Oh, fuck. I should have known. I've spent enough time in deep cover to understand how hard it is to be someone you're not. "You are the strongest woman I've ever met, Sloane. I understand why you never told her, but...she's a good person. In my line of work, you learn to read people. Marina's got your back. And so do I. You're not alone anymore."

She rests her head on my shoulder for a long moment, and I worry I just said the wrong thing, but when she finally meets my gaze again, some of that bone-deep sadness has faded. "I know. Really. I do. But I've kept secrets so long...I don't know how *not* to."

"You'll learn, sweetheart. It'll take time, but you'll learn."

Sloane

Marina hands me a cup of coffee, and I can't even form words until I take a deep whiff. "You are a godsend."

"I," she says on a yawn, "am hungover. That party last night was off the hook."

Griff snags his glasses, pours himself a cup of coffee, and heads for the bath off the main room of the suite. "I need to shave. Sloane? When room service knocks, come get me. Don't answer the bell—either of you."

He doesn't shut the door completely, and Marina takes a seat next to me on the couch. "So?" she whispers. "Did the two of you...?"

"No!" The water's running, and we're far enough away that I don't *think* Griff's glasses will pick up what we're saying, but I still keep my voice as low as possible. "He held me. That's it. You know I don't...do that sort of thing."

"Why not?" Marina's bloodshot green eyes tell me exactly how much fun she had last night at the party, and I arch my brows. She wouldn't...

"You didn't bring anyone back here, did you?"

With a snort, she shakes her head. "As if Mr. British Stick-in-the-Mud would have let me." At my horrified expression, she starts to roll her eyes, then winces. "Dammit. I need at least another couple of ibuprofen. But Sloane, even if I'd wanted to, I wouldn't have actually done it. Not with someone after you." Scooting closer, she drapes her arm around my shoulders. "You come first, sweetie. Always."

I release the breath I didn't know I was holding, set the china cup down and wrap my arms around her. "I'm sorry. I'm not myself right now. This whole situation..."

Except it's not the situation. Not being in danger, anyway. Griff's right. I can't let Dimitri and Rodney—or even Max—stop me from trusting everyone for the rest of my life. I made one bad choice when I was eighteen. And since then, every potential friend was someone who could—and would —betray me.

Pulling back, I retrieve my coffee and take a fortifying sip. "Marina? I've never had *sex*." My eyes burn, but I won't let myself cry. "Not...after I escaped Dimitri. I don't know if I can."

She chokes on a sip of her coffee, then lunges for a napkin and holds it against her nose. "Oh, God. I didn't think...I'm an idiot. We've known each other for how long? More than ten years. We've never talked about your love life. I should have...I don't know. Put the pieces together? Or asked. Something. I'm so sorry."

"Don't apologize." The cup rattles in the saucer, and I take a deep breath to try to steady my nerves. I've taken more Xanax in the past week than I usually do in a month, and if I'm not careful, I'll make my tardive dyskinesia even worse right before a show where all eyes—and all cameras—are on me. "I didn't let anyone get close to me. I thought it was better that way. But I'm tired of being alone. Of not trusting anyone."

Marina rests her hand on my thigh and gives it a quick squeeze before lowering her voice to a whisper. "Does Griff know?"

"I told him last night. After I freaked out on him for grabbing my ass." My cheeks flush hot, and I cast a quick glance at the bathroom. I'm about to tell her this fake relationship isn't so fake anymore when the suite's bell rings, saving me from more "girl talk."

It feels good to trust someone. To confide in Marina. But it's also harder than I thought it would be, and the distraction of breakfast is exactly what I need.

CHAPTER TWENTY-THREE

Sloane

When I emerge from the bedroom, Griff is down on one knee strapping the knife to his calf. He smiles, but something's off.

"What is it?" I tug at the sleeves of the loose black dress and chew on my lower lip. I *just* took a Xanax, but it hasn't kicked in yet, and my anxiety is through the roof.

"You look stunning," he says as he smooths the leg of his dark gray trousers. "You always look stunning. But—"

"This dress doesn't look like me?" I laugh, and some of the tension gathered between my shoulders fades away. "I hate it. The shoes too. But I can't wear anything that might leave a single mark on my skin."

Griff taps the temple of his glasses, then frowns. "No marks?"

"No bra, only the smoothest panties on the market, no socks, nothing with elastic..." I wave my hand up and down my body. "I'll have at least six outfit changes for the show this afternoon. I won't see what they are until I get down there, but wardrobe could put me in anything from a skimpy negligée to a bathing suit to a ball gown. Since I don't know what parts of me are going to be on full display, I can't have any seams pressing against my skin. Those marks can take up to an hour to fade. Hence, this *thing*. I could cut a hole in a pillow case and feel more stylish."

He slides his right arm around my waist—gently, so he won't crease the ultra-soft dress to my skin—and up close, he smells so good. A feeling I think might be arousal warms me from the inside out, and I sigh.

"What's wrong?"

"Nothing." A smile tugs at my lips when he starts to argue with me, and I kiss him. Both to silence his protests and because I want to. It's nothing compared to the heat of last night's make-out session. Just a little flick of my tongue against his lips, but the half moan, half growl he makes? It sends goose-bumps racing over my skin. "I like this. When you hold me, I feel safe."

"You *are* safe with me." The rough edge to his voice comforts me even more, though he can't promise me safety and he knows it.

Change the subject. Otherwise, you're going to end up having a panic attack before you leave the room.

"How do your glasses work?" At his furrowed brow, I add, "You tapped the temple when I came into the room. Does that turn them on?"

Griff releases me and removes the black frames. "There's a touch sensor on each side. The one on the left temple turns the glasses into a camera. As long as I have my phone on me—and a signal—the video streams directly to the cloud—and my team.. If I'm somewhere with no cell service, the recording maxes out at ten minutes. The sensor on the right switches between three different modes. Off, on, and alerts only."

"Alerts?"

"The software recognizes sounds like alarm bells, fire and police sirens, someone knocking, even laughter and crying. Royce—he's the hardware guy who came up with the idea for these things—is working on a version for the public that'll identify all kinds of ambient noises. Things like approaching cars, footsteps, dogs barking, cats meowing, birdsong." As he speaks, his shoulders straighten slightly. "The man is a genius. He designed the panic button too."

Oh, crap. I haven't told him. "Um, about that. I can't keep it on me today."

Griff's casual, relaxed expression vanishes in an instant. "Then I'm not leaving your side."

"You can't be in the dressing room with me. Only models and staff are allowed. *Beauty and Style* is *very* strict about their runway shows." With every word, Griff's deep blue eyes grow harder.

"We'll see about that." He pulls out his phone and taps the screen half a dozen times. "Austin, I need Wren or Ripper to find a way to get me backstage with Sloane for today's runway show. She can't wear the tracker, and over a hundred people will be going in and out of that room over four hours. I know it's the middle of the night in Seattle, but anything you can do..."

The speech-to-text software translates his words, and he texts them to his boss. "Are you ready to go?" His easy, warm tone is gone, and in its place, the hardened CIA agent I met two nights ago right after I found Max's body.

"No. But we don't have a choice. If I don't show up, not only will I be in breach of contract, but Dimitri will find out—somehow—and he'll know something's wrong." With a sigh, I run a hand through my long locks. Without any makeup, wearing a dress that's two sizes bigger than I need, with soft, black moccasins on my feet, I look nothing like Sloane Sanders, the Christmas Book cover model and the global face of *Beauty and Style.*

And when I take Griff's left hand, I catch sight of the two of us in the large mirror on the wall. For a long moment, I can't move, can't tear my gaze away. His suit is just as smart and stylish as yesterday's, and he slicked his hair back today, the longer strands on top reminiscent of James Dean.

"Sloane?" Griff steps in front of me, breaking the spell that had me so entranced. "We have to go."

I'd give anything to hide out in the suite for the rest of the day. Or hell, the rest of the weekend. To pretend Dimitri had never found me again. To succumb to the magic I saw for just a moment in that mirror and be a "normal" couple.

Instead, I plaster on my fake smile and follow Griff out the door.

***

Griff

"You can't go in with her, sir," the security guard says when I try to accompany Sloane into the dressing area off the main ballroom. "Only models and *Beauty and Style* staff."

"I'm Sloane's agent, and I'm responsible for her safety and happiness at this event," I say, leaning forward so I can get right in the man's face.

"If you continue to make a scene, I'll have you removed from the hotel, sir." The second guard pulls a handheld radio from his belt, an obvious threat to call in backup.

"Griff." The single word in red text scrolls across my lenses, and Sloane's warm hand cups my cheek. "I'll be fine. There should be a seat with your name on it in the front row of the ballroom."

Fuck. Austin hasn't returned my text, and while I could take these assholes—they're not much better than Rent-A-Cops—that would ruin the whole show for Sloane. "I don't like this, sweetheart."

"I know." She draws me away from the desk so one of the other models can check in, then wraps her arms around me and leans in to kiss my neck. "Can your glasses pick up my words if I whisper?"

"Assuming that's what you're doing right now? Yes." To anyone watching, we're two people in love, and she's doing her best to calm me down.

"Good." Another kiss and she scores her teeth over my earlobe. "Trust me. I don't like this any more than you do, but this is my job, and I'm really good at it. If *anything* goes wrong, Marina will know, and she'll use her panic button."

These pants are getting tight, and it hits me. We haven't said the words. Hell, I don't know if she'll ever be able to say them. But the picture we're painting for the world? It's not a lie. Sloane has my heart, and she always will.

When she draws back enough for me to see her lips again, I tuck a lock of hair behind her ear. "What's one supposed to say to a model before a show? Is it like Broadway where you can't say—"

"Good luck?" She laughs, and for the first time since we left the hotel room, her smile is completely genuine. This is the real Sloane Sanders. The same woman who walked the *Bahnhofs-trasse* with me last night. "Maybe just cross your fingers that all the tape stays where it's supposed to."

"Make sure it does." Threading my fingers through her hair, I slant my mouth over hers, and time stops. Kissing her is my new favorite pastime, and from how her body responds to me? She feels the same. Her nipples tighten into hard nubs, and it hits me. No marks on her body. Nothing tight. She's not wearing a bra.

Pressing closer, she slides her hand down my back to my ass. All the blood in my body heads south, and if I don't stop this soon, I won't be able to walk into that ballroom.

"Sloane." All I can manage is a single word, and thank fuck Marina pokes her head out of the dressing room door.

"If you don't get your butt in here right now, Sloane, you're going to be last in line for hair and makeup, and you know what that means!"

Her breathing not quite steady, Sloane sags against me. "I should go. Marina doesn't make idle threats."

"Wait. What would it mean? If I kept kissing you for another five...maybe ten minutes?" I ask.

Besides the biggest case of blue balls I've ever had.

She throws her head back and laughs, and it fills her entire body with a lightness I want to see again and again. "The last time I was late for one of these multi-model shows, Marina put so much setting spray in my hair, I had to take three showers that night to get it all out. And even then, it was still crunchy."

"Ouch. You'd better get in there, sweetheart. And remember your promise."

She squeezes my fingers, then traces a line across my palm with her thumb. The sensation makes me feel alive and whole, and even in this cocoon of never-ending silence, I know I'm not alone. Not anymore.

Sloane

From the moment I walk into the dressing room, personal privacy goes out the window. Most of the models are half naked, given that they all have a turn on the runway before me. As the Christmas Book cover model, I get top billing, but that means I have more time for my nerves to take over.

Thank God for Marina. In under ten minutes, she has my hair piled into a messy bun and starts on my makeup. The show runs for almost an hour—much longer than normal. Before every model's appearance, one of the *Beauty and Style* executives will introduce us and share a personal tidbit or two about our lives, and after the first three rotations, the conglomerate's CEO has a thirty-minute speech during which Marina will have to completely redo our makeup and hair as we switch from day to evening looks.

I don't know how Marina keeps everything straight given that her notes look like a doctor tried to scribble instructions while riding a roller coaster. But she always does.

"Tonight, you need to eye mask for at least an hour," she chides, dabbing concealer on the dark circles. "Between the stress and whatever you and McMuscles are doing behind closed doors, you're going to look like you have two black eyes tomorrow if you're not careful."

"Gee, thanks for the vote of confidence, best friend forever," I mutter. "I thought you were always supposed to be on my side?"

"I am." She leans down to whisper in my ear. "I'm trying to *sell* the whole relationship story."

"Thank you." Meeting her gaze in the mirror, I smile and try to match her hushed tone. "But it's not a story. Not anymore."

"Sloane!" Marina beams as she picks up her foundation

sponge. "When this is all over, " her expression sobers, "we're going to have a nice long girls' weekend where we can catch up on everything we haven't talked about over the years."

Shame crawls up my neck, and I reach back and rub at the rough skin where Dimitri's tattoo used to be. "I'd like that. I'm sorry I haven't been a great friend."

"Oh, hush. That is not what I meant. Eyes closed now, please."

As Marina dusts my lids with gold, I think of all the times I deflected, answered with half-truths—or even flat-out lied to her—and suddenly, I'm close to tears again. Dammit. I'm never *this* emotional.

Because you never let yourself feel anything.

My inner voice has always told me the truth, even when I refused to listen.

"Sloane? Sweetie, take a deep breath for me. Right now," Marina snaps. "You are *not* allowed to cry. This is waterproof liner, but no one's going to be able to see it if your eyes swell up."

"I'm okay." I clasp Marina's hand on my shoulder as I count backwards from forty-seven, again. By the time I reach forty, I'm calm. "Really. Once this junket is over, everything's going to change. It has to."

STANDING JUST BEHIND THE CURTAIN, I try not to destroy the shimmering golden lip gloss Marina touched up just seconds ago.

Donna, the head of the *Beauty and Style* Christmas Book selection committee, stands at the far end of the T-shaped runway at the microphone. "Our next model has been the global face of our brand for the past five years. Her poise, dedication, and passion are unmatched in the industry, and we're so very proud to feature her on the cover of this year's Christmas Book. Please welcome Sloane Sanders!"

The applause is enough to send my heart racing, but I school my expression into one of casual detachment as I stride slowly and confidently onto the stage. With one hand shoved into the pocket of the tailored "business" capris, the dark blue jacket reveals a fitted bralette in the same midnight linen.

Donna goes on and on about what I'm wearing—the designer, the material, how I can go from a business meeting to a night on the town simply by unbuttoning the jacket—and I reach the end of the runway, turn, pose, turn, and pose again, desperately wishing the lights weren't so bright so I could see Griff.

But it's no use, and when Donna concludes her little spiel, I offer up a demure smile, let a few more flashbulbs go off, and then make the long trip up the stage until I'm safely back in the wings.

Jill—the young model with the caffeine pill habit—is waiting for her second turn, and she's bouncing on the balls of her feet. "This is *the best!*" she gushes, reaching out to capture my hand and give it a quick squeeze. "Don't you just love every freaking minute?"

I almost say no until I realize this could be the last runway show of my career. Despite the strict and "boring as fuck" diet, the endless hours of workouts, the long shoots under hot lights, this job has given me so much.

"I do," I say and offer her a genuine smile. "Don't take a single minute of this experience for granted. Soak it all in, and when you have to show up on set at 5:00 a.m. because some photographer wants the 'perfect' light or when you're wearing a bikini on the beach in January and freezing your ass off, remember how you feel right now."

And then Donna's calling Jill's name, and the young woman beams at me and heads out for her spotlight.

By the time I'm back in the care of Marina's capable hands, I'm almost calm. Happy even. If this really is my last show, I need to give it my all and enjoy every second of it.

CHAPTER TWENTY-FOUR

Griff

Even in the front row, I can't make out what's being said about each of the models. My glasses don't do shit in a crowd this large—or this boisterous. Between the applause, the conversations happening all around me, and the music pumping loud enough I can *feel* the beat, my normally silent world is filled with a dull, constant roar.

Until Sloane emerges from the wings. I can't take my eyes off her. The outfits? They're *interesting*. Most show off a fair bit of skin, more now that apparently the show's transitioned from daytime to evening wear. Pretty sure that negligée she wore for her last appearance was held up by string and prayers.

Whenever Sloane isn't on stage, I text back and forth with Austin and Ripper—the other computer genius out in Seattle.

Ripper: Got a lead on Rodney Carriger. He moved down to Mexico not long after Sloane signed with the Ulstrum Agency. He paid for a new identity—name of Ricardo Cortez—and was living mostly off the grid. Only reason we found him at all? His dental records matched those of a dead body discovered outside of Cancun two weeks ago.

Shit. Another of Volkov's victims? As one of the blond male models I saw at the cocktail party the other night walks the stage wearing a pair of billowy pajama pants and a cropped silk shirt, I thumb out a reply.

Any sign of Volkov near Cancun?

There are only two models left before Sloane's final appearance, and though she'll need to stay and mingle at the cocktail party immediately following the runway show, I'll be by her side. Every hour that passes without another threat—or a confirmed location on Andrei or Volkov—grates on my nerves.

Ripper: Nope. But I doubt the man does his own dirty work. The guy who broke into Sloane's house? Based on her description and traffic cameras in the area around the time of the attack, he's not affiliated with anyone. Local muscle for hire. Inara and the new probie are headed down to San Diego. They'll make sure the asshole knows to stay away from Sloane if he wants to continue breathing.

The idea of Sloane returning to the place she was attacked has my every protective instinct flaring to life. Austin and Dax thought we'd have Volkov by now, that my assignment would end with the gala party tomorrow night. But I'm not leaving Sloane's side with any threat to her safety still out there.

The beat of the music changes, and the lights dim, a spotlight on the *Beauty and Style* CEO behind the microphone. It takes all my concentration to read his lips.

"And now, dressed in the very gown that she's wearing on the cover of our beloved Christmas Book, our darling star, Sloane Sanders!"

The second she emerges, I stop breathing. Red silk crosses over her breasts, wraps around her shoulders, and tapers down to her waist. The gown billows with every step, and Sloane spins, showing off one long, toned thigh before continuing to sashay down the runway.

She's an angel in crimson, sparkling silver heels glinting in the lights, and the audience bursts into applause so loud, it fills the room, even to my damaged ears.

At the end of the stage, Sloane curtseys, spins one last time, and joins the rest of the models who've all come out to applaud her. The CEO says something—I can make out the timber of his voice, but not his words—and the world behind me dissolves into a sea of flash bulbs.

THE TEN MINUTES it takes Sloane to make her way off the stage are the longest of my life. "You amaze me," I say in her ear as I embrace her. I can feel the vibrations in her chest as she says something in reply and add, "My glasses don't work with the music this loud."

When she draws back, the light in her eyes, even through the contact lenses, brings a peace to her entire being I don't know that I've seen in "Sloane Sanders, the model." All through the cocktail party, the press conference, and even during her first walk down the runway, she's been guarded. Acting the consummate professional while practically falling apart on the inside.

But now, she's different. Happier.

"I need some water—or sparkling cider. The lights take a lot out of me. But, I need something else first." Before I can ask what, her fingers stroke the back of my head, and she's kissing me. The intimate contact settles me, giving me the peace I've craved my entire life but didn't know it.

This woman is it for me. The urge to tell her *right fucking now* is so strong, I don't know how much longer I can wait. She takes the lead, her tongue tracing the seam of my lips, and I let her in, let her control the speed, the urgency…all of it.

Flashbulbs explode around us, and I can feel the press of bodies getting closer. Sloane stiffens and breaks off the kiss, and the only thing in her eyes? Fear.

"Hands around my neck, sweetheart. Now." Scooping my right arm under her knees and using my left as best I can to support her back, I rush her to the far side of the room where the security guards who refused to admit me to the dressing room stand at attention. "Hey. If the two of you want to do your fucking jobs, you could make sure *Beauty and Style's* star model isn't crushed to death by the media."

They stare over my shoulder at the approaching mob of photographers, and after a beat, leap into action. One radios for backup, and I escape out the double doors of the Pavilion with Sloane still held in my arms.

"Are you okay?" I ask when we're safely out in the hall where the air's cooler and it's quiet enough for me to lower Sloane to her feet and turn my glasses on.

"Y-yes," she stammers, her hand pressed to her heart. "I've been mobbed before at events like this, but never that quickly."

"Do you want to leave? Go back up to the room?"

Sloane's still shaken, and reaches for my hand, linking our fingers and squeezing gently. "No. I'm expected to stay through the party. Once the press are escorted out, it'll be calmer."

Angling a glance back inside the Pavilion, I know she's right. It's already considerably less crowded, and the music isn't so loud I can feel it through the soles of my feet.

"Sloane?" The word scrolls across my lenses in black, tagged as Unknown, and I follow Sloane's gaze to find the *Beauty and Style* CEO, Franklin Meadows, standing a few feet away. "My apologies for interrupting. And for the abhorrent behavior of some of the media. They've been escorted from the premises. Will you rejoin us inside? I'd love to introduce you to some of our investors who weren't able to make it to the opening cocktail party."

Sloane releases my hand and steps forward. "We'd be happy to. This is Harry Griffin. My boyfriend. He's also standing in for my agent from the Ulstrum Agency."

She signs my name, along with "boyfriend," and something in my heart cracks open. I didn't know how much I needed her to say the word. Even though we're in public, the look in her eyes? I think—I hope—it's love. She just might not realize it yet.

I offer Meadows my hand, and he shakes it, though he doesn't look me in the eyes. "It's a pleasure, Mr. Meadows. Your team put on a phenomenal show this afternoon."

The man shifts uncomfortably on his feet, his gaze bouncing between me and Sloane. "I'm afraid I don't sign," he says to her with an apologetic shrug.

I'm used to this. Being dismissed. Having people talk around me rather than to me. So used to it that I can easily shove down the annoyance. "I read lips well enough. Signing is easier in a crowd, but as long as you speak slowly, I can understand you."

"Oh." If anything, Meadows looks even more off balance now, and I offer Sloane my arm.

"See you inside," she says, her lips tight. Once we're through the doors, she leans closer to me. "I'm so sorry."

"For what?" The bass beat of the music thrums in my ears, providing me with a hint of normalcy in my fucked up life.

"Franklin didn't talk to *you*." Her brow creases, and I cup the back of her head and plant a gentle kiss to the furrow.

"I'm used to it, sweetheart. Mostly. It's why I'm so fucking thankful for these glasses. One-on-one, I don't have to be just 'the deaf guy.' I can be Griff, 'the guy who happens to read lips.'" I force out a laugh, even though I doubt it sounds completely genuine.

"How can you be so...calm?" she asks. "He didn't even try..."

"Because you're much more important to me than putting some guy in a four-thousand dollar suit in his place. And this is your night. Your whole weekend. Doesn't mean I'm not angry. Or that I'll give Meadows a pass if he tries to talk around me again, but..." After a deep breath, I take both of her hands and bring them to my lips before I hold her gaze. She has to know what she's signing up for. With me. "This is a part of my life, Sloane. The anger. The frustration. Feeling like I'm 'less than' because of my arm or what I can and can't hear. I live with that every single day."

Her frown doesn't reassure me, and the idea that I shot our relationship in the foot makes me wonder why I thought I could have something *real*. No woman—especially not one as smart, as brave, and as drop-dead gorgeous as Sloane—would sign up for this shit.

"Griff?" Her hand on my cheek draws me out of my misery, and when I look up, the understanding written all over her face is the most beautiful thing I've ever seen. "If you're trying to scare me away, it won't work."

"Saw right through me, did you?" I run a hand through my hair, forgetting that I'd slicked it back before we left the room. "Shit. I ruined it."

Sloane's laugh reassures me that while my hair is probably a mess, whatever this is between us? It's still intact.

Sloane

Despite being on my feet—and in heels—going on five hours, I feel like I'm floating as Griff and I step into the elevator. The moment the doors close, he tangles his fingers in my hair and kisses me so thoroughly, I'm out of breath by the time we reach the fourth floor.

"Wow." The word escapes on a sigh, and I lean against him as we make our way to our room. Marina—with Jacob as her escort—left the party over an hour ago, still nursing her hangover from last night.

Once we're safely back in the suite, I sink down onto the couch and carefully remove the glittering silver heels. "When this weekend is over, I don't want to even *see* a pair of heels for at least a month."

"No heels. Noted," Griff says, loosening the top few buttons on his black dress shirt. "Anything else?"

"Strawberry ice cream. A whole pint of it." My stomach growls loudly, reminding me I haven't had a single bite to eat since the dry-scrambled egg whites and fresh fruit Marina ordered me for breakfast. "Are you hungry?"

"For strawberry ice cream?" His laugh is so warm and genuine, I join in as he picks up the room service menu and flips through it. "Or an actual meal?"

"Tomorrow night's dress leaves very little to the imagination. I'll stick to a salad. But maybe if *you* ordered something more...substantial, I could have a bite?" Crap. I sound so pathetic. But this is the job.

"Where I'm concerned, Sloane? You can have whatever you want." Griff winks one of those deep blue eyes and sets the menu in front of me. "Will you order? I could use a break from the glasses. I'll take the orecchiette pasta with duck confit."

Pasta. I'd kill for a plate of pasta.

One more night, then I can eat whatever the heck I want.

"I'll order. But…where are you going?" Griff stops halfway across the room and turns back to me. "Making sure Marina didn't lock the door. Jacob walked her back here and made her promise she wouldn't go out, but in this business, Sloane, you trust, but verify." The latch turns easily, and the moment he cracks the door, I can hear Marina snoring over the sound of some violent action movie.

"She won't stir until morning. Marina never gets drunk, so her hangovers are *epic*." After I order our food, I push to my feet, wincing as my cramped toes protest. "I need to get out of this dress. If room service rings, I'll let you know."

Griff looks like he wants to say something, but instead, nods and heads for the bathroom. And then it hits me. He slept with me last night. We both admitted this wasn't pretend. Yet his clothes, his toiletries? The case for his arm? They're all still in the main room. Relegated to corners like he's some sort of afterthought.

"Griff?" I call from the doorway. He's staring out at the lake again, but he still has his glasses on, thank goodness.

Whipping around, he goes from almost relaxed to on full alert in a single breath. "What's wrong?"

"Nothing. I just thought maybe…you could move your stuff in here?"

"Are you sure?" Staring at me like he can't quite figure me out, he waits for me to nod. "Okay. You want to change first?"

"No. I'm not afraid of you seeing me, Griff. Of everything that comes after? Yes. But not of you seeing *me*. The real me." It's the truth—mostly. I am scared, but not in the way he probably thinks.

To prove my point—both to myself and to Griff, I stand in front of the mirrored bathroom door and start taking off the dress one hook, zipper, and strap at a time. Wardrobe put me in a one-piece bodysuit underneath all the layers of silk and chiffon, so even when the dress falls to the floor at my feet, I'm still wearing the equivalent of a nude strapless bathing suit. Albeit one with a push-up bra built in.

Griff stops in the doorway, his duffel bag slung over his shoulder, and his jaw half-open.

"You realize more of me is covered now than when I was in that lace negligée, right?" I ask after I turn to face him.

"Doesn't...uh. Shit." He clears his throat. "Yeah. But you were also twenty feet away, in public, and now you're not."

"You're kind of cute when you're embarrassed." Picking up my dress—*Beauty and Style* gave me this as a gift for participating in this show—I toss it over my arm and head into the bathroom. I wasn't lying. Being naked in front of Griff wouldn't bother me. If this were still a cover story, a fake relationship I knew would end the moment I'm no longer in danger? I'd strip down in a heartbeat, just to see his reaction.

But it's not. This is real. And if we get naked, we'll do it together. Even if we don't do a damn thing more than that—tonight or ever—I want this to be special. For both of us.

CHAPTER TWENTY-FIVE

Sloane

The room feels different now. Griff doesn't have a lot of "stuff." His tux and suits hang in the closet, the case for his arm sits next to the dresser, and he left his duffel bag in the corner. But having his things mingling with mine? I didn't think the added intimacy would be so very powerful.

Over dinner—where I steal more than a couple bites of his pasta—I tell him a little about what happens in a runway dressing room, and he shows me the video of the audience he took with his glasses.

Dimitri isn't there. Neither is Pavel Andrei. Not a single person looks out of place, but apparently his team is running some sort of facial recognition program on everyone "just in case."

After Griff sets the tray back outside the door, he flips the switch for the gas fireplace and sits close enough our thighs touch. "Ripper texted me during the show. Rodney Carriger was killed down in Mexico two weeks after Volkov got out of prison."

I should feel...*something*. Pity? Shock? Anything. But I'm numb.

"Sloane?" Griff rests his hand on my arm. "Say something."

"Like what? I don't even know if I'm sorry he's dead. He made me feel even more 'invisible' than Dimitri. At least when I was trapped in that life, I wasn't alone. The other girls and I... we were together. Not friends, because he never would have allowed that. He rotated us between houses all the time so we couldn't get too close to anyone. But Rodney...he told me every day how I had nothing—was nothing—without him."

"You were *never* nothing," Griff says, his tone so possessive and full of anger, I'd be afraid if he weren't looking at me like I was his whole world.

"I was." He starts to protest, but I shake my head. "Let me get this out. Please."

If we're going to try to make this work, he has to know all my dirty secrets and broken pieces. Even if telling him kills me.

Taking his hand, I guide his fingers to the back of my neck. "Do you feel this?"

I'd let my hair down after the party, and Griff brushes it to the side. For a long moment, he doesn't say anything, and my heart hammers against my ribs. Until he turns me back to face him. He knows. It's in his eyes. In the furrow between his brows. In the way a muscle in his temple throbs. "A tattoo. One you had removed."

"Wait here. I'll be right back."

Griff calls my name, probably worried I'm running away. That couldn't be further from the truth.

When I return with a pen and one of the hotel notepads, he breathes a sigh of relief. On the small piece of Baur au Lac stationery, I draw the crown, an approximation of the barcode, and the series of numbers Dimitri said would forever mark me as his. I still remember them. Even after all these years.

"The barcode isn't right. I never figured out how the numbers and those stupid lines paired up," I whisper. "We all had one. Every girl...the first night...was shown what he expected of us. Then, after we were too broken to fight back, one of his men would tie us down on a rough wood table and mark us."

I'd give anything to erase the horrors of those nights from my memories, but I'll carry them with me forever.

"When he brought a new 'shipment' of girls into the house, we all had to watch. His way of making sure we never forgot what we were."

Griff takes the paper and balls it up with such force, I'm surprised the fibers don't simply disintegrate in his hand. Stalking over to the gas fireplace, he tosses the remains inside and watches them burn, his shoulders heaving with every breath.

I can't talk to him until he turns back to face me, and with how tense he is, I'm actively afraid of touching him without warning. Unable to stand it any longer, I stamp my foot twice, hoping the vibrations will register.

He whirls around, and as his gaze locks with mine, I know without a doubt, this man would kill to keep me safe.

"We're going to find him. No one is good enough to hide forever." His right hand shakes, and even his prosthetic is balled into a tight fist. "I don't care how smart he thinks he is or how well funded, he's going to make a mistake—soon—and my team will make sure he never hurts anyone again."

The absolute conviction in his voice is almost enough to reassure me, but in a little over forty-eight hours, I'm supposed to fly home. Back to San Diego. What then? I can't ask. Because what am I supposed to do with the answer?

Griff crosses the room in three steps, then skims a knuckle along my cheek, slowing my racing thoughts. I try to smile. "I'm sorry I ruined our night."

"Don't apologize. You didn't ruin a thing."

I lean into his touch, needing more. "What now?"

"Whatever you want, sweetheart. We could get in bed and talk or sleep or—"

"Kiss me?" After dredging up so much of my past, I need to know Griff's feelings for me haven't changed, and I'm too much of a coward to ask.

His smile reassures me more than any words, and when our lips meet, everything else in the world falls away, and it's just the two of us. He hasn't taken off his prosthetic, and his left hand molds to my hip, strong, yet gentle too.

Smoothing my palms down his back, I savor the feel of his muscles shifting under my touch. He keeps his kisses short, soft, letting me set the pace, and when I capture his lower lip between my teeth for just a second, a low moan rumbles in his chest. I have no idea what I'm doing. My entire education in kissing came from soap operas and movies over the years, but with Griff, my body—or at least my mouth—seems to know exactly what to do.

Warmth blooms in my core, then tightens into a ball of pure need. My fingers dig into the hard muscles of his ass, and he tears his lips from mine. "Bedroom," he says, his voice rough. "Or tell me to stop."

"Bedroom." I don't want this to end. Griff leads me into our room, shuts the door, and yanks off his t-shirt. As soon as he catches sight of the metal running from his wrist to the sleeve covering the prosthetic, his confidence fades, his shoulders slumping unevenly. "Griff." My fingers trail across his chest to his shoulders and all the way down both arms. "What's wrong?"

"I haven't been with anyone since," he gestures to his left arm. "All my 'moves'? I need both arms. I'm not even sure I can be on top, and this...your first time—if we get there—should be perfect." His voice cracks, and he stares directly at my lips. I'm not sure he's even breathing.

"It will be." I wish I knew the right words, but I've never had...romance. Or tenderness. Or anything but violence and pain. "I trust you, Griff. And I don't trust anyone. Or didn't until my life fell apart a week ago. Not truly. My mama and sisters don't even know everything that happened to me. You do. Most of it, anyway. And the rest? I'll tell you. Not tonight, but tomorrow. Or the next day. Or whenever you ask."

My eyes burn and water, but I won't let myself cry. I want this one night. To reclaim a piece of myself that was taken away so long ago with this man who looks at me like I'm his only tether in a storm.

"Please. Kissing you is exciting and thrilling, and when I'm in your arms—with or without your prosthetic—I'm safe in a way I've never been before. You touch me, and I want more. Every time."

"Get on the bed," he says quietly. "There were condoms in the mini-bar. I'll be right back."

He rushes from the room, and I pull back the covers. After so many hours in that form fitting dress, I put on a loose pair of shorts and a tank top. My nipples strain against the fabric, and every movement highlights just how sensitive they are.

You'd think I'd have some idea of what to expect, but I don't, so I sit with my feet on the floor, my fingers tapping my thighs so I don't start chewing on my bottom lip.

When Griff returns, his dark blue eyes blaze with intensity. The door closes, and he strides toward me without breaking his gaze. I expect him to touch me, to push me down or even kiss me, but instead, he sinks to his knees and takes my hands in both of his. "Sloane, this is probably too soon. But what I feel for you? This stopped being a job for me the moment I talked to you in the bar before you even knew who I was. I want you more than I've ever wanted another woman in my entire life. But I meant what I said. If you can't...if we don't end up having sex tonight—or ever—I don't care. As crude as it sounds? I can get myself off if I need to. But finding a woman I don't have to hide from? Who accepts me the way I am?" He shakes his head, staring down at our joined hands. "Nothing in this world is more important to me than you. Nothing."

If I try to speak, I'm scared I'll burst into tears. The longer I stay silent, though, the more worried Griff looks. "I used to hate myself for trusting bad men," I whisper. "Then I hated myself for not trusting...anyone. Maybe...maybe I wasn't supposed to until now."

He surges up and cups my cheeks, kissing me until I'm breathless. "If anything I do," he pants when we come up for air, "makes you uncomfortable..."

"You'll know." I hold his gaze until he nods.

Gently, he eases me down onto my back and stretches out next to me. "We'll go slow, sweetheart." Lifting the hem of my tank top just enough to expose my stomach, he kisses a line down the center of my body until he reaches the top of my shorts.

Every time his lips touch my skin, there's a spark of electricity that makes my breasts ache and my core clench. Griff slides his right hand under the soft fabric until he's cupping the bottom of one of my breasts, then pauses, his blue eyes meeting mine. God, I want more. Need it.

"I'm okay, Griff. Truly."

The first skate of his thumb over my nipple makes me gasp. The second tears a whimper from my lips. No man has ever brought me pleasure by just...touching me. "More?" he asks.

"More." I'm squirming, clutching the sheet tightly in my fingers, my toes curling as Griff nudges the tank top higher until the breast he hasn't yet touched is exposed to the cool air in the room. His lips brush the tight nub, and oh my God. Pleasure shoots straight down, and goosebumps race along my skin.

"You taste like honey," he says, then bites down gently. "Fuck. I wish I could hear you."

It takes everything in me to release my death grip on the sheet so I can touch his cheek and get him to look at me. "You hear my heart."

His eyes shimmer, and he scoots up so we're face to face. "And you hear mine."

"Take off your shorts." I don't know where this sudden boldness comes from, but I need to see him. All of him.

"It's hard...unless I stand up." With a grunt, he rolls off the bed, and his arousal is already *very* obvious. A pair of black boxer briefs hide under his shorts, and he arches his brows, asking for permission.

"Those too. Y-yes."

Deep breaths. He'll stop if you need him to.

Griff hooks his right thumb under the elastic band, and after a couple of attempts to make his left work the way he wants, I get to my feet and stand in front of him.

"Sometimes...when I'm nervous, my hand...I can't..." The shame in his eyes is too much for me to bear, and I cover his hands with mine.

"Then let me." I can't believe I'm doing this. Stripping a man naked. Willingly. The Calvin Kleins fall to the floor, and I swallow hard as I take a step back. He's as big as I'd imagined—feeling him pressed up against me the previous night gave me some idea what to expect—but it's more than his size. It's the *v* that angles to a neatly trimmed patch of hair surrounding his cock, the way the tip glistens, and his thighs. The man has thighs like a Greek god.

"Say something." He doesn't move, and I force myself to meet his gaze. "Sloane? We can stop. Right now."

"No." Before I lose my nerve, I strip off my tank top. The low, appreciative rumble in Griff's throat makes me shiver, and I pull down my shorts too, leaving me in nothing but a pair of nude panties. "I know they're not...um...sexy. But they're no-show under just about any outfit and—"

Griff clears his throat. "Sloane? You are the sexiest woman I have ever seen in my entire life and all I want in the world right now is to hold you."

Stepping into his embrace, I wait for the panic. The memories. The fear. But his heat calms me. And his scent? It's intoxicating. Bergamot and oak, like being out in the woods. "Wh-what now?" I ask once I tip my head back so he can see my lips.

Scooping me up with his right arm, he carries me the three steps to the bed and lays me down with a stifled grunt of pain. Before he joins me, he squeezes his left shoulder—hard—a couple of times, but before I can ask him if he's okay, he shakes it off and kneels next to me. "Can I touch you, sweetheart? Take off those panties and taste you?"

I've come this far, and Griff hasn't pushed me, hasn't done a single thing but be patient, understanding, and...perfect. So I remove the last barrier between us.

"Fuck. You smell like heaven."

With my knees bent, I'm completely exposed, and Griff stretches out on the bed between my thighs. "Once I go down on you, I won't be able to hear you if you need me to stop. Promise me something, okay?"

"What?" No man has touched me down there in years, and while I know about oral sex—when I hurt my knee, I read all sorts of romance novels—I'm terrified. Not of Griff. Not of experiencing pleasure. But of how I'll react. Whether I'll freak out and ruin what I think could be beautiful.

"Tap my head. Grab my hair. If *anything* feels wrong, if you need a minute, if it's all too much."

As soon as I agree, he wraps his right arm around my leg gently and presses a kiss to the inside of my thigh. Excitement and fear tangle in my head when he trails his lips closer to my mound.

With two fingers, he spreads my lower lips open. "I'll never get enough of you, Sloane," Griff murmurs, and the vibrations so close to my clit are almost too much. Thrusting my hips slightly, I ask him for more without words and he understands.

The first pass of his tongue has my back arching, and I stifle my yelp. Every stroke sends waves of pleasure through me. They threaten to drown me, but if I die like this, it will be worth it. Griff anchors me with his arm, but he's not holding me down. He's holding on.

Digging the heel of my free leg into the mattress, desperate for leverage to get closer, I stare down at the man who's changed my life in so many ways in only a few days. His hair falls over his forehead, but every few seconds, he flicks his gaze to mine, and though I can't see his lips, his eyes give him away. He's smiling.

I don't think—can't with all the amazing sensations taking over my body—and wrap my fingers around his forearm. The second I touch him, his head snaps up, lips glistening with my arousal. "I'll stop," he says, but I shake my head.

"No. I..." How do I explain what I need and why when my mind is drunk on what he's doing to me. "I need to hold on to you. Don't stop." My voice isn't steady, but the feel of his forearm muscles shifting under my hand is the extra connection I was craving, and I nod, my lips tugging up at the corners despite my complete inability to catch my breath.

When he returns to whatever magical thing he was doing with his tongue—somewhere in the back of my mind, I swear there's a pattern, but hell if I care to figure it out—my body catches fire. The ball of need in my core grows, spreading to my limbs, my chest...everywhere.

Time stops. The rest of the world falls away, and I keep my gaze locked on his. I'm terrified and thrilled at the same time until my core clenches so hard, it takes over my entire body. My whimpers turn into a moan, and then there's nothing but blinding light, a dull roar in my ears, and waves of pleasure.

Griff

I feel the moment she lets go, and my God, she's beautiful. Drinking her in, slowing the letters I'm tracing on her clit, the ones that spell out the three words I long to say to her, I treasure the gift she gives me.

Not her release, though I'll never forget how she looked, sounded, tasted...

Her trust. After so many men hurt her, after almost two decades with her heart under lock and key, she's so open with me, it's staggering.

Her chest heaves with each breath, and she's trembling. The ache from my dick spreads all the way to my balls, but I manage to extricate myself from between her thighs so I can pull her against me under the covers.

"You were—you are—so beautiful." Kissing the top of her head, I settle her with her leg draped over me. In this position, I can't see her lips or her face, but after a few moments, a tear hits my chest, and I tense.

"Did I hurt you, sweetheart? Talk to me. Tell me what you need."

Sloane lifts her head, her eyes unfocused, and a lazy, contented smile gracing her lips. "You were...that was...wow."

It feels so natural to laugh with this woman. Like we've shared these moments for years, not days.

"We should get some sleep." Carding my fingers through her hair, I try to memorize everything about this night. Her taste. The feel of each sound she made as her entire body vibrated. The way she coiled so tight, ready to fly, and the arch of her back as she finally let go.

"No." This time when I meet her gaze, those brown eyes are clear, determined. "I want all of you, Griff. Or...I want to try. Please. Don't leave me wondering what it would feel like with you inside me."

Fuck. She's not a virgin. I know that. But this is still her first time. What if I hurt her? What if I can't balance myself over her? My left arm and shoulder ache, and dammit. If they'd been able to save more of my arm, I'd take this metal monstrosity off. I don't want her to see it. *I* don't want to see it. But I need it, and that's killing me.

Holding her hasn't lessened my desire—or my hard on—in the least so I'm ready for more, but is she? Truly?

Our gazes collide again, and the gut punch of raw need hits me hard enough to knock the breath from my lungs. The only sound I can make when her delicate fingers stroke over my dick is a strangled groan.

"Is this okay?" she asks. A tiny frown deepens between her brows, and she starts chewing on her lip.

"Sloane, there's nothing you could do to me that would be anything but."

Covering her hand with my prosthetic fingers, I feel her

warmth as she continues to touch me. After the barest skim of her palm over my crown, she sucks in a sharp breath.

Sloane stares down at her hand, her eyes fixed on the glistening precum with a mixture of fear and anticipation.

"Kiss me, sweetheart. I won't hurt you. We can stop—"

She doesn't listen to me, just brings her hand to her lips and tastes me.

I've never been so turned on in my life. Her nerves fade away in an instant, and she sighs, the corners of her mouth tugging into a shy smile.

"I didn't know if I could..."

In my silent world, a shout and a whisper look much the same, but the way her shoulders curve, the soft and slow movement of her lips—I think she meant those words for her—not for me.

"You can do anything. You're the strongest, bravest, and most amazing woman I've ever known."

Rolling onto my side, I snag the strip of condoms from the nightstand and tear the foil with my teeth. I'm too raw, too on the edge to even try using my left hand, something Sloane immediately understands.

"This, I know," she says. "Let me help you."

Her fingers tremble, but she rolls the latex over my shaft slowly, her eyes never leaving my gaze.

"Go slow." Her nerves are back, but just below the surface, there's also desire. Confidence. Determination.

Carefully, I straddle her, supporting myself on my elbows. The position puts pressure on my stump, but I'll endure the pain for this chance to be her first. Maybe even her only. If she'll have me.

Nudging at her entrance, I don't look anywhere but at her. Lips. Eyes. Lips again.

"Kiss me?" she asks, her brows lifting in a gentle arch.

"Anytime." Our lips meet, and she tenses briefly.

Shit. What did I do?

"Sloane?"

She opens for me, her tongue darting out to dance with mine before she reaches for my ass to draw me closer. The head of my dick pushes into her, and she's still kissing me—now with more fervor, biting down on the corner of my lower lip.

I feel every vibration when she moans and pulls me deeper. Letting her control my entrance, I lose myself to the feel of her. Slick, tight, hot as fuck. For this one perfect moment, I'm completely hers, and I think she's all mine as well.

When I'm as deep as I can go, I break off the kiss. "You're perfect. Have I said that yet?"

Sloane laughs, and the movement makes her inner walls tense around me. "Maybe a couple of times."

"I mean it. I'll keep saying it for as long as you let me."

I'm dangerously close to the precipice—not of my climax, but of going from "I'm falling in love with her" to "I'm completely, totally, hopelessly *in* love with her."

Moving my hips slowly, I watch Sloane's face for any sign of pain, but she's staring back at me with such intensity, need, and honest-to-God wonder that I take a risk and thrust harder.

"Again." Her swollen lips are so easy to read, or maybe that's her heart speaking directly to mine. "Harder."

If I do what she asks, I'll come in under a minute, and I balance on my left arm, ignoring the sparks racing up my shoulder so I can capture a lock of her hair in my fingers. "I want this to last," I manage before I kiss her again.

She tastes of both of us, and the room is filled with our combined scents. Not only arousal, but her lotion, my cologne, the unique, fresh as rain fragrance that always surrounds her.

Reaching for me, she digs her fingers into my ass cheeks, hard enough she'll probably leave bruises, but I don't care. I rock my hips faster, and she joins me, matching my rhythm until we're moving as one.

I'm so close, but from the way her channel grips me harder, so is she. My fingers skate over her hip, down to our union where her slick heat intensifies. Her clit practically begs to be touched, and when I circle the tight nub, she cries out into our kiss, loud enough the sound registers just as she implodes, and I let myself go with her.

CHAPTER TWENTY-SIX

Griff held me all night, and none of my nightmares come for me when he's close.

Lying still so I don't wake him, I marvel over the events of the past twenty-four hours.

I had sex. I *enjoyed* having sex.

The word seems too plain for what we did, but I've always hated the term "making love," as if you could manufacture those feelings through penetration alone. I know for a fact: you can't.

Afterwards, we soaked in the large, jetted tub for almost an hour, and that experience was every bit as intimate as our more...vigorous activities.

He didn't hide from me. Didn't turn to keep his arm out of my line of sight. Even put his glasses on so we could still talk while I leaned against him.

"I know you're awake," he says, his voice rough with sleep. "Roll over?"

I do, and he traces my cheek with a knuckle. "How do you feel?"

The uncertainty written all over his face hurts my heart. "Griff, don't."

"Don't what?" His shoulders tense, and he's about to sit up when I rest my fingers on what remains of his left arm.

"Worry? I'm not a broken vase held together by bubble gum and a prayer." Shifting my legs under the sheet, I smile. "I'm a little sore. But not in a bad way." Relief smooths out the furrow between his brows, and I reach for him, my fingers curling over his hip. "There's nothing on the schedule today. Marina said something about massages, and I probably should spend some time with her. One-on-one. This was supposed to be our 'girls' weekend. Amid all the parties and work, anyway. But…"

How do I tell him I don't want to leave his side if he's not coming home to San Diego with me? That I'm scared what's going to happen when we break this magic bubble of the fancy resort and the very obvious danger following me everywhere.

I don't realize I'm chewing on my lip until he brushes his thumb over my mouth. "Relax, sweetheart. As long as you let me check out the spa first—make sure there aren't any hidden entrances or places someone could get to you—spend as much time with Marina as you want. I'm not going anywhere."

Swallowing hard, I screw up the courage to just ask. "Tomorrow? When I'm supposed to fly home? You're not going back to Virginia?"

"Until we know the threat's neutralized, you're stuck with me." He grins, but my heart cracks in two. "Sloane? What did I say?"

"What about after?" I'm not proud of how weak my voice is. And for the first time, I wish Griff could hear it. I don't know how to tell him what he means to me.

"Fuck. I'm sorry, Sloane. I didn't think." He sits up, starts to reach for me, and then drops his left arm with a heavy sigh. "Dammit. I can't even hold you properly." The raw emotion bleeds through his tone and he shuts down like a switch flipped. "I need a minute."

"Griff!" But he's already out of bed and striding for the bathroom. He's not wearing his glasses and all I can do is watch as he shuts the door without a backward glance.

Five minutes later, when he hasn't emerged and I'm close to tears, I shrug into the velvet and silk robe, belt it tightly, and flee into the main room. Thank God. Marina's already up and the rich scent of coffee fills the space.

She doesn't say a word as I pour myself a cup and stare out the french doors to the lake.

"What did he do?" she asks. "Because I can call Clive's mom right now. Well, okay. Maybe not right now. It's like 4:00 a.m. in Boston and she's in her seventies."

"Nothing." If I tell her, I'll end up bawling, and then I'll look like I got punched in the face. Again. There's only so much makeup can do, and there'll be a red carpet for tonight's gala. My life is enough of a disaster as it is. I don't need more rumors about my love life, my weight, my face, my mental health...

"Bullshit." Marina pushes up from the couch and stands directly in front of me. She's a good four inches shorter than I am, and clears her throat when I don't immediately look at her. "Sloane."

With a huff, I try to side step her, but she moves with me. "Fine. I asked him what was going to happen after he and his team found Dimitri and I wasn't in danger anymore, and he said, 'fuck,' then locked himself in the bathroom."

"What?" She stares at the closed bedroom door like she can shoot daggers out of her eyes, and if anyone could, it'd be Marina. "Is he naked? Because I don't think I could handle all those muscles naked. But if he's not, I'm going to bust in there and—"

"Sloane." Griff's deep voice silences Marina mid-rant, but I don't turn until he's at my side, clad in one of the hotel robes with the belt tied crookedly and not very effectively around his waist. "I said a minute. I know it was a hell of a lot closer to ten. I'm sorry."

"You don't have to apologize." Taking a sip of coffee to hide the wobble in my lower lip, I focus on the serene, shimmering waters of Lake Zurich and try to ignore how the most perfect night of my life turned to ruins when the sun came up. "You'll stay with me until I'm safe, then go back to your life."

"Fuck no." He hasn't touched me, and when I finally do face him, his right hand is clenched into a fist and his knuckles are bone white. "I'm shit at expressing my feelings. I've gone through three shrinks in the past five months because they keep telling me they can't help if I'm not honest with them. I lost my goddamn arm, can't hear a thing unless it's loud as fuck, and some days, the only thing that gets me out of bed? Needing to take a piss."

Marina backs away, shutting the door to her room quietly while Griff's pleading gaze bores into me.

"I'm fucked up, Sloane. Not just my body. My head too. You shouldn't want to be with me."

I start to protest, but he shakes his head.

"Let me finish before I say something stupid—again—and hurt you. When I said I needed a minute, it was because I didn't know how to tell you that even when my life feels like it's falling apart, when I can't do something as fucking simple as holding you with both arms or tying this stupid belt, *you* make me feel whole. I'm not leaving you, Sloane. Not unless you ask me to. You're all I've ever wanted in this world and so much more than I deserve."

The moment I reach for him, he breaks, crushing me to his chest as I wrap my arms around his waist. Sobs wrack his body, the hoarse sounds pure, raw agony. We stay locked together for so long, I expect Marina to sneak back in the room for more coffee.

"Griff? Look at me." His entire body shudders as he takes a deep breath, and I draw back so he can see my face. I don't want him to read my words on his glasses. Tapping the right temple twice, I smile up at him. "Are they off?"

"You remembered." With a nod, he loosens his death grip on my waist. "They're off."

"Good." Taking his hand, I lead him over to the french doors, unlock them—which requires me to release him to unwind a very thick rubber band from around the two handles. "What the heck is this?"

"A precaution. Can't do much about the glass being easy to break, but those locks could be picked in under a minute. With the band, you'd probably hear someone breaking in. There's another one around the doors in our room."

Our room.

We're both barefoot, but I gesture for him to follow me out to the balcony. The cool, crisp November air makes my skin prickle, but I haven't once seen Griff in the sun, and I need to feel free for the rest of this conversation.

He takes off his glasses and drops them into his pocket. But the motion is too much for the loosely tied belt, and he curses under his breath as he holds the robe closed.

"Let me help."

From the tension rolling off him in waves, he doesn't like the idea.

"If this is going to work—us—you can't choose when and when not to trust me. It's all or nothing." Griff drops his arm with a sigh. After I secure the belt, I rest my hands on his shoulders. "You've kept me sane from the moment we met. Protected me. And you never judged me. You charmed the *Beauty and Style* executives last night, handled the press when I couldn't, and most of all, you showed me what it means to be...loved. You aren't broken. No more than I am."

"Sloane, you're perfect," he says, and I laugh.

"I'd never had sex before last night. I'm almost thirty-five years old, and I'd never had...never...*come* before. You're the only one who knows my real name—other than Dimitri and, I suppose, your team now." My cheeks warm, the sun intensifying the flush from my secret shame.

"I haven't told them. Though, as good as they are, they might have figured it out." The man I'm falling in love with is back with me, no longer a shell, though his pain lingers just under his skin, in his eyes and the set of his jaw. At my shock, he shrugs. "It wouldn't help us find Volkov. He paid off his parole officer—or someone in law enforcement—and got himself a fake ID so he could leave the country. A man like that isn't going to put an ad in the paper asking if anyone has information on Sophiana Lebedev."

Hearing Griff say my name—my *real* name—stirs something in my soul. I'm not Sophiana any longer. And even though I could take back my name if—when—Dimitri is no longer a threat, I don't want to.

"Thank you." Reaching up, I cup his cheek, and he closes his eyes for a brief moment. "Come have coffee. I'll order breakfast. If you're feeling adventurous, you can try some of my green smoothie."

His chuckle puts us on solid ground again. We're not done. I'm not sure we'll ever be done reassuring one another. But maybe two broken souls can fit together and make each other whole.

Griff

One sip of Sloane's smoothie and I slide my plate across the table to her. "Eat something real. That shit tastes like wheatgrass and spinach and the death of all hope in this world."

She laughs so hard, she snorts a little bit of the green liquid out her nose, and my glasses pick up a couple of very colorful curse words. "Don't *do* that to me! And I am *not* eating hash browns and bacon." With a final, longing look, she nudges the plate back toward me, then adds, "Until tomorrow. Tomorrow I can eat whatever I want."

"My flight is at 5:00 p.m.," Marina says as she polishes off her croissant. "You're not flying back through New York, right?"

Reaching for Sloane's hand, I link our fingers and squeeze gently. "We might stay until Monday. It'll give my team time to upgrade her home security system and find us seats *together* all the way to San Diego."

"Someone's going to be in my house?" Sloane asks.

Shit.

"I...uh. I should have told you. When you ordered breakfast, I asked Austin to set things up. Hidden Agenda—that's the firm out in Seattle—partners with the best home security company in the country. No one's breaking in ever again."

And if they try? I'll be there to stop them.

Sloane chews on her lip, and Marina shoots me a look that says, "*You're being a dumbass.*"

"Fuck, Sloane. If you want to wait until we get back to San Diego, I'll call Austin right now."

"No, it's okay. You're right. Better to have the work done while I'm gone. But...won't they need my keys?"

I pause with a forkful of hash browns halfway to my mouth. "No, sweetheart. They don't need your key. And they're discrete." At her wide eyes, I realize there's a lot about my life and my work I haven't told Sloane, and if I expect her to trust me—to love me—I can't keep secrets from her anymore.

Leaning in, I whisper in her ear, "Are you okay staying here one more night? We could see more of Zurich. Have that *real* vacation you wanted?"

Sloane's eyes shimmer with tears, but they're not from fear or shame. No, that's pure joy in the brown depths. "I'd love that. If it's safe."

"I'll keep you safe, sweetheart. On my life, I'll keep you safe."

CHAPTER TWENTY-SEVEN

Sloane

The past three hours were exactly what I needed. Even if I spent the first thirty minutes constantly checking the treatment room doors. Marina chided me more than once, but she doesn't know Dimitri. He was quiet all day yesterday, and that makes me nervous.

After our body scrubs and mud baths—ew, but Marina insisted—Jacob comes to escort her back to her room.

"Be careful," I say, giving her a tight hug.

She rolls her eyes. "I'm going up to the room, then to the makeup and hair station on the second floor to help any of the models who want a professional look for tonight. That's it. And Mr. British Shadow will be there the whole time."

"I know. But I worry. I can't help it." Shit. Once Marina leaves tomorrow, she'll be unprotected, and my heart starts racing until Griff pushes through the door to the spa's reception area. He spent the morning rubbing his left shoulder, and I convinced him to join me for a massage.

"I can't believe I let you talk me into this," he mutters in my ear when we embrace. "I am *not* getting naked."

He's so worried about not being able to protect me, he insisted on knowing the names of the two therapists who would be working on us so his people could run a thorough background check.

Griff refuses to use the locker rooms to change into a robe, but accompanies me into the couple's massage room, locks the door, and kisses me. "I'm still not sure this is a good idea. It's hard for me to protect you without my prosthetic—or a weapon—but I did fantasize about doing this with you that first night."

"Oh, now the truth comes out!" Laughing, I strip him of his t-shirt and run my hands over his muscled chest. "You took every precaution. It's fifty minutes. Telling the staff you were worried about the press forcing their way in here was brilliant."

I shed my wrap, and Griff makes an appreciative, low growl as his gaze roves over my body. "Before the party, I want you, Sloane. If you're not too sore."

The blush starts at my belly and spreads all the way to my neck and cheeks in seconds. "I'm not."

"Good." The glint in his eyes dims. "I can't wear my glasses for this. I won't hear the masseuse if they ask me questions."

"Just keep your eyes on me. I can repeat anything. Or try to sign, if it's a simple question." Cupping his cheek, I smile. "It'll be okay."

"You should be able to relax," he protests.

"I'll relax. Staring at you for the next hour? Totally not a hardship." Winking, I get under the sheet. "Ready whenever you are."

Griff unlocks the door to find the two massage therapists—a man and a woman—waiting outside in the hall. As soon as they enter, he clears his throat. "The front desk assured me we could keep the door locked. The press have been hounding Ms. Sanders this whole weekend."

"Of course, Mr. Griffin," the man says. "I am Francois and this is Orna. What would you both like out of this session?"

Griff sinks onto the table next to mine and rubs his left shoulder. "I wear a prosthetic. Stay away from everything below my left deltoid. If my arm swells, I can be in a world of hurt. Back, neck, and shoulders are all fair game. I'm also mostly deaf, but I read lips. If you need to talk to me during the session, Ms. Sanders will either repeat whatever you say or she'll sign."

"Very well. Lie on your stomach."

After Orna goes over my preferences, Griff and I face one another, and after the first ten minutes or so, I think he starts to relax. The change in his face is so breathtaking. Enough so, I want to draw him again. To memorize this moment. I'm still terrified about what will happen tomorrow, the next day, the next week, but at least for one afternoon, everything is as perfect as it can be.

Griff

The massage was so amazing, I dread having to put my prosthetic back on. My shoulders and neck haven't been this loose and pain free in months. But I can't protect Sloane with only one arm.

I have at least another two hours before I have to don the monstrosity, and Marina ordered a spread of fresh fruit, nuts, and sparkling cider so we relax on the couch, Sloane leaning against my chest. Until my watch and phone vibrate in the distinctive pattern I created for Austin.

Propping my tablet up on the table, I answer the call. "You're on speaker. Sloane's with me."

"Good. I'm conferencing Ripper in."

"Ripper?" Sloane asks.

"His nickname. Call sign, really. From the Special Forces. He and Wren are experts on the dark web. And...well, finding information. About anything."

"You can just call us geniuses," Rip says. On the tablet, his name precedes the transcription. "Because we have a line on Volkov."

Sloane sits up so quickly, her knee bangs into the table, and the thin flute glass with her sparkling cider threatens to tip over until I steady it. "What? Where is he?"

"Well, his money is in Milan, Italy. Three days ago. We have a facial recognition match to the last known photo of the asshole outside of the Banco di Milano," Ripper says, and the tablet screen splits in two with a grainy photo of Volkov on the street in the sun.

Sloane covers her mouth with her hand. We're close enough, I know she made a noise, and from the look on her face, it wasn't a good one. "A little warning next time," I snap and drape my right arm around her shoulders. "Sweetheart, breathe for me, okay."

She nods and turns away from the screen. "That's him. He's bigger. Older, but...shit."

"Take the photo down. Now." Sloane doesn't need to spend another second looking at that piece of shit, and the screen shifts back to transcription only. "Any idea what he's been doing for the past three days?"

"No." This from Austin. "He disappeared in a sea of people at a piazza two blocks from the bank. We're watching the airports in Zurich and Milan, but he could *drive* to Zurich in a little over three hours."

Not helping, Pritchard.

With every word, Sloane's expression shutters further, and soon, I don't know if I'll be able to reach her.

"We have the gala tonight. You have control of the hotel security cameras, right?"

"Affirmative. And Wren's facial recognition program will send an alert to your phone and watch if any of Volkov's known associates—or Volkov himself—show up," Austin says. "Dax worked some of his magic with the local police, and if you need *anything*, ask for Officer Eric Keller."

After Austin rattles off the number, Sloane and I both save the number to our phones.

"One piece of good news." Ripper's words scroll across the screen. "The guy who broke into your house, Sloane? He's in custody, and he's talking."

"Talking?" she asks, reaching for my hand. Her fingers flutter, and her lips press together, then purse before she clenches her jaw and squeezes her eyes shut.

"Yep," Austin replies. "We sent Inara and Graham—they work with Ripper out in Seattle—to find the asswipe and *persuade* him to forget where you lived."

Sloane shoots me a confused look, and I squeeze her hand. "I'll explain later."

"Well, they found him. Breaking into a surf shop in Coronado. He was all too happy to tell the District Attorney everything he knew about Volkov in exchange for the DA's office 'losing' one of his previous strikes. The plea deal still sends him to prison for two years, but that's a hell of a lot less than the twenty-five to life he would have earned."

The screen splits again, and the right side cycles through half a dozen camera feeds. "Got the travel arrangements and security system taken care of too," Ripper adds. "E-tickets, schematics and instructions were sent to both of your phones.

The system's armed, so make sure you know how it works before you try to unlock the front door."

"Will do. Thanks. How's Wren feeling?" Second Sight's hacker—or genius, per Ripper's earlier declaration—handed most of this case to Ripper after another wicked bout of morning sickness, and when I messaged Dax yesterday, he was worried.

"Better," Ripper replies. "Ryker finally found the right combo of ice cream, potato chips, and oddly...spinach."

"So the kid is going to be Popeye?" Ryker McCabe is close to seven feet tall, and while I've never met the man, his reputation in the intelligence community is fucking terrifying.

On screen, the word *laughter* appears after Ripper's name. "Maybe. Except they're having a girl."

Austin joins in with the laughter. "I can't wait to see McCabe try to figure out how to hold a newborn. Might have to fly out to Seattle for that. Listen, Griff? You and Sloane have fun tonight. We're doing everything we can on our end. If we get any updates, we'll let you know."

We say our goodbyes, and I wrap my arm around Sloane's waist and hold her close. "They're the best in the world, sweetheart. *We're* the best in the world."

Even though I'm not sure I should lump myself into that category any longer, I do it for Sloane, and in her gaze, I find such unwavering confidence that I vow to put my issues aside and be the man she thinks I am.

"CAN I TRY...BEING ON TOP?" Sloane asks, her eyes half-hooded after the climax I wrung from her body only a few minutes ago.

Smiling, I roll onto my back, cup her neck, and pull her

close for a tender kiss. "You can have whatever you want, sweetheart."

She chews on her lip for a moment, clearly nervous. "You'll tell me if I'm not doing it right?"

Locking eyes with her, I try to impress on her just how serious I am with my tone. "There is nothing you could possibly do wrong. Go slow, and stop if you need to."

With a nod, she picks up the foil packet and rips it open. Her warm fingers stroke down my dick, and once I'm sheathed, she straddles me, her hands on either sides of my shoulders so a curtain of her blond hair falls all around our heads.

"Just ease yourself down."

She does, and I wrap my fingers around the base of my shaft to hold myself steady for her.

"You feel so damn good, Sloane." Her inner walls are so tight, so hot and wet, and from this angle, fuck me. This is nothing like our first coupling. Her confidence grows as she seats herself fully and then kisses me.

Slowly, I start to move my hips under her. I can't hear the sound she makes, but I can feel it, and that's enough. Some things don't need to be heard. And maybe...I haven't lost as much as I thought.

Rising up enough so I can see her face, she smiles, her lips swollen. "Harder," she says.

My hand curls around her hip, and I raise my brows, asking for permission before I move any further. "Can I grab your ass, sweetheart? It'll give me better...leverage."

She answers by covering my hand with hers, guiding me right to the spot that will give me the most control. Her trust is so fucking amazing, such a gift, and I'll never, *ever* take it for granted.

Digging my fingers into the tight muscle, I start to move

faster, and she matches my rhythm, riding me so hard I won't last much longer.

"Sloane," I manage. "I want you to come again. Before I let go. Can you touch yourself?"

She sucks in a sharp breath, but it's not in fear. No. Excitement is all I find in the depths of her eyes. Trailing her fingers down her flat stomach, she finds her clit, and I know the instant she starts to feel pleasure. Her eyelids flutter, and her channel tightens around me. "Oh, God." She throws her head back and her entire body implodes, squeezing my dick with each wave of her release.

I only have one single thought as I let myself fly with her.

She's it for me. And soon...I'm going to tell her.

CHAPTER TWENTY-EIGHT

Sloane

After I help Griff with his bowtie and a pair of cufflinks that are quite literally tiny pocket knives attached to the post and toggle, I shoo him out of the room so Marina can zip, tape, and tuck me into my gown.

Griff's seen me naked—several times now—but there's something magical about this dress, and I want to surprise him.

"After tonight, I don't ever want to see a pair of nipple covers again," I mutter, smoothing the silicone over the sensitive skin. The adhesive *hurts* no matter how I try to remove them, but with this dress? The bodice is designed to lift my boobs as far as they'll go, while the silk provides no protection should I get cold—or aroused. And with Griff at my side, aroused is a distinct possibility.

"Promise me you won't just disappear," Marina says quietly, the dress draped over her arm. "If you need to run, I get it. But find some way to let me know?"

A tear threatens, and even though I'm still mostly naked

save for a pair of nude panties and those cursed silicon stickers, I hug her so hard, she squeaks. "The point of running," I whisper in her ear, "is so no one can find me."

"Sloane—"

"Shh. It's my last resort only. Griff will do everything he can to make sure I never have to 'just disappear.'"

Marina wriggles free of my embrace and holds my gaze. "That's not a promise."

Sighing, I hold out my right hand, making a fist with every finger but my pinky. "I swear."

<hr>

"YOU'RE GORGEOUS, Sloane. And I've outdone myself." Marina turns me toward the full-length mirror on the wall, and holy shit. She's right. The lavender gown comes to a peak at my left shoulder with a sparkling strap of rhinestones that follows the S curve of the bodice down to my waist.

Taking a couple of steps, then spinning around, I marvel at the design. The gown is split all the way to my hip, but thanks to Marina's superior taping skills, even dancing won't reveal anything inappropriate.

I gently pluck at one of the dozens of curls tumbling from behind a sparkling headband, and it bounces back almost immediately. "I've never felt more like a movie star—or a princess—than I do right now."

"Well, then go meet your prince." Marina beams, but then her eyes widen. "Oh, but can you do up the top hooks on the back of this thing?"

As soon as I fasten the last few hook and eye closures on her silk and lace ball gown, we take a few selfies out on the patio. "I'm sorry this hasn't been as much of a 'girls' weekend' as it was supposed to be."

"Sloane, I'm in one of the fanciest hotels on the planet, had an amazing spa day with my best friend, and now? I'm going to the party of the year. In a dress that probably costs more than *Beauty and Style* paid me this weekend. Except for the whole danger and death portion of the trip...I've had the time of my life."

"Me too." We hug once more—albeit gently so we don't wrinkle—and she nods at the door.

"Go. I'll hang back here for a couple of minutes so the two of you can smooch a bit. Plus, Jacob isn't supposed to be here for another ten minutes."

With one last squeeze of her hand, I head for the door and my very handsome, very protective date.

Griff

Don't tug at your bow tie.

The damn thing feels like it's choking me. This is only the fourth time in my life I've put on a tux, and while this one—a midnight blue number with a deep-cut vest—was tailored to my exact measurements, the bow tie still chafes.

Or maybe what chafes is that I needed help with it. And the cufflinks. Sloane didn't make a big deal of it, but I hate having to rely on anyone for something so basic.

While I wait for Sloane to finish getting ready, I double check the knife strapped to my calf and practice drawing the gun from a special pocket sewn into the inside of the vest. With the rest of the team trying to zero in on Volkov's location, tonight should be nothing but a party full of pompous executives, music, and the official unveiling of this year's Christmas Book.

Glasses, watch, phone...all fully charged. I'm as prepared as I can be. Until the bedroom door opens and Sloane glides toward me.

"Holy fuck."

She spins, causing the dress to flare out around her and show me a long, toned expanse of leg, then laughs. God, I wish I could hear the sound.

"You're not going to be able to sit down all night, are you?" I slide my hand along her waist, the fabric soft under my fingers.

"Probably not." She presses a quick kiss to my lips before retrieving her clutch from the table.

"Are you wearing your panic button?" I hate asking. Hate that she has to even worry about that when we're supposed to be going to a party and having fun.

Sloane touches a spot under her left arm, her gaze fixed on the floor. "This is the only place I could put it."

"Hey." Skimming a knuckle along her jaw, I wait for her to look up at me. "What's wrong? You're wearing it. That's the important thing. We shouldn't need it. It's a party. I'm not planning on leaving your side."

"We haven't heard from Dimitri in two days. I'm scared, Griff."

Her breath ghosts over my cheek, warm, scented with mint, and the urge to keep her here, to carry her back to our bedroom and figure out how to get her out of that dress—once I kick Marina out—is almost too strong to ignore.

"Maybe no one's heard from him because he knows we're close to tracking him down and he's in hiding. Hold on to that hope, Sloane. This is your night. The unveiling of the Christmas Book. You should be able to enjoy it."

"I will. As long as you're with me," she says, and I wish these glasses had the ability to save the words scrolling across the lenses. My heart belongs to Sloane. Now and forever if she'll have me, and soon, I won't be able to stop myself from confessing just how far I've fallen for her.

Pulling her close enough she can probably feel the solid weight of the gun in my vest pocket, I cup the back of her neck. My fingers—my real ones—graze the rough skin where she once bore that shitstain's mark, and she shudders.

Dammit. Being reminded of him is the last thing she needs right now.

"Don't go there," I whisper. "You survived. Hell, you did more than that." Turning us so we're facing the full-length mirror on the wall next to the door, I nod at the reflection. "Look at yourself. What do you see?"

She lifts her gaze, and her lower lip wobbles until she traps it between her teeth. After a long moment, she sighs, the motion causing her chest to heave. "I see an imposter."

"No." Fuck. This isn't going the way I intended. "*No.* You are *not* an imposter. I see a woman with poise and confidence. A woman who knows exactly who she is and what she wants. I see *you*, Sloane. The real you. And I love you."

She sucks in a sharp breath, and if I could kick myself as hard as I wanted to, I'd end up in next week.

"Don't say anything, sweetheart. I know it's too soon. Until five seconds ago, I'd promised myself I wouldn't tell you until we were home. Back in San Diego. But, dammit. I can't help it. You're it for me, and tonight, you're going to shine in front of everyone." Carefully, so I don't mess up her makeup, I touch my lips to hers, then kiss the sensitive spot behind her ear and lower my voice. "We'll dance. We'll mingle. And when the party's over, we'll come back here and I'll hold you all night. Every night, if you'll let me."

Digging in her clutch, she pulls out one of my handkerchiefs and dabs at her shimmering eyes. "Griff...I...there's so much I want to say. I just don't have the words."

"Shh. We have time. I'm not going anywhere. Except down to the ballroom with the most beautiful woman in the world."

With one last, lingering look in the mirror, Sloane nods. "Okay. Let's go." She only manages a half smile, but it's genuine, and I offer her my left arm. I don't have any sensation above the wrist, but the weight on my shoulder as she wraps her fingers around my elbow reassures me enough to unlock the door.

When we're back in the States, I need to tell Austin just how right he was. About everything.

THE BALLROOM IS LIT with thousands of tiny white lights, tall silver "trees" decorated with bright blue ornaments line the room, and every post is wrapped in silver and white tulle. Along the far wall, six tables hold hundreds of copies of the Christmas Book, but the stacks are hidden under blue velvet drapes until the *Beauty and Style* CEO gives his big speech in a couple of hours.

After the security guards check my name against the list on their tablets, we're allowed in.

"It's so beautiful," she says, leaning closer to me and resting her head on my shoulder for a brief moment.

"Not compared to you." I cover her hand with mine, fully intending to kiss her when Donna Mills, the head of the *Beauty and Style* Christmas Book selection committee rushes over to us.

"Sloane, my dear. You are a vision. That *dress!*" Donna leans in to air kiss both of Sloane's cheeks.

"You're too kind," Sloane says with a small smile. "This is my boyfriend, Harry Griffin. He's standing in as my agent for the weekend as well."

"Mr. Griffin. It's a pleasure." Leaning in, presumably to whisper, she adds, "I heard about the little mob scene after the runway show. I was backstage at the time, but you were mentioned several times during the cocktail party—carrying Sloane to safety like some gallant white knight."

"All part of the job, Ms. Mills." Clearly, the woman doesn't know I can't hear her, or if she does, she hasn't let on. "I presume we won't have the same problem tonight."

"Oh, no. Not at all. The only photographers allowed in are with *Beauty and Style*. You'll be quite safe from any mobs—beyond Sloane's fans, of course, and she has many among our staff."

"Working with you has been my honor," Sloane says, and from the look on her face, she means it. Ever since the middle of the runway show yesterday, she's been comfortable and relaxed when not worried about Volkov, and I intend to do whatever I can to ensure she stays that way. To let her enjoy the evening so if she does decide to retire, she can do so with no regrets.

She deserves it. And so much more.

Sloane

The hours pass quickly, a flurry of congratulations from investors and executives alike, idle chitchat with some of the models—including Jill, who stares at Griff like she wants to eat him for dessert—and dancing.

Marina, with Jacob her constant shadow, flits by at regular intervals, the last time with a glass of champagne in her hand. "Only one," she says, winking at me. "Otherwise I'll turn into a pumpkin with a massive headache long before midnight."

"I'm sure Jacob would dance with you." I adjust my hand on Griff's shoulder, the straps holding his prosthetic in place noticeable only because I know about them. "You can't leave without one dance under these gorgeous lights."

My best friend rolls her eyes. "I asked. He said he 'doesn't dance.'"

Guiding us to the edge of the dance floor, Griff stares daggers at Jacob until the former-SAS officer joins us. "Dance with the woman, for fuck's sake. It's a slow song. You're not going to have to pull out any 'moves.'"

"Fine. But I will not be held responsible for any broken toes," he mutters and offers Marina his hand.

With a huge smile, she sets her champagne flute down on a tulle-wrapped table and practically floats to the middle of the ballroom.

"Thank you." I press a quick kiss to Griff's lips, and his hand tightens on my waist. "She loves to dance, and I don't know why no one else in the place is asking her."

His laugh warms me from head to toe. "Because everyone's afraid of Jacob and how he's watching her." Shaking his head, he adds, "It's purely professional, but men like him—like us— we train to be intimidating."

"Well, I like you intimidating."

We sashay back to the dance floor, where Griff takes my hand, spins me out and back, then dips me. He's perfect. Serious and protective to his very core, but capable of these wonderful, light, surprising moments where he can make me laugh and forget about all of my problems.

"Liked that, did you?" he asks, grinning as he pulls me close to trail kisses along the curve of my neck.

"I did. You're quite an accomplished dancer. Better than I am, and I've taken more lessons than I can count."

"My mom insisted I know how to dance properly before I

went off to college. Most humiliating six months of my teenage life—ballroom dancing classes with my mother." He chuckles, his blue-eyed gaze turning a little wistful. "She moved to Florida six years ago, and I've only seen her once since I got back from Pakistan."

"Are you close?" Thoughts of Mama and my sisters elbow their way through my earlier joy, and I hope I can call them soon.

"We email every week or two. Before this assignment, I was planning on spending Christmas with her." He stops so he can cup my cheek. "If it's safe—if Volkov is no longer a threat—will you come with me?"

The emotions rushing over me clog my throat, making speech impossible, but I nod, then swallow hard. "Yes. I'd...yes."

If I needed any more proof that I was in love with this man, I'd be an idiot. He understands me in a way no one else ever has. I need to tell him—right now.

"Ladies and gentlemen!"

The music fades away, and the *Beauty and Style* CEO, Franklin Meadows, stands at a microphone on a raised platform next to the tables of still-hidden catalogues.

"Thank you all for coming out tonight. For making this year's Christmas Book launch our best, most successful event in the history of *Beauty and Style Limited*. You've been patient as we've teased you time and time again, but I won't keep you waiting a second longer!"

Uniformed Baur au Lac employees stand next to each one of the covered tables and whip off the velvet drapes with identical flourishes.

"It is truly my honor to present this year's Christmas Book to the world!" Franklin bows to a round of thunderous applause, then holds up the book, revealing me mid-spin, the red dress flaring around me, a fiery plume of silk and satin, and a look of pure and utter joy on my face. I remember that shot. The photographer had just said something to make me laugh, and I was convinced the photo would catch me with the strangest expression.

"Oh my God. Sloane, you're..." Griff shakes his head. "It's stunning. Perfect, even."

I can't find the words to answer him because he's right. It's perfect. My final cover. My exit from this industry, from hiding away, from always fearing someone would learn my secret.

This is the best ending I could have imagined. Better still with Griff at my side. Turning to him, I take both of his hands, making sure to run my fingers over the palm of his prosthetic, a move I've started to realize makes him feel whole. "I lo—"

"Sloane! Congratulations!" Before I can confess my true feelings for him, half a dozen people surround us—models, executives, investors—and I have to thank every single one of them. Griff steps back, giving me space, and I glance over my shoulder, hoping he knows what I was about to say.

From the look in his eyes, he does, and I let the rest of the crowd have their piece of Sloane Sanders, the model. Sloane Sanders, the woman? She's all mine. Except for the piece of her heart that now belongs to Griff.

BY THE TIME I've made the rounds—twice—I'm dead on my feet, and Griff looks decidedly uncomfortable. "What's wrong?" I ask, taking his arm.

"Nothing a quick trip to the men's room won't fix." He scans the room with a frown. "I don't see Jacob and Marina."

"They could have gone outside for some fresh air." Gesturing to the glass doors surrounding the ballroom, I squint, but while I can tell the patio is crowded, I can't make out any faces. "I see at least six more investors I should talk to before we leave. If we don't visit the powder rooms now? It could be more than an hour before we have another chance."

Griff keeps his arm around my waist the entire way to the back corner of the room where a short hallway leads to the lavish bathrooms. Griff knocks on the door to the ladies' room, then pokes his head inside. "Security check," he calls out.

"Griff!"

"Not taking any chances with your safety," he says quietly, cupping my arm and leading me into the outer lounge area, then checking the stalls. Amazingly, they're all empty. "I'll be waiting right outside when you're done, sweetheart. If there's a line in the men's room, I'll text you. Got it?"

"Okay." Even after the events of the past week, his protectiveness still surprises me—and makes me feel safe. With a quick brush of his lips to my cheek, he's gone. It takes me a full ten minutes to take care of my own needs and rearrange my dress, but before I leave the powder room, I pause at one of the mirrors in the lounge.

My lips are a mess. Though my TD hasn't bothered me tonight, the lip stain I put on before the party is mostly gone. Digging in my bag, I pull out the tube and reapply, waiting the full minute for the liquid to dry to a perfect matte shade.

My phone buzzes, Marina's photo on the screen, and I tap the FaceTime button. "Hey, where are—?"

Sweat dampens my palms. My heart pounds so hard against my ribs, I can barely breathe. Marina's tear-stained face peers back at me, a strip of duct tape over her lips. The image zooms out, and I swallow my sob. She's slumped against weathered wood, her hands tied behind her back, ankles bound too, and her eyes are swollen and rimmed with red.

"No," I whisper.

"Hello, Sophiana." Dimitri's raspy voice is like an icy sword piercing my heart. He turns the phone, and I lock on to his cold, brown eyes. "It is good to see your face."

Wheezing, I start to stumble for the door.

"Stop!" The image shifts again, and the man from the press conference—Pavel—yanks Marina against him and presses a knife to her side. She whimpers, and a small red spot stains her dusky pink dress.

Dimitri makes a *tsk tsk* sound over the line. "If you take another step, Pavel will start cutting. We can make her bleed in many ways." His heavy footsteps echo over the call, and the camera angle changes. Is that...is she in a boat? "What happens to her now depends on you, Sophiana. Do exactly as I say, and your friend will remain *mostly* intact. Disobey me, and not only will Pavel hurt her, but we will set the boat adrift. Lake Zurich is so big, she will bleed out before anyone finds her."

"P-please. Don't hurt her," I manage. "She doesn't know anything about you! I kept quiet, just like you told me to. I didn't tell anyone! I swear on my life!"

"On your life?" He laughs. "Or on hers? Listen very carefully, *shlyukha*. You will keep your video on, but I will not. Can't have anyone seeing Ms. Marsh in this state, after all. You will not return to the party. Go out the door and to your left. At the end of the hall, there is an exit that leads outside. Tell that cocky American you are sleeping with that you need some air. Say only that. Nothing more. I have no doubt he will insist on coming with you. But that is okay. My men are waiting, and they will stop him from interfering."

"Promise me you won't kill him!" My voice breaks, and my chest feels like someone is squeezing it with a giant pair of pliers. "I'll do what you want. But let Griff and Marina live."

My mind is reeling. If I can't talk to Griff, if Dimitri is

watching everything, how can I tell him what's about to happen?

The panic button.

Carefully, trying not to let Dimitri see my movements, I reach for the button taped just under my arm. But no matter how hard I push, I don't feel the center of the device move. The boning in the dress runs right over the quarter-sized circle of metal. Shit.

"I am a reasonable man, Sophiana. And I have no reason to kill this...*Griff.* He did not take you from me. He did not lead the police to my door. No. That was you."

"Do you promise he'll live?" Each word is harder to force out than the last, and all I can focus on is the terror written all over Marina's face. Until Dimitri turns the phone again so I'm staring right at him.

"You have my word. Provided you do not try to warn him or deviate from my instructions in any way. Remember to keep the phone held high so I can see your face. Oh, and keep talking to Ms. Marsh as if she is up in her room with a bad hangover. That way I know you have not put the call on mute. Go. Now. Before Pavel decides he wants to have some fun."

Marina screams, the sound muffled, but full of pain, until the audio falls silent and the video turns black. All I can see on the screen now is my own face and Marina's name.

Once Dimitri has me...he'll kill me. And I didn't even tell Griff I love him.

CHAPTER TWENTY-NINE

Griff

What is taking her so long?

The dress, you idiot. She told you it was taped in at least six different places.

Checking my watch and my phone, I'm about to text her when the door to the ladies' powder room opens and Sloane emerges, holding her phone up in front of her.

"You should have stopped with one glass of champagne," she says. "We'll be back to the room in an hour or so." As she reaches my side, the phone almost slips out of her hand, but she rights it quickly. "Drink lots of water. And hang on a second, Griff's here." Her gaze flicks to mine for a brief moment, worry in her eyes behind the contacts. "I need some fresh air. Can we go outside? There's a door at the end of the hall. Dealing with this dress was...difficult."

"Outside?" Her fingers curl around my prosthetic, and she holds on so tightly as she tugs me with her, I know something's wrong. "Sloane, wait."

"Please? I didn't take a Xanax before the party and knowing Marina's sick...I'll be fine once we get outside." A tear shimmers in her eyes. I'd do anything for this woman, but my instincts are screaming at me to stop her.

"Marina?" I ask. "Are you okay?"

We're at the door now, and Sloane stops, staring up at me. Her fingers tremble as she touches my cheek, then the left temple of my glasses, activating the camera—and the recording ability.

Fuck. She's warning me.

"I'm sorry," she whispers, then opens the door and bursts out into the night.

"Sloane!" I call as I race after her, but the second the door closes, my head explodes in pain, and a beefy arm wraps around my neck, cutting off my air. I drive my right elbow back into my attacker's gut, but he's huge—and fat—and it does little to dislodge his iron grip.

A second man, no more than a shadow, grabs my arms and wrenches them painfully behind my back.

"Don't fight them," she sobs as a third asshole wraps massive fingers around her bare arm and jerks her against him. "Don't fight and you'll live. He promised."

My vision dims. "Sloane..." I croak, but she's already fifty feet away, sobbing until the big, dark-haired thug slaps her across the face.

Letting my body go limp, I only have time for a single thought before the world goes dark. *Volkov. She's talking about Volkov.*

Sloane

My cheek throbs, fiery pain that snakes all the way to my temple. Anton—one of Dimitri's generals who shuttled his girls back and forth from the hotel to the basement in Philadelphia—grips my arm hard enough to bring tears to my eyes, and I can't stop looking over my shoulder to try to catch a glimpse of Griff.

A black car with tinted windows idles at the curb at the end of the block, and I dig my heels into the soft grass, but all that gets me are two bare feet and a growl to "Stop fighting or you will be sorry."

I'm already sorry.

"What are they doing to Griff?" I ask.

"Shut up, *cyka*," he snaps. Opening the back door, he shoves me into the car. The urge to try the opposite door is almost overwhelming, but if I run, Dimitri will kill Marina, and I have no idea where she is. Or Jacob. What happened to him?

Anton's large body squeezes in next to me, and the man in the front seat—one I don't recognize, but who's just as big and ugly—tosses him a roll of duct tape.

"Hands."

I don't fight. Don't do anything but cross my wrists in front of me and let him wrap the tape around them. Six times. I count, though I don't know why. What does it matter? I'm dead. Griff...maybe he'll survive. Dimitri is a monster, but though he'd string his girls along with promises of fast food, hot showers, or a fix to take the pain away, the very few times he uttered the phrase "you have my word," he followed through.

No one speaks on the drive. Anton ordered me to keep my bound hands in my lap, so I sit quietly, my fingers drumming on my knees while I chew on my lips until I taste blood.

Rain starts to fall, and the lights of Zurich turn to blurry streaks of bright colors outside the windows. One turn, two, three, and the car slows, making a final turn and rolling through a deserted parking lot.

Why didn't I pay attention to the route we took?

Because you won't survive this. He won't let you. What's the point?

Cool air hits my skin as Anton yanks me from the car, and my feet land in a puddle. The hem of my dress drags along the wet asphalt as I'm dragged down a long wooden dock. Lake Zurich stretches out before us, an inky black void behind an old wooden boat house with light spilling from a crack in the side door.

"Eto ya," Anton calls out. The reply is muffled thanks to my heartbeat roaring in my ears, but a second later, the big asshole throws me to the ground just inside the boathouse.

Throwing my bound hands out to break my fall is almost useless, and pain sings all the way from my palms to my shoulders. *Marina. Where's Marina?*

My eyes water, but I scramble back against the closest wall, blinking rapidly until I can focus on my best friend. The boathouse opens out onto the lake with a long wooden platform running down the center. On the far side, Marina lies in a small boat—no engine, barely even a canoe—with blood staining the whole left side of her dress.

"Marina!" Before I can get to my feet, Dimitri aims a kick to my ribs, knocking all the air from my lungs.

"My little Sophiana is all grown up," he says. I struggle to breathe, curling inwards as nausea crawls up my throat. Air rushes back into my lungs in a whoosh. His scent is the same. Vodka and *kvasya* and sweat. "I thought maybe I would take you from the *Bahnhofstrasse.* You were all alone then. You and that stupid American. It would have been simple. But...you were always my favorite."

"Bullshit," I croak. "Your favorite was whichever girl you thought needed to be taught a *lesson* that night."

He grabs me by the hair and throws me against the old wooden wall. Marina screams, the sound muffled, but full of pain and terror. My head hits hard, and my vision blurs. This is it. This is when he kills me.

"Maybe I should keep you alive for a bit," Dimitri says as he crouches in front of me. "Teach you to be grateful for what I have given you."

"You...gave me...nothing but pain."

"I gave you one final night to bask in your glory, *Sloane*. You were the darling of the whole evening. I paid one of the hotel staff a thousand francs to send me photos." He pulls out his phone and waves it back and forth. On the screen, Griff and I are laughing, his arm around my waist, my hand on his chest.

"Is he alive? Is Griff alive?" I ask. Tears tumble down my cheeks, and behind Dimitri, Pavel holds Marina against his broad chest and traces the sharp point of his knife along her cheek, under her chin, and down to her breasts. She whimpers and tries to pull away, but he chuckles and plunges the blade into her side. "No! Stop! I did what you wanted! *Everything* you wanted! Let her go!"

"Not everything." Dimitri stands, towering over me, and holds out his hand. "You have not suffered as I have these past fifteen years."

Does he seriously think I'm going to let him help me up?

"Pavel, Anton? My little Sophie needs more *motivation*."

"No! Please, no!" I thrust my bound hands up, but it's too late. Anton curls his fingers around the back of my dress and yanks me to my feet, dragging me halfway down the walkway so I'm standing right in front of Marina. She's struggling to breathe, her chest stuttering, and she's so pale. Blood seeps from around the blade embedded in her side, less than I expect, but still too much.

Pavel chuckles and pulls a second, smaller knife from his boot.

"Don't," I whisper, then lock eyes with Marina. "Look at me, Marina. Only at me. I love you. You're my best friend. We still need to have that girls' weekend."

She sobs behind the gag, shaking her head and trying to shrink back from Pavel, who's spinning the small knife around and around in his thick, fat fingers.

"Stop this, Dimitri! Please! You can do whatever you want to me. Cut me, rape me, send all those terrible photos of me to the media. I don't care. But Marina did nothing to you!" I hold up my bound hands, pleading, but he just laughs and nods at Pavel.

The tip of the knife pierces her skin just under her collarbone, and Marina's weak scream is echoed by my own. Pavel yanks the blade from her body, and blood flows freely down her breast. Her eyes roll back in her head as Anton releases me, and I fall to my knees, desperately reaching for her, but Pavel leaps out of the boat, shoves at it, and I watch, helpless, as Marina floats away, unconscious, bound, and bleeding.

"Come here, Sophiana," Dimitri says, his tone full of triumph. "Crawl. On your knees. Now!"

Pavel and Anton stand side by side, ready to hurt me if I don't obey. But Dimitri's already taken everything from me. My one chance at true happiness with Griff. My best friend. My freedom. He doesn't get to take *anything* else.

Bracing my hands on the rough wooden planks, I get to my knees, then to my feet. Pavel and Anton take two steps closer, and I retreat the same distance. I'm perilously close to the end of the wooden platform, but I'd rather jump into Lake Zurich and drown than let Dimitri get his hands on me again.

"I will never kneel for you again." Marina's dying. Griff... for all I know, he could be dead too. I'll die before I let him take anything else away from me.

Dimitri throws his head back and laughs. "Oh, we will see about that."

Griff

It's dark, the stench of fertilizer and dirt surrounding me. I'm on my stomach, grass tickling my left ear. My head aches, and my arms...fuck. Stretching the fingers of my right hand as far as they'll go, I find the hard, plastic zip tie binding my wrists.

Voices. Not too far away. Laughing. The few minutes before I passed out play on a loop. Sloane tapping my glasses. Tears in her eyes.

"Don't fight and you'll live. He promised."

Volkov. He found a way to get to her.

Think!

Raising my head, even two inches, makes the world spin and tilt on its axis. My left shoulder protests the movement, sending electric sparks shooting all the way down my back. Cufflinks. Dax gave them to me because, in his words, "They're distinctive. But also useful. Just in case."

I need useful. But Sloane had to help me put them on. The fingers of my left hand are useless. My stump is completely numb, and that includes the rewired nerves that control my prosthetic.

The first cufflink pops off and rolls away. Goddammit. It's too dark in here for me to see, and even if I could...the fucking thing is somewhere behind me. Those shitstains zip tied my ankles as well, so leverage is at a premium.

One last hope. I find the other one, flip the toggle, and it lands in my palm. Thank fucking God. Pressing on the post, I breathe a sigh of relief at the feel of the *snap*. What's not so pleasant? When I stab myself in the wrist sawing at the zip tie. Ignoring the pain, I tighten my grip, working the tiny pocket knife back and forth until the plastic snaps in two, and my arms fall limply to my sides.

Stifling my groan, I whisper, "Austin? Tell me you're still listening. I'm fucked, man. Sloane's gone. Volkov took her."

The glasses flicker once, and the sight of text scrolling across the lenses is the second most beautiful sight in the world.

Police on their way. Ten minutes max. Have a lock on Sloane's tracker. Marina's went dead minutes before your glasses started transmitting.

Ten minutes? Sloane doesn't have that long. Slowly, an inch at a time, I get to my feet, and though my left arm is still useless, I rip at my right pant leg and slide the dagger from its sheath.

I'm in some sort of gardening shed. Still on Baur au Lac property if I had to guess. And those two Russian thugs are making sure I don't wake up and cause a scene.

They'll have no problem killing me if I do. Hell, they'll probably kill me anyway. Unless I get to them first.

Adjusting my grip, I creep toward the door. Asshole #1 and Asshole #2 are pointing at the bright lights inside the hotel, chuckling and making jokes about all the *pretty people*. How they haven't even noticed the star of the evening vanished under their noses.

Rustling from behind me stops me in my tracks. Fuck. Not another threat. But when I turn, my eyes now adjusted to the darkness, I make out another prone form. Jacob. Dropping to one knee, I feel for his wrists and ankles and cut him loose. But he's still barely conscious. They must have hit him a lot harder than they hit me. Or he didn't try to play "out cold" like I did.

Five minutes.

The bright green words flash once on screen, then disappear. "Not waiting," I whisper.

With one final glance out the crack in the doors, I know what I have to do. A well-placed kick sends the left-hand door crashing into Asshole #1, and he hits the ground knees first. Spinning around, I sink the knife deep into #2's throat, my position at his side the only thing saving me from being drenched in the arterial spray.

He's dead in under a minute, so I return my focus to the first guy. He's on his feet again, a gun pointed at my head. "Dimitri said you could live. As long as you were no trouble. Now? You are trouble."

"Dickhead, do you really want to fire a gun two hundred feet from one of the biggest and most secure parties in Europe? The police would be on you in a heartbeat." His moment of hesitation is all I need. Rushing him with my left shoulder dropped, I jerk up at the last minute, sending my titanium elbow joint into his chin.

A bone cracks, he whimpers in pain, and my knife finishes him off, sinking deep into his chest over his heart. "Shoulda' thought about body armor, man. I did."

Under this shirt? A thin layer of Kevlar. Not even Sloane knows about that.

"Send me directions to Sloane's tracker," I snap as I take off at a run towards the front of the hotel.

Wait for the police.

"Fuck no. The second I find a cab, I'm going. Send me the goddamn address. Now!"

Bootsvermietung und Seelounge. Utoquai 6.

"Jacob's in the shed. Where I just was. I think he'll need

medical. Send the police to Sloane's location, but I'm not waiting for them if I get there first. And for fuck's sake, tell them if they make a move without me being there...they're going to regret the day they were born."

Rounding the front of the hotel, I spot a line of cabs all waiting to take partygoers home. One of them...yep. There's that distinctive scrape on the front bumper. Elias.

I yank his passenger door open and drop into the seat next to him. "*Bootsvermietung und Seelounge. Utoquai* 6. Get me there in half the time it would take *anyone* else and it's a five-hundred franc tip."

"Yes, Mr. Griffin. Right away. But..." His lined face takes on a few more wrinkles as he stares at my bloodstained white shirt. "Do you need medical treatment?"

"Not my blood. Drive, man! The woman I love is in danger, and if we don't get there in the next few minutes..."

Elias answers by wrenching the wheel hard to the left and peeling out like he just earned a spot in the Indy 500. Maybe—if we're fast enough—I can still save Sloane's life. If not, I'm taking Dimitri down. Even if that means I go down with him.

CHAPTER THIRTY

Griff

Exactly four minutes later, Elias points. "It's up ahead on the right."

"Cut the lights." After a beat, when he doesn't answer, I growl, "Headlights. Off. Now."

My phone buzzes in my inner vest pocket, and I tap my watch to answer the call as the cab comes to a stop just outside a mostly empty parking lot.

Rain falls lightly, and I scan our surroundings until Ripper's words appear on my lenses. "Pulled the FaceTime call Sloane was on when things went pear-shaped. Sending the relevant bits to your phone now."

"Mr. Griffin?" Elias asks. "Are you all right?"

"Not in the least." Turning to him, I rub my left shoulder. Pins and needles. That's all I have. Until I can get full sensation back, my left hand's useless. "There's a former human trafficker asshole somewhere on these docks. He's kidnapped my girl-friend *and* her best friend, killed her agent, and probably a whole lot of other people over the years, and I have no idea how many people he has with him."

The taxi driver's eyes widen. "You are not serious."

"Do I look like I'm kidding? I'm CIA. Highly trained, but right now? I'm compromised." Yanking up my left sleeve to reveal the titanium forearm, I fight the frustration, the anger at how fucked up I am. "Two of the asshole's men knocked me out and tied me up back at the hotel, and my left arm—what's remains of it—is numb. I can't do a damn thing with it until I regain full sensation, and Sloane doesn't have much time left."

"Uh, Griff? Who are you talking to?" Ripper asks. "The police found Jacob. He's got a concussion and at least three broken ribs. He fought—hard—when they took Marina."

Pulling out my phone, I show Elias the screen before I respond. "Rip, I took a cab to the boat rental place. We're just outside the parking lot. There's a single car—license plate ZH 443999—parked close to the docks with a guy sitting behind the wheel."

Elias taps my left shoulder. Thank God the sensation's coming back.

"Hang on, Rip," I say.

"I was not always a cab driver, Mr. Griffin," Elias says with a sly grin. "I have done many things in my life. And I have loved. My wife and son? They are my whole world."

"Which is why as soon as I finish talking to my team—" I wave the phone, "—you're leaving."

"No." He sits up a little straighter. "I was a member of the Swiss Armed Forces for seven years and was trained as a medic. May I touch you?"

"Yeah." I'm not sure what he's about to do, but my phone tells me the video has finished downloading, so I tap to open it. The words scroll across the bottom of the screen. Is that...a boat Marina's in? Shit. Setting her adrift so she can bleed to death?

I'm about to tell Elias I can't wait any longer when his hands wrap around my left shoulder. Strong fingers dig into my upper back, and I feel a subtle pop, then a zing of pain, like sparks dancing along my skin. But seconds later, the pins and needles fade, and though the arm still feels weak as fuck, my thumb twitches at my command.

"What the hell was that?" I ask, turning to face the man.

He smiles. "Something I learned from another medic. Pressure points to increase circulation. The cots we had to sleep on were not comfortable. Many soldiers complained of their arms going numb at night."

"Thank you." Shoving my phone back inside my vest pocket, I pull out my wallet. My left hand is just functional enough to cradle the leather billfold so I can grasp the wad of francs with my right. I don't know how much is there. At least five hundred. Thrusting the money at Elias, I nod. "You're a good man. Go home to your family."

He starts to protest, but as soon as my wallet's back in my pocket, I get out of the car, give him a little wave, and head for the shadows along a chain link fence.

There's no cover. No trees, only the one car. How the hell am I supposed to get down the dock? Lights glow from inside a building at the end, and I'd bet my life that's where Volkov has Sloane and Marina.

Trapped in my world of near-total silence, I don't hear the cab until it passes me, heading right for the only other car in sight. Shit.

Elias, no!

But the cab blocks my view of the other car—blocking their view of me as well—and I take off at a run. Elias drives slowly enough I can catch up easily. Staying low, I keep my right hand pressed to the side for balance, and when the cab stops, we're less than twenty feet from the other car.

"Who are you?" The words scroll across my lenses, the unknown voice appearing in italics with a #1 in front of it.

"I am supposed to pick up a fare here," Elias says. "A woman? Have you seen her?"

The man is brave as fuck, and I don't know how I'll ever thank him. Besides doing whatever I can to make sure he stays alive. Pulling the knife from its sheath once more, I round the back of the cab and spring for the big Russian with his hands on his hips.

Balling up my left fist, I swing, catching him in the jaw, and the solid impact reverberates all the way to my chest. Titanium packs a hell of a punch, and blood spurts from his lips, along with at least one tooth.

I'm not interested in keeping anyone alive. Not knowing what Volkov's done. But I'm on foreign soil, so I keep the knife as a last resort. Landing a second jab to the asshole's cheek, I stagger back as he collapses to the ground.

"Go," Elias says, waving me toward the dock. "I have ropes. He will stay down."

Only taking the time to spare the cab driver a brief nod of thanks, I rush down the long wooden dock, my steps as light as possible. God, I wish I could hear. Could tell if I'm being quiet or sound like a herd of elephants.

Close enough to make out shadows moving inside the boathouse, I slow, creeping forward one careful step at a time.

Red text on my lenses. Fuck. Sloane. "I will never kneel for you again."

"Oh, we will see about that." An unknown voice. Volkov. It has to be. The door's mostly closed, and I take out my phone, turn on the camera, and angle it just enough to see the inside of the boathouse.

Ice runs through my veins, and I shove my emotions down so far, I might never be able to find them again. It's the only way I'll survive this—that Sloane will survive this. She stands tall at the end of a long wooden platform, her hands duct taped in front of her. Two men advance on her with Volkov standing fifteen feet away, his cold stare fixed on the woman I love.

Marina's nowhere to be seen. Shit. I send Ripper a quick text.

Get search and rescue to the lake. Marina's not here.

Three large, very angry, very powerful men. One strong-as-fuck woman with her hands bound, and me.

"Don't come any closer," Sloane says.

No!

If she jumps, she'll drown. That dress. Unable to use her hands.

Screaming.

The word flashes three times before it disappears, and I shove the phone into my back pocket. Now or never. I test the weight of the knife in my hand. I can do this. For Sloane. Because no one is *ever* going to hurt her again.

Angling a quick gaze around the door, I pinpoint my two targets. Volkov stands too close to a wooden beam for me to get a clean shot, and the other two—Pavel Andrei and another dude I don't recognize—carry Sloane by the arms as she kicks wildly. "Let me go! Or just kill me already!"

Oh, *hell* no. As the three round the end of the wooden platform and turn towards Volkov, I throw the knife. It sails end-over end until it finds its target. In the unknown man's lower back. He drops Sloane's arm, falls to his knees, and struggles to reach the knife.

Off balance, Andrei shoves Sloane towards Volkov, and pulls a gun from his shoulder holster. Two shots splinter the wood inches from my head, and now...all I have left is the small pistol inside my vest. And ten bullets.

"Griff! Run!"

I ignore the red text and pull the weapon from the holster. Backing up, I wait for Andrei to charge. And he will. The man's been suspected of a dozen crimes because without someone else in control, he's too fucking stupid to pull off anything more complicated than assault and battery.

The moment he rushes through the door, I fire, and though my left hand is only good enough to help steady my right, the bullet hits its mark. The back of his head. He's flat on his face—what's left of it anyway—in less than five seconds.

"If you want Sophiana to live, you'll put down the gun."

Volkov.

If I drop my weapon, we're both dead. "Sloane? Talk to me."

Fuck. No reply. Ripper sends a message to my glasses telling me the police are five minutes out, but that's four minutes Sloane doesn't have.

Stepping out from behind the door, the gun aimed where I last saw Volkov, I draw on all the anger I've kept locked up since the attack that stole so much from me.

The fucker has one arm around Sloane's torso, pinning her arms in front of her. With his other hand, he presses a knife to her throat. She strains, her head pressed against Volkov's shoulder to try to escape the sharp blade, but it's no use. Blood seeps around the shiny metal. He hasn't hit her carotids yet, but one flinch—hers or his—and he will.

"You won't get away with this." I don't dare take another step closer. "The police are on their way. Search and rescue will find Marina, and you're all alone now."

The other thug is still alive—technically—but he's barely moving, and a large pool of blood spreads out around his prone body.

"You can kill me, American," Volkov says with a smile that

makes me want to kick his teeth in. "But this whore will die with me."

"Call her that again and I'll make you suffer before I end you. Let her go, and I'll put one between your eyes. Nice and quick." My left arm throbs with every beat of my heart, but my anger and desperate focus give me the fine control of my prosthetic fingers I need to line up my shot.

The knife glints in the overhead lights, and Sloane's lips move even as pain flits across her face and more blood trickles from her neck to her chest.

"I love you."

Seeing those words—knowing she feels the same way I do—it lets me believe I can do this. I have to do this. For her. So we can have our forever. "Trust me, sweetheart. I'm going to get us out of this."

Volkov laughs and drags Sloane back another few steps. But he can't do that with the knife held as tightly to her neck, and the second it lifts slightly, she swallows hard and shudders against the big man.

Dropping my left hand to my side, I spell out, *"Gag. Vomit,"* and hope Volkov doesn't notice the movements—or understand what they mean. But he's too preoccupied with what he's about to do to Sloane.

"You are half a man, Mr. Harry Griffin. And while I clearly underestimated your skills and your background, nothing can make up for only having *one arm*." Grinning, he angles the knife against her neck. Sloane makes a sound—it has to be a low wail for me to be able to hear even the faintest hint of it—and tears cascade down her cheeks. But then she starts to gag and choke, sucking her stomach in hard.

"You fucking bitch," Volkov says with a sneer. His gaze trails to his captive for the briefest of moments.

"Now!" I shout. Sloane slams her head back, catching

Volkov in the nose, and I fire. The knife jerks, but her move forced her up onto the balls of her feet, and the slice catches her close to her collarbone, safely away from any major arteries. He still has a hold on her, though, and they fall together, landing in the water with a massive splash.

No!

I toss the gun aside, racing for the end of the dock. Sloane kicks wildly, trying to stay afloat. I drop to my knees and grab her wrists with both hands to pull her up. It's awkward as fuck, and we topple over together, me on my back with her on top of me, but she's safe. In my arms.

Her bound hands slip over my head, and she holds on for dear life, her sobs loud enough even I can hear them. "You're safe, sweetheart. He'll never hurt you again."

CHAPTER THIRTY-ONE

I'm cold. So cold. But I hold on to Griff and let myself break. I'm so out of it, so numb, I'm only dimly aware of him helping me sit up. But when he tries to get me to let go of him, I can't.

"N-no..." I stammer.

"Sloane, I need to get this tape off your wrists. And check those cuts on your neck. Please, sweetheart."

His voice sounds so strange. Like he can barely get the words out, and that startles me enough to let him guide my hands over his head. He unwinds the tape, and I wince as he reaches the last layer. My wrists are red and raw underneath, and the skin burns in stark contrast to the rest of my body.

Tugging at his tie with a grunt, he rips it from around his neck and presses it to my throat. "You're still bleeding, but I don't think he hit anything vital." His voice cracks on his last word.

Hearing this strong, protective man close to losing it helps me focus, but the second I do, I feel *everything*. The pain in my ribs from where Dimitri kicked me. My swollen cheek, split lip, bruised hands, and my neck. Oh, God. My neck burns.

Sirens. I hear sirens. "Marina..." I whisper. Even talking hurts. Dimitri kept the flat of the knife pressed so hard to my windpipe, I could barely breathe, and now...it's like someone punched me in the throat.

"Search and rescue are already out on the lake," Griff says, still trying to stop the bleeding from the deepest cut by my collarbone. "They'll find her, Sloane. I promise."

"She...she needs an ambulance." My entire body trembles, the panic attack hitting me so hard and fast, I can't warn Griff before I'm wheezing and shoving at him, desperate to dislodge this boulder that feels like it just dropped onto the center of my chest.

"Sloane! Stay with me," he murmurs softly, his hands framing my cheeks and forcing me to look into his eyes. "Ninety-one. Ninety. Eighty-nine. Eighty-eight. Count with me, baby."

"Eigh-eighty-s-seven," I manage, but can't go any further. Eighty-six is stuck, playing on a loop in my head, and as desperate as I am to force the words from my lips, I can't.

A strong arm wraps around my back, and Griff kisses me. He's so warm. So solid and *real*. So *alive*. I'm alive. Dimitri... isn't.

"Come back now," he whispers against my mouth before kissing me again. This time, I part for him, letting the bold strokes of his tongue ground me, even though my split lip sends electric shocks of pain all the way to my chin. I don't care. Pain means I'm still here. Still breathing. With the man I love kissing me.

Winding my arms around his waist, I hold on tight, losing

myself to his warmth. We survived. He saved me, and we survived.

When he finally pulls back to look at me, I find so much love in his gaze, it brings fresh tears to my eyes.

"I thought I was going to lose you," he whispers.

"I'm sorry." Through my sobs, I try to explain, but I don't even know if he can understand me as emotional as I am. "I couldn't tell you. The camera...he was listening. I didn't have any time to think. Marina...he showed me Marina. Threatened to kill her if I didn't... Told me to get outside..."

"Shh, sweetheart." Griff touches a finger to my lips. "I saw the video. Ripper pulled it from your phone. I understand. You did everything right. Turning on my glasses, staying alive. *Everything.*"

Footsteps thud down the dock, and I tense, grabbing onto him with a whimper.

"It's the police." He pulls me into his lap and holds me close as six men burst into the boathouse.

"Griffin Hargrove?" one of them asks while another checks Anton for a pulse.

"This one's dead," the second officer says, and I release a shuddering breath.

"Yes. I'm Griff. Sloane needs medical attention. Who has contact with Search and Rescue?" He's all business now, though he hasn't moved or let go of me.

"I'll call in. I'm Officer Keller." The first man into the boathouse kneels next to us. "You are quite fortunate, Mr. Hargrove. Dax Holloway vouched for you. My older brother worked with him a time or two in Afghanistan. Otherwise...we would have to take you in for this...mess."

"I'm the luckiest man in the world," he says, reaching up to tuck one of my wet curls behind my ear. "Because I'm alive, but more importantly, so is the woman I love."

My heart belongs this man holding me, and if there weren't so many people around, if I weren't still so worried about Marina, I'd tell him exactly that and so much more. But for now, all I can do is rest my head on his shoulder and whisper, "I love you."

TWELVE HOURS LATER, a doctor emerges from behind a set of swinging doors. "Ms. Sanders? Mr. Hargrove?"

"Here," I call, my voice hoarse. We've been at the hospital all night waiting for news on my best friend. When Search and Rescue found her, she was unconscious, and they lost her heartbeat twice in the ambulance.

Griff helps me to my feet, keeping his arm around my waist. My entire body aches. No broken bones, but three bruised ribs, a sprained wrist, and five deep cuts—three of which required sutures—have left me weak and unsteady. But Jacob, who refused to be admitted, despite his concussion, brought us food a couple of hours ago. I ate an entire serving of french fries and half a hamburger before my nerves took over and refused to let me take another bite.

"Ms. Marsh should make a full recovery. She lost approximately one third of her liver, but she was quite lucky. If anyone had pulled that knife out before we started surgery, there would have been nothing we could have done. She will have to stay here for at least a week, and I do not recommend she fly back to the United States for at least three weeks. But you can see her once the anesthesia wears off."

My legs give out from relief, and only Griff's arm keeps me upright. "Thank you," I manage before I bury my face against his chest, crying softly.

"We'll arrange for her to recover somewhere close by," Griff says, and the way his voice rumbles under my ear settles me like nothing else can. "We'll be staying in Zurich until she's able to fly back to New York with us."

"What?" My head snaps up, and I meet his gaze. "We're staying?"

"She's your best friend. Of course, we're staying. She shouldn't be alone." Confusion creases his brow. "Did you really think—?"

"I don't know what I thought," I whisper.

"We're going to get that vacation we deserve, sweetheart. And you and Marina will have your girls' time. Even if she's confined to her bed for most of it. We're safe. She's safe. Everything else...we can figure out as we go. Together."

Looking around for the doctor, I see him disappear through the swinging doors, and Jacob sinks down into a chair behind Griff, his head in his hands, muttering, "Thank fuck."

Standing under my own power, I run my fingers through Griff's hair. "I love you. For so long I didn't think I'd ever find another person I was willing to trust. To let in. It was too dangerous. But with you? It was so easy. You made me feel safe from the very first time we talked—even before I knew who you were. You saved my life. And now this? I don't know what to say. How to tell you just how much you mean to me."

"You don't have to, Sloane." He smiles, soft and gentle, his deep blue eyes locked on mine. "Because I feel the same way. You see me. All of me." Griff shrugs his left shoulder. He took his prosthetic off hours ago, and it's wrapped in his tux jacket on the chair next to Jacob. "All my flaws. All my damage. And you accept it. Even when I don't."

Leaning in, he claims my lips in a possessive, but tender kiss, and for the first time in forever, I know I have a future. One with an amazing, protective, and strong man who loves me despite my flaws, my history, and the lies I lived for so long.

We found one another, and whatever happens next, we'll face it together.

EPILOGUE

Griff

Leaving the two-bedroom flat that's been our home for the past month was harder than I thought. So much healing took place there. Sloane tossed away all of her contact lenses, and told Marina everything. Including her former name.

She also switched up her anxiety meds. The dizzy spells scared the fuck out of me, but her tardive dyskinesia tics have faded dramatically, and more importantly, when her anxiety flares, she stays present. Talks to me. Lets me help her through the worst of it.

With Austin, Dax, Wren, and Ripper's help, there's now a paper trail showing her legal name change from Sophiana Lebedev to Sloane Sanders. I don't know how they did it, but no one will question Sloane's dual Russian and American citizenship now, and she can finally be whoever she wants to be.

In the spring, we'll visit her mother and sisters, but for today, it's enough that Wren was able to siphon off more than three million from Volkov's bank accounts and distribute it to Sloane's family.

Her mom and youngest sister are moving to Moscow, along with the oldest, Sasha, who left her abusive husband after more than twenty years of living in fear. Sloane's third sister, Irina, loves the man she married, but soon, they plan on moving as well, so the whole family will be safe and never want for anything again.

The car service turns onto a quiet, tree-lined street, and Sloane grips my hand tightly. "You can't see the house from the road, but park at the end of the cul-de-sac," she says, leaning forward, a wide smile on her face.

As we walk under a green, leafy canopy, she pulls out her phone and shows me the screen.

Marina: My doctor cleared me to go back to work right after Christmas. Thank God. Any longer without something to do besides read, watch movies, and gossip, and I would have started to lose my mind. Miss you! Can't wait for our spa week in February!

We stop at her front door, and Sloane digs in her purse and comes back with a small, rectangular box tied with a red ribbon. "Open it," she says, smiling.

Cradling it in my left hand, I pull the string and lift the lid. A silver key on a Zurich, Switzerland keychain rests inside. "Sloane..."

"I loved spending the last month with you, Griff. Well, besides the bruises and worry over Marina and all the stress." She laughs, but I can tell the memories of what we all went through will stay with her forever. "But that wasn't...real life. Not exactly. This is. I want us to be together. Long term. Maybe even..." She lifts her gaze to mine, and her brown eyes hold so many emotions. Fear. Anticipation. Love. "Maybe forever. I don't care if we stay in San Diego or move somewhere else, but for now...this is my home. And I want it to be yours too."

Pulling her against me, I kiss her, loving how she fits perfectly in my arms. How she opens for me. I can feel the vibrations of her moan, and I want her naked. Just as soon as I figure out where her bedroom—our bedroom—is.

"I have something for you too," I say. Reaching into my bag, I withdraw the framed sketch of the two of us from that magical night on the *Bahnhofstrasse.* Sloane gasps as she touches it, running her fingers over her eyes. I snuck out one night when she and Marina were watching a movie and found the artist who drew it. He was quite happy to change her eye color for me.

"You...my eyes... This really is us now."

"I love you, sweetheart. Now and forever. My home is wherever you are and always will be."

HOURS LATER, with a fire burning in the hearth, Sloane curls against me on the sofa. Her breathing changed a few minutes ago, slowing when she finally fell asleep, and I stretch out my right arm to snag my phone from the side table.

"Griff," Austin says when the call connects. The word scrolls across my lenses, and I keep my voice to a whisper.

"Sloane's asleep. We're home. In San Diego. This can wait if you're busy."

"Mik's making us a late dinner. I got back from Texas an hour ago."

"How is Connor?" Austin's latest recruit just finished his first assignment, and from the updates Austin sent me, it wasn't an easy one.

"Better than I expected. A hell of a lot better, actually."

Stifling my laugh so I won't wake Sloane, I press a kiss to the top of her head. "You have a knack, man. I don't know how you do it, but you could advertise a whole other set of skills, you know."

The word *laughter* appears on my lenses, and I continue. "Listen, I never thanked you properly for what you did for me. For Sloane. All of it."

"We're family," he says. "That's what we do."

Family. The word rattles around in my head for so long, Austin asks if I'm still on the call.

"Yeah. I'm here. Just...processing."

More laughter. "When Dax said those same words to me, I didn't believe him. Not until I almost lost Mik and he and Ronan came through for both of us. I meant it, you know. Family is more than the people we're related to by blood. So much more."

He's right. Sloane's my family. And Austin. Dax and his team too. "Look, I won't keep you. But what you said? 'You're the only one who can decide if she's worth forever'?"

"I remember."

Staring down at the woman sleeping against me, I marvel at how lucky we both were—and are—to have found one another. "She is, man. She absolutely is."

THANK you for reading Rogue Officer. Griff' refused to talk to me for a long time. The man was just in so much pain—mostly mental—from his injuries and the loss of everything he knew that he didn't want to let me tell his story.

But once he opened up to me, it was like a dam broke. And suddenly, I couldn't stop him.

I hope Griff and Sloane's story left you with all the feels for both of them. You'll see these two again. You know I can never quite leave my couples alone after they find their forevers. I always want to bring them back for cameos in other books.

My next release is Protecting His Target, Book 9 in the *Away From Keyboard* series. After that, you can read Connor's story. Remember him? If not, I'll refresh your memory. He was Q's brother in Braving His Past. Connor has a lot to atone for, and you can read all about his redemption next year in Rogue Survivor.

Of course, you can feel free to preorder both Protecting His Target and Rogue Survivor now. It would certainly make me happy. But don't worry. My Facebook group, page, and newsletter will give you plenty of reminders before those books go live.

Thank you again for reading. I know there are thousands of authors you have to choose from, and I'm honored every time you pick up a book of mine.

Love, Patricia

ALSO BY PATRICIA D. EDDY

Away From Keyboard

Dive into a steamy mix of geekery and military prowess with the men and women of Hidden Agenda and Second Sight.

Breaking His Code

In Her Sights

On His Six

Second Sight

By Lethal Force

Fighting For Valor

Finding Their Forevers (a holiday short story)

Call Sign: Redemption

Braving His Past

Protecting His Target

Gone Rogue (an Away From Keyboard spinoff series)

Rogue Protector

Rogue Officer

Rogue Survivor

Dark PNR

These novellas will take you into the darker side of the paranormal with vampires, witches, angels, demons, and more.

Forever Kept

Immortal Hunter

Wicked Omens

Storm of Sin

By the Fates

Check out the COMPLETE By the Fates series if you love dark and steamy tales of witches, devils, and an epic battle between good and evil.

By the Fates, Freed

Destined: A By the Fates Story

By the Fates, Fought

By the Fates, Fulfilled

In Blood

If you love hot Italian vampires and and a human who can hold her own against beings far stronger, then the In Blood series is for you.

Secrets in Blood

Revelations in Blood

Holidays and Heroes

Beauty isn't only skin deep and not all scars heal. Come swoon over sexy vets and the men and women who love them.

Mistletoe and Mochas

Love and Libations

Restrained

Do you like to be tied up? Or read about characters who do? Enjoy a fresh COMPLETE BDSM series that will leave you begging for more.

In His Silks

Christmas Silks

All Tied Up For New Year's

In His Collar

ABOUT THE AUTHOR

I've always made up stories. Sometimes I even acted them out. I probably shouldn't admit that my childhood best friend and I used to run around the backyard pretending to fly in our Invisible Jet and rescue Steve Trevor. Oops.

Now that I'm too old to spin around in circles with felt magic bracelets on my wrists, I put "pen to paper" instead. Figuratively, at least. Fingers to keyboard is more accurate.

Outside of my writing, I'm a professional editor, a software geek, a singer (in the shower only), and a runner. I love red wine, scotch (neat, please), and cider. Seattle is my home, and I share an old house with my husband and cats.

I'm on my fourth—fifth?—rewatching of the modern *Doctor Who*, and I think one particular quote from that show sums up my entire life.

"We're all stories, in the end. Make it a good one, eh?" — *The Eleventh Doctor, Doctor Who*

I hope your story is brilliant.

You can reach me all over the web...
patriciadeddy.com
patricia@patriciadeddy.com

facebook.com/patriciadeddyauthor
twitter.com/patriciadeddy
instagram.com/patriciadeddy
bookbub.com/profile/patricia-d-eddy

www.ingramcontent.com/pod-product-compliance
Lightning Source LLC
Chambersburg PA
CBHW070435170726
48291CB00002B/518